STATIC

L.A. WITT

RIPTIDE
PUBLISHING

Riptide Publishing
PO Box 6652
Hillsborough, NJ 08844
www.riptidepublishing.com

Static
Copyright © 2014 by L.A. Witt

Cover Art by L.C. Chase, http://lcchase.com/design.htm
Editor: Carole-Ann Galloway
Layout: L.C. Chase, http://lcchase.com/design.htm

ISBN: 978-1-62649-103-8

Second edition
January, 2014

Also available in ebook:
ISBN: 978-1-62649-102-1

STATIC

L.A. WITT

☌ TABLE OF ♀
CONTENTS

Chapter 1 1
Chapter 2 11
Chapter 3 21
Chapter 4 31
Chapter 5 41
Chapter 6 47
Chapter 7 61
Chapter 8 73
Chapter 9 81
Chapter 10 89
Chapter 11 101
Chapter 12 107
Chapter 13 119
Chapter 14 131
Chapter 15 141
Chapter 16 149
Chapter 17 159
Chapter 18 165
Chapter 19 181
Chapter 20 187
Chapter 21 193
Chapter 22 199
Chapter 23 205
Chapter 24 211
Author's Note 219
Also by L.A. Witt 223
About the Author 225
Sneak Peek: A Chip in His Shoulder 229
Sneak Peek: Hostile Ground 239

☿ CHAPTER 1 ♀
DAMON

When my girlfriend's cell phone went straight to voice mail for the fourth time in twenty-four hours, "worried" didn't even begin to describe it.

I paced beside my kitchen table, eyeing my phone like it might suddenly spring to life with her ringtone the way I'd been begging it to. Alex had planned to visit her estranged parents yesterday, and after those get-togethers, it wasn't unusual for her to hole up in the house and block out the world for a while. I always worried myself sick when she did that—the woman could drink like nobody's business when she was upset—but the next morning always meant a text message saying she was okay. Hungover, probably depressed as hell, but okay.

This morning, that text hadn't come.

More than likely, things hadn't gone well. They never did. I'd told myself all day long that she just needed some space, some time. I didn't want to crowd her, but damn it, something about this raised the hairs on the back of my neck.

I looked at my watch. It was almost eight. Over thirty-six hours since she was supposed to meet them. Almost forty-eight since I'd heard from her at all. Something was wrong. It had to be.

I grabbed my phone and keys. Hopefully she'd be irritated with me showing up at her door. Annoyed by the intrusion, aggravated by me coming to her before she was ready to interact with the outside world again. At least that would mean she was home safe.

I pulled out of the driveway and ignored the posted speed limit. We lived about twenty minutes apart, and I was determined to get there in under fifteen. Ten if I could swing it.

I'd never met Alex's family. She'd told me little about them, but just the way her hackles went up at the mere mention of her parents' existence spoke volumes. It wouldn't have surprised me if they had abused her when she was young, and not just in the emotional, manipulative ways I assumed they still did. She was prone to unpredictable bouts of deep depression, which had been more frequent and severe in the last six months or so, and not just after she'd seen her family. She went through phases—hours, days, *weeks*—when she'd balk at any suggestion of physical intimacy. Sometimes she didn't mind an affectionate touch, but recoiled at the first hint of anything sexual. An arm around her could make her melt against me or shrink away like a beaten dog, and I never knew when to give her space and when to give her a shoulder.

Then, almost overnight, she'd be insatiable in bed. Whenever I asked her about it, she clammed up. Apologized, avoided my eyes, changed the subject.

What did they do to you, baby?

Turning down Alex's street, I took a few deep breaths and willed my pounding heart to slow down. She was fine. Probably drunk and upset, but no more worse for wear than the last time she'd seen her mother and stepfather. I was overreacting. I was being too protective.

Or maybe I wasn't.

Her house came into view up ahead. Her car was parked in front of the garage, and the faint glow of a single lamp illuminated her living room window. There were no other cars in the driveway or on the street, so presumably she was alone. Assuming, of course, that she was home. Someone else could have driven her somewhere, or she—

Easy, Damon. Don't jump to conclusions yet.

Heart still pounding, I parked beside her car. On my way up to the porch, I hesitated, wondering for the hundredth time if she'd be upset with me showing up when she clearly didn't want to see anyone.

After almost turning back twice, I made myself get all the way to the front porch, and before I could find another reason to talk myself out of it, I knocked. Waited. Craned my neck a little, listening for movement on the other side of the door.

Nothing.

My heart beat faster. I knocked again, harder this time.

Still nothing.

I rocked back and forth from my heels to the balls of my feet, staring at the door and wondering if I should give it one more try or leave. In my coat pocket, my keys ground against each other as I ran my thumb back and forth over them. Her house key was on the ring. I could let myself in. Damn it, where was the line between caution and intrusion?

One more try, and if she doesn't answer, I'll go.

Knock. Knock. Knock. Silence.

I exhaled hard, a knot twisting in my gut. She wasn't here. Or she wasn't answering. Whatever the case, I wasn't going to stand here all night, so I turned to go.

Movement inside the house stopped me in my tracks. I froze, listening, and the muffled sound of approaching footsteps sent a cool rush of relief through my veins.

The dead bolt turned. I exhaled.

Then the door opened, and that relief turned to something else. Something much colder.

"Who the—" Confusion and fury slithered through my veins as I stared at the man on the other side of the threshold. He leaned on the door and rested his arm on the doorframe. Vague surprise flickered across his expression and straightened his posture, but the heavy fatigue in his eyes kept his reaction subdued. I wondered if he was drunk. Or maybe he'd been asleep. In my girlfriend's bed. That was all too likely, I realized. He was pale, sleepy-eyed, dressed only in a pair of gray sweatpants, and his short hair was disheveled enough to imply far more than I ever wanted to know.

Alex, baby, tell me you didn't . . .

I found my voice again. "Who the fuck are you?"

Barely whispering, barely even keeping his eyes open, he said, "You might want to sit down for this. Come in and—"

"Just tell me what the fuck is going on."

He flinched, closing his eyes. "I can explain." His voice was quiet. "This isn't what it looks like. Not even close."

I laughed bitterly. "Oh, I'm sure it's not." With every word, the barely contained fury rose, as did my volume. "I suppose you're just keeping her company? Where the fuck is she? Where—"

"*Damon.*"

"You . . . you know who I am?"

"Yes, I do." His hand went to his temple, and he grimaced as he whispered, "Please don't shout. You're upset. I get it. I understand, and I'll explain, but . . ." He winced. "Please. Don't. Shout."

Anger made me want to grab his shoulders and show him the meaning of the word "shout," but I held back. Quieter now, I said, "What's going on?"

He stepped back and gestured for me to come in. I hesitated, but then followed him into Alex's house. He closed the door and leaned against it, rubbing his eyes with the heels of his hands. A low, pained sound escaped his throat. The light in here was dim, but not enough to hide just how pale he was.

"Are you—" I eyed him. "Are you all right?"

"No." Lowering his hands, he rested his head against the door. Dark circles under his eyes and a dusting of five-o'clock shadow along his jaw only served to emphasize his alarming pallor. After a moment, he opened his eyes. He winced and brought his hands up again. "This is going to sound weird, but bear with me. I need to lie down."

"Why?"

"Because when I stand, my head hurts so bad I can't see straight." With what looked like a hell of an effort, he pushed himself off the door, paused when his balance wavered, then started toward the living room. I wasn't sure if I should be impatient or concerned. But at this point, he was the only one who might know where Alex was, so I followed him.

As he walked ahead of me, I noticed a small white bandage in the middle of his back. Perhaps two inches square, taped in place over his spine a few inches above his waistband. My own spine prickled with goose bumps. Contrasting sharply with his pale skin was a smear of something brownish-red. I thought it might be blood at first, but even in the dim light, it looked too orange. Iodine, maybe? The remnants of something used to sterilize skin before a medical procedure?

Eyeing the bandage and the iodine and this stranger in my girlfriend's house, I wasn't sure this situation could get any weirder.

He eased himself onto Alex's couch like he had every right to do so, and I took a seat in the recliner. For a long moment, he kept a hand over his eyes and didn't speak. He took a few long, deep breaths, jaw clenched and cheek rippling as if trying to keep himself from getting sick. I might have suspected he was severely hungover, had it not been for that bandage.

I waited. A million demands, accusations, and pleas for information were on the tip of my tongue, but I waited.

Without lifting his hand, he finally spoke in a low, slurred monotone. "None of this is going to be easy for you to hear, and I'm sorry I didn't explain it a long time ago."

I blinked. A long time ago? I'd never seen this guy in my life. Just how long had this been going on? Was he the reason she didn't want to get married? I bit my tongue, though. *Let him explain,* then *get pissed.*

"Damon, I'm a shifter."

My heart stopped. "What?"

He swallowed. "I'm a shifter. This"—he gestured at himself with the hand that wasn't shielding his eyes—"is my male form."

Confusion kept the pieces from falling into place for several long seconds. Then those pieces did fall into place, and the air left my lungs in a single exhalation.

No way. No fucking way. But, how? She was . . .

I somehow managed to pull in another breath.

"Alex?" I whispered, almost choking on her name.

With a single, slow nod, he jerked the world out from under my feet. Had I not already been sitting, my knees would have buckled. I sat back against the recliner. Two years. Two damned years together, and I'd never caught on. She'd never said a word.

Fuck, this wasn't going to fit into my head. Not for a while, anyway. I didn't know how to feel. Furious? More confused than before? Relieved to find out she was all right—well, sort of—and she hadn't been cheating? Deceived? I didn't know. I was simply . . . numb. Stunned.

He took a deep breath. "This isn't how I wanted you to find out."

"You're . . ." Skepticism, suspicion, maybe a little denial worked their way into the tangle of emotions. "How do I know it's you?"

The hand over his eyes didn't move. "Giving a foot massage relaxes you almost as much as it does whoever's getting the massage." His bare foot rubbed against the other, toes curling like Alex's always did whenever I suggested giving her such a massage.

I gulped. Leaning forward and resting my elbows on my knees, I said, "She could have told you that."

"The night we met, you were so scared to ask me to dance, by the time you'd worked up the nerve, you were almost too drunk to string a coherent sentence together."

Normally that memory made me laugh. Alex, too. No one in the room cracked a smile.

I cleared my throat. "She could have told you that, too."

He drew a ragged breath. In an equally unsteady voice, he said, "You just found out why I've changed the subject whenever you've brought up getting married, and right now, you have your hands folded so tight in front of your lips that your knuckles are turning white." He lifted his hand off his eyes and looked at me.

I unfolded my hands and let them fall to my lap, pretending not to notice as the blood rushed back into my fingers.

He rested his forearm over his eyes. "I'm sorry, Damon. I'm sorry I didn't tell you."

I swallowed hard. "But, why now? You've always been female around me, but . . ."

Alex clenched his jaw, his lips thinning into a taut line. When he spoke, his voice threatened to crack. "Because I *can't* shift now."

A sick feeling churned in my gut. "Why not?"

"An implant," he said through his teeth. "In my spine." The bandage on his back flashed through my mind. "My parents, they . . ."

Oh, God . . . "What?"

"They forced me to get it. Drugged me. Said it was for my own good. By the time I knew what was going on, I was too doped up to fight back."

"Oh, my God. But, why would they force it on you?"

"Because I'm an abomination," he growled. For the first time since I'd arrived, he abandoned the quiet monotone he must have maintained to keep the pain at bay. "Ever since the implants came out on the market, my parents have been trying to badger me into getting one. They've always hated what I am, and it's—" He swallowed hard and then took a deep breath. Held it. Let it out. Drew another. Then he muttered, "Shit," and put a hand to his mouth. He flew to his feet and down the hall, and when he got to the bathroom, I cringed at the sound of him getting sick.

I rubbed the back of my neck, grimacing for him and trying to get my head around all of this. It didn't help that his condition had him unusually subdued and, aside from the sprint to the bathroom, moving in damn near slow motion. I could only imagine the emotional toll this was taking on him, and my presence was no doubt compounding his stress, but he was in too much pain to show it. It would have been hard enough to reconcile the Alex I knew with the one in front of me *without* pain muting her personality.

A moment later, about the time I'd stood to go see if he was okay, Alex returned. When he stepped into the faint light, my stomach flipped. His alarming pallor was worse than earlier.

"You okay?" I asked.

"Yeah," he said. "Fuck, sorry about that."

"Nothing to be sorry about." I stepped toward him. "Need a hand?"

He made a dismissive gesture and pushed himself away from the wall. "No, I can make it."

"Is this a normal side effect? Of . . . what they did?"

"I don't know. It's been—" He stumbled, catching himself on an end table. I grabbed his arm. When he'd more or less regained his balance, I held him steady while he eased himself back onto the couch.

"You sure you're all right?"

"I don't know," he whispered hollowly. "This headache, it's unreal. It started last night, and it just keeps getting worse." He cleared his throat and winced. "It's like the worst migraine I've ever had, times ten."

I winced. "Jesus. Can you take anything?"

"Nothing's helped. Anything I've been able to hold down hasn't done a damned thing." He laughed humorlessly. "I thought about drinking, but figured I shouldn't add a hangover to the mix."

I pursed my lips. That was a hint of the Alex I knew. Her drinking had worried me for some time, and it didn't surprise me at all to hear she—he—was tempted to drink now. The fact that he hadn't given in to that temptation was more than a little worrisome.

"At least when I lay perfectly still and flat, it's better," he said. "Not much, but better. But every time I get up . . ."

"Would turning off the rest of the lights help?"

"Doubt it. I've been in the bedroom all day with the lights off, and it hasn't done much."

"Maybe we should take you to the emergency room. Just to make sure it's nothing serious."

I expected him to fight it. The Alex I'd known the last couple of years had to be dragged kicking and screaming to the doctor, never mind the ER. This Alex just released a breath and gave a subtle nod. Either this was a sign that the man in front of me wasn't really Alex, or this headache was bad enough to make even Alex think something was wrong. Neither option loosened the knots in my gut.

"Let's go then," I said softly. "Can you make it out to the car?"

"Yeah, I think so." He started to get up but groaned and lay back again.

"I can call an ambulance. That might—"

"No. I can make it. Just . . ." He swallowed. "Just let me lay here for a minute."

He was right, he made it. By the time he got from the couch to the car, he was near tears from pain, and I wondered a few times if an ambulance was a better idea after all. As he stretched across the backseat, though, it occurred to me that waiting for an ambulance would mean *waiting*. By the time the paramedics got here, we could have been halfway to the ER. That, and he was in the car now. No sense dragging him back into the house.

No paramedics, then. I turned on the engine and backed out of Alex's driveway. I drove as fast as I could without jarring him, cringing on his behalf whenever I had to make a turn or slow to a stop.

The whole way to the emergency room, neither of us spoke. Aside from the occasional groan, Alex was completely silent. A few times, I thought he might ask me to pull over so he could puke again, but he didn't.

In between worrying about him and watching the road, I tried to comprehend this whole situation.

A shifter? Alex? All this time, I'd assumed she was a woman. And she was. A woman *and* a man. It wasn't that I'd never known a shifter, or that I assumed every shifter was out in the open about it, but after two years together, I didn't know?

Part of me wanted to be pissed that she'd lied to me about it. Part of me felt guilty, wondering why she hadn't thought she could tell me. And the rest of me just didn't have a fucking clue what to think, what to feel, or what to do. Tonight was simple enough: get him to the emergency room and make sure he was physically okay.

But was he okay emotionally?

Could *we* be okay?

I shook my head and exhaled. All of that could wait. It had to. I glanced in the rearview, which I'd tilted down slightly. The passing streetlights flickered across him like an old black and white film, illuminating at split second intervals the hand draped over his stomach. The other hand was probably over his eyes, shielding them from the shards of light that threatened to worsen his pain.

I turned my attention back to the road. The headache was worrying in its own right. Alex was prone to the occasional migraine, including one or two that had knocked her on her ass for days. Never like this, though. Coming so close on the heels of some medical procedure with which I wasn't at all familiar, and putting her—*him*—in enough pain to warrant going to the ER without a fight, this one scared me.

This whole situation scared me.

☿ CHAPTER 2 ♀
ALEX

Lying on the hard bed in the emergency room, I breathed as slowly and deeply as I could. The lights were off and I was alone, and with every breath, the nausea and headache receded ever so slightly.

This wasn't a migraine. The pain was similar—a couple of white-hot blades digging in behind my eyes and trying to pry off the top of my skull while a steel band wrapped tighter and tighter around my head—but I'd never experienced anything so intense. Light, noise, movement, everything made it worse. Sitting up? Agony. Standing up? Kill me.

For the moment, at least, everything was still and quiet. The triage nurse had taken me back to a room immediately once Damon told her what was wrong. Thank God. Another minute in the waiting area with all its lights and sounds would have had me on my knees and begging for death.

Meanwhile, Damon had gone to park the car. I cringed, and not from the pain this time. He must have been appalled. Disgusted. I tried to tell myself he'd understand. Eventually, somehow, he'd understand. The fact that he hadn't turned tail and run after learning the truth said something. Then again, Damon was the type who'd take a stranger to the hospital if he thought they needed help. That didn't mean he'd stick around once the danger had passed. He could walk away without worrying he'd abandoned me to a life-threatening injury.

Fuck. Why hadn't I told him? All this time. All those opportunities. Maybe if I'd told him sooner, he'd have been gone sooner. Months ago. A year ago. Long before I'd had a chance to fall for him like I had.

I blew out a breath. Go, me. The queen of making things difficult for myself.

A light tap on the door sent pain ricocheting off the insides of my skull. The door opened, spilling blinding fluorescent light into the room for a few seconds before once again shutting me into darkness.

"Sorry I took so long." Damon's voice was soft, and the relief it sent through me would have made me shiver if my body had dared move enough to allow it. "Couldn't find a place to park."

"Don't worry about it." My own voice echoed painfully inside my head.

"You doing okay?"

"Don't know yet," I murmured.

Something rustled softly. "They want you to put this on?"

I didn't look up. "The hospital gown?"

"Yeah."

"Probably. And when I can move without wanting to die, I'll gladly put it on. For now, no."

He didn't push the issue. A chair creaked and his jacket whispered as he got comfortable. Neither of us spoke. It was easily one of the most awkward silences that had ever fallen between us. So many questions, so many answers to which he was very much entitled regardless of whether or not I could find the words. The silence soothed my head to a more bearable throb, but it didn't do much for settling my nerves.

Another knock on the door made me flinch. Then the door opened again, letting in some of the light and sounds from the hallway before clicking shut and restoring the room to a tolerable noise level. Shoes tapped on the hard floor. Paper hissed across paper.

"Mr. Nichols?" The male voice was mercifully quiet.

I licked my dry lips. "Yes?"

"I'm Dr. Erickson," he said. "I understand you have a severe headache after an intraspinal implant?"

"Severe headache doesn't quite describe it, but yes."

"Can you sit up? I'd like to have a look at the implant site."

I groaned. "Would now be a bad time to mention that sitting up makes it hurt like hell?"

"That doesn't surprise me if it is what I think it is." He paused. "Can you shift onto your stomach?"

Shift. Now there was something I'd have been *thrilled* to do. I nearly rolled my eyes at my own thought. The throbbing in my head suggested that wasn't such a hot idea, so I concentrated on changing position.

I managed to get partway up, but the room listed violently, and when I grabbed the edge of the gurney for balance, more pain shot up into my skull.

"Easy," Dr. Erickson said. "Here, I'll check it as quickly as I can, then you can lie back again. Can you sit up a little more?"

Bracing against the pain, I did as he asked. The room spun and tilted and jerked, and I held my breath as the back of my head threatened to cleave right open. Something clicked. A handheld light, I guessed. I was distantly aware of him peeling away the bandage. There may have been some gentle pressure from his fingers, but the only pressure I was acutely aware of was above my neck and increasing by the second.

God, please, hurry up, please, please, this hurts so bad I can't fucking breathe. Please—

"Okay, go ahead and lie down again." He kept a hand on my shoulder and guided me back onto the gurney. "You all right?"

"Peachy," I muttered. "That's why I'm here."

He patted my arm gently. "Still have your sense of humor, I see."

I just breathed while the pain receded to a more bearable level.

Dr. Erickson cleared his throat. "Anyway, the incision looks fine. No immediate signs of infection, which is a good thing. As for the pain, you have what's commonly called a spinal headache. During the insertion procedure, the dura mater around your spinal cord was punctured, and it's leaking cerebrospinal fluid. The decrease in pressure from the loss of fluid around your brain creates a severe headache."

My eyes flew open for a split second before a flash from his penlight forced me to close them. "Come again?"

"It's fairly common after lumbar punctures and spinal anesthesia, and I've seen it on occasion with recipients of these implants."

"Can anything be done about it?"

"Yes, yes, of course," Dr. Erickson said. "There's a procedure called a blood patch. We'll take a small amount of your own blood and inject it into the same site. The clot will stop the leak, and the pain should stop shortly after, once the cerebrospinal fluid around your brain returns to its normal pressure."

On *so* many levels, that made my skin crawl.

Forcing back a fresh wave of nausea, I said, "It's not... dangerous?"

"The procedure?" he asked. "Or the headache?"

"Either, now that you mention it."

"No, the blood patch is a very simple procedure, and while the headache is extremely painful, it isn't life threatening."

I exhaled. "I swear, I thought it was going to kill me." Something in my chest sank a little. Jesus, was I *disappointed* that this thing wouldn't kill me?

Oblivious to the inner workings of my twisted mind, the doctor went on. "A lot of people feel like they're going to die with something like this, but you'll be fine. Once we get that blood patch in place and make sure you're in the clear as far as infection goes, you'll recover quickly."

"What about taking the implant out?" I asked.

"You just had it put in. Once the fluid leak is taken care of, you shouldn't experience any further discomfort. This is a side effect of the insertion procedure itself, so there's no need to remove the device."

"It's not that. I don't want it. I want it out."

He cleared his throat. "Well, it's not unusual to experience some regret after an elective procedure, but—"

"It wasn't an elective procedure," I growled through clenched teeth. "I wasn't given a choice, and I want. It. *Out*."

"You were forced to get the implant?"

"Yes."

He pulled in a breath. "That could be a problem."

"How so?"

"If whoever performed it was willing to do so without consent, then there's a good chance it wasn't done under sterile conditions. Back alley procedures usually aren't, so the risk of developing an infection, even if it looks clean at this point, is markedly higher than if it had been performed in a proper surgical environment. That, and there's a significant possibility the implant is one of the unsafe black market devices."

Ice water filled my veins. It hadn't even occurred to me that the implant itself could be dangerous. "So, how do I get it removed?"

"This isn't my area of expertise, but I can recommend a few neurosurgeons in the area. They'd know better than I would what the procedure involves." He paused. "Where was the surgery performed?"

"I don't know. I don't even remember leaving my parents' house."
Fingers tapped on a hard surface, echoing painfully along my
nerve endings, but it was Dr. Erickson's words that made my breath
catch. "You may not have left their house."

"What?"

"There are a few black market, back alley 'surgeons' performing
these procedures anywhere with a flat surface. I've had a few of
their patients come in with complications, including what you're
experiencing." Something made a quiet scratching sound, so I guessed
he was writing. "If it was performed without your consent, I wouldn't
be at all surprised if it was done under such conditions. With that in
mind, I think we'd be wise to admit you overnight."

"Great," I muttered.

"It's just a precaution. There are no signs of a problem at this
point, but I'd rather err on the side of caution. And as long as you're
admitted, we can also see if IV analgesics will help with the pain. Then
we can get you that blood patch first thing in the morning."

"How long will I need to stay?"

"Assuming no infection develops or any other complications,"
he said, "you'll most likely be discharged tomorrow afternoon with a
prescription for antibiotics."

"Even after having something put into his spine?" Damon asked.

"The insertion itself is a minor procedure. Alex should be back to
normal within twenty-four hours or so."

"Aside from the part where I can't shift, right?" I asked dryly.

"Right. Aside from that." He muffled a cough. "Anyway, I'll have
a nurse come down and take you up to your room. For now, just hang
tight in here."

"Don't think I'm going anywhere."

After the doctor left, Damon's chair squeaked softly. "Your parents
seriously drugged you, put this thing in your back, and then dumped
you off at home?"

I shrugged in the near-darkness. "I guess. I vaguely remember
coming around at my folks' house. Next thing I knew, I was at home.
My mom was still there. She said she was supposed to stay with me for
twenty-four hours to make sure I was all right."

"But she didn't?"

"I kicked her out."

"You kicked her out? Alex, what if something had happened while you were alone?"

Another pointless shrug. "Then maybe I'd be dead."

He didn't say anything. He'd seen me through a few depressive phases that had me teetering on a suicidal edge, and maybe he thought this could drive me over that edge. Maybe it would.

After a while, he asked, "I just don't understand why they would do this to you. I mean, if it's so painful . . ."

"I told you. I'm an abomination. They hate what I am. They're part of one of those crazy denominations that think shifters, gays, transgendered people—anyone who isn't heterosexual and static male or female—is hell-bound."

"What a lovely thing to think about your own child," he muttered.

"Tell me about it. They've spent the last ten years or so trying to save me from myself." I rubbed my forehead to soothe the relentless throbbing. "Remember how I told you I ran away from home a few times and tried to get my aunt in Los Angeles to let me live with her?"

"Yeah."

"This is why." I swallowed. "She's the most devout Catholic you'd ever know, has a picture of the Pope in three different rooms, but she's never said an ill word about 'my kind.' As far as she's concerned, God doesn't make mistakes."

"And your parents' sect believes differently?"

"Quite. They believe this was caused by sin. It's not God's mistake, it's ours. Or some bullshit like that." I scowled into the darkness. "On the bright side, at least they were considerate enough to do it on a Friday. Mom wanted to make sure I was recovered enough to go back to work on Monday."

"You really think you'll be up for that?"

"I have to eat."

"You have sick time."

"Which I should probably save up until I know how long I'll be down after getting the stupid thing out."

"True," he said quietly.

Silence fell. Fortunately, it didn't last long because a nurse came in to take me up to my room.

Though I kept my eyes closed the entire way out of the emergency room and up to the other floor, the trip was anything but pleasant. Worse than the drive in. Every sound—and, Christ, there were plenty of them—made the pain worse. Clattering wheels, beeping monitors, ringing phones, slamming file drawers, voices talking over voices. Quieter sounds I never would have noticed before added to the unbearable cacophony: clicking pens, shuffling papers, scraping chair legs, crinkling wrappers, rattling pill bottles. Fuck, I was in hell.

At some point, the noise faded. Then a door closed with a heavy thud and cut off every sound except the gurney's rattling and squeaking. A moment later, that too stopped. Something clicked, and a steady, quiet beep penetrated the stillness.

Beep. Beep. Beep.

On and on, while the nurse adjusted this or that machine, hooked me up to God only knew what, the beeping persisted.

Beep. Beep. Beep.

So this is what Chinese water torture feels like.

I took a few long, deep breaths to settle my stomach, and the headache slowly receded to something a little closer to tolerable.

"Alex?" A high female voice met my ear like the sharp end of an ice pick. "I just need to—" She stopped abruptly. Damon said something I couldn't hear. Then, almost whispering, the nurse said, "Oh, sorry, hon. Listen, I just need to hook up an IV and go over a few things with you about the blood patch procedure."

I nodded.

"Is there any way we could turn the lights down?" Damon asked softly. "I think he's still sensitive to light."

"Sure, sure, let me take care of that," the woman said. Footsteps tapped on the floor. Something clicked. Then her footsteps returned. "Is that better?"

Cautiously, I opened my eyes. The room was dim. Not dark, but not excruciatingly bright. It was long past nightfall, so no blinding beams of sunlight poured in through the windows.

"Does that help?" she asked.

"Yeah. Thanks."

Beep. Beep. Beep.

"I don't suppose there's any way to turn that off?" I asked.

"What?" she said. "The monitor?"

"Yeah."

"I can mute it." With a click, the beeping ceased. "Better?"

I released my breath. "God, yes. Thank you."

"Do you have someone who can drive you home after the procedure tomorrow?" The nurse glanced at Damon, then turned to me, eyebrows raised.

I looked up at Damon.

He cleared his throat and turned to the nurse. "Yeah, I can do that. When?"

"Depends on when the procedure is scheduled. He'll need to spend some time in recovery, but I would guess we can discharge him late in the afternoon. Give us a call in the morning, and we'll let you know what time."

"Sure, yeah, I'll be here."

A mix of relief and guilt twisted in the pit of my stomach. He wasn't deserting me, thank God, but was he staying out of pity? Obligation? I doubted he wanted to be the dick who ditched me while I was in the hospital in agony. Heaven knew he wouldn't be the first to walk away after finding out what I was.

Maybe that was why I'd never told him. Deep down, I knew he'd leave.

"Alex?" The nurse's voice pulled me back into the present.

"Sorry, what?"

"I asked if you'd eaten anything in the last twelve hours."

"Nothing that's stayed down, no."

"Well, we'll get some fluids in you to keep you hydrated," she said. "Nothing by mouth until after tomorrow's procedure, though."

"I'll live." I supposed I was hungry. Maybe. My stomach had been pretty busy kicking back anything I'd tried to eat since yesterday. Hell if I knew when I'd last tried to get anything down.

While she put in the IV, I closed my eyes. The light was as bearable as it was going to get. I just couldn't bring myself to look at Damon.

The nurse finished getting the IV going and fiddled with some of the various monitors. Then she left.

And there we were again, alone in this awkward silence.

Damon took a breath. "I, um, I guess I should let you get some sleep."

"I don't see that happening any time soon." My voice was more slurred than I'd expected. I forced my eyes open. "Who knows, though? This shit might be kicking in."

He laughed halfheartedly. "Well, do you want me to stay a bit longer? Or let you try to sleep?"

Don't go. "You don't have to stay." *Please, Damon, don't leave.* "Thanks for, um, everything."

"Anytime." He paused. "I'll get out of your hair, then. I'll be here to pick you up tomorrow afternoon. Call me if you need me to be here sooner."

"Okay, I will." *No, no, don't leave.* "Thanks."

Our eyes met briefly. He dropped his gaze. I looked away. Under normal circumstances, he'd never leave without a kiss, but I didn't expect it this time. Probably not in the foreseeable future, if ever. My skin crawled. Nothing quite like being something your own boyfriend wouldn't touch.

With murmured good-byes and fleeting eye contact, Damon left.

I closed my eyes and sighed. I couldn't really justify being disappointed. He'd stayed with me longer than I'd expected. Certainly longer than I had any business asking him to. The fact that he hadn't run for the hills—yet—was something I was grateful for.

Damon wasn't phobic of shifters, transgendered people, gays, or anything like that. Quite the opposite. He was good friends with at least one coworker who was a shifter, and he didn't bat an eye at the people who came to the everyone-friendly bar where I worked. I'd hoped a few times he'd get a clue from the fact that I worked there. Foolish me, when he'd asked, I'd said I liked the atmosphere.

I wasn't a dishonest person. Just scared. Once bitten and all that. And out of all the guys I'd dated, Damon was the one I'd been most afraid of losing. I'd sworn up and down I'd tell him, but every time I tried, I choked.

Come on, Alex. It's not like he's never heard of shifters. But then, anyone who hadn't been living under a rock had heard of us, even if we were a rarity. Plenty of people carried the gene but couldn't shift. Many shifters were completely stealth, living as one gender and shifting only behind closed doors. They told no one and didn't answer censuses with their true status for fear of persecution. And why would we? Fuck the census and everyone else if revealing ourselves meant being targets for torches and pitchforks.

Or repulsing loved ones.

Chances were, most people knew a handful of us without even knowing it. I doubted anyone at my day job had a clue about me. Oh, weren't *they* in for a shock when I came strolling in on Monday?

If I could have done so without causing myself more pain, I'd have groaned. Monday wasn't going to go well at all. I had one coworker who knew. And, damn it, I'd promised him and his wife I'd watch their kids on Wednesday night while they went to some church function. Somehow I doubted I'd be up for that. Hopefully they'd understand if I bailed on them this one time.

Hopefully a lot of people would understand a lot of things. One person in particular, though I wasn't holding my breath.

Between the pain banging around in my head and the guilt and fear twisting in my gut, I didn't expect to get much sleep. The painkillers had other plans, though, and I eventually drifted off.

I dreamed, and by morning, wished I hadn't.

☿ CHAPTER 3 ♀
DAMON

Fingers laced behind my head, I stared up at my bedroom ceiling. I hadn't slept last night because I was worried about Alex, and in spite of my body aching for sleep, tonight was shaping up to go the same way for the same reason.

Alex was safe for the time being. That headache had scared the hell out of me, and I didn't envy the pain she—he?—was undoubtedly in, but he wasn't in danger because of it.

Our relationship, though? Fuck.

I wanted to be pissed at Alex for not telling me, but I couldn't be. I knew too much about how society viewed shifters to be upset she'd kept it a secret. I'd known a few over the years, some who were completely out, others who confided in a handful of select, trusted friends. They took a lot of shit for what they were. I empathized, I sympathized, but how the hell was I supposed to handle this?

And what about between now and when the implant came out? Alex was a man. I could be there and help him through this, but I wasn't gay.

My own thought made me cringe.

No, Damon. What you are is a dick.

I rubbed my eyes and swore under my breath. Alex was still the same person. When the implant came out, she'd be able to resume her female form, but I wasn't sure how I felt about being with someone who was also a male. I wasn't sure how dual genders affected her sexuality. Did she need someone to satisfy her male side as well as her female side? I had no idea.

Sorting this out would be anything but simple.

At least she was more or less okay. Damage control on our relationship wouldn't be pleasant, but I'd rather sit through some awkward conversations than attend Alex's funeral.

I rolled onto my side and let that cold comfort, combined with sheer exhaustion, carry me off to restless sleep.

By the time I got to the hospital the next day with a double shot espresso in hand, Alex had already gone into the operating room. The nurse had permission to update me on Alex's condition, and apparently the pain had worsened this morning, so they'd gotten her—*him*—in sooner rather than later.

"Is that a bad sign?" I asked. "The pain getting worse?"

"It's not uncommon for spinal headaches to worsen," she assured me. "It's not dangerous, just miserable for the patient. Most patients come out of this procedure feeling much better, though, so hopefully it'll help him."

"Hopefully. Thanks."

"You're welcome." She squinted at something on her computer screen. "Oh, and it looks like he's in recovery now. The waiting room's a little crowded, so if you'd prefer to wait in his room, he should be down within the hour."

As she suggested, I waited in Alex's empty room, jumping out of my skin every time a gurney rolled by outside. Even if this was a relatively minor procedure, I was worried. Every minute that went by without Alex being wheeled in unnerved me a little more.

And who was I kidding? The prospect of any one of those passing gurneys being his also wound me up. I was nervous about seeing her. Him. About the conversations we needed to have. Would I say the wrong thing? Were things between us supposed to stay the way they'd always been? Christ, this wasn't going to fit in my brain.

Forty-five minutes or so after I'd arrived, one of the passing gurneys slowed, turned, and rolled into the room. Alex's eyes were closed, but there was a hell of a lot more color in his face today.

"Looks like you have a visitor," the nurse said to Alex as she pushed the gurney into place.

Alex opened his eyes, and when he saw me, his eyebrows jumped slightly. "Damon."

I forced a playful lilt into my voice. "Who else were you expecting?"

He started to speak, but then just closed his eyes and shook his head. "Didn't think you'd be here." He paused, then quickly added, "This early, I mean."

"Do you even know what time it is?"

He managed a tired laugh. "Now that you mention it, I don't even know what day it is."

"It's Sunday, for the record."

He looked up at me with wide eyes. "It is?"

"Yeah, it is."

"So much for my weekend," he muttered, rubbing his forehead.

"How are you feeling?" I asked.

"Tired, but a million times better than I did last night."

"Sounds like a good sign."

"It's a very good sign," the nurse said. "The doctor wants you to stay in here for a couple more hours, Alex, and then you can go home. Is there anything I can get you to make you more comfortable?"

"I don't suppose a scotch on the rocks is an option."

She laughed. "No, I'm afraid not." She patted his arm. "Just press the nurse call button if you need anything."

"Thanks."

The sedative they'd given him for the blood patch procedure had him fading in and out for the next hour or so. At least it was an excuse not to have a serious conversation. We talked about nothing in particular when he was awake. When he was asleep, I'd kick back with a magazine.

I also stole a few glances at him while he was out, searching his features for the woman I knew. He'd kept his hand over his eyes most of the time last night, and even when he hadn't, we'd been in darkness or close to it. Besides, I'd been too shocked last night to take in any details, so this was the first time I'd been able to really look at him.

Daylight illuminated a stranger who was startlingly familiar. If I hadn't known who he was, I'd have sworn he was related to Alex. A brother, a cousin, someone who shared enough DNA to have the same shape nose, distinctive cheekbones, and, I realized whenever he was awake, blue eyes. She was fairly tall as a female; I was almost six-two, and only had three or four inches on her. As a male, he was the same height—I assumed, since I'd really only seen him struggling to stay standing at all, never mind straightening up to his full height—and his bone structure was slightly heavier than his female form, but on the finer end of the spectrum for a man. Not feminine per se, but uncannily similar to the Alex I knew.

I couldn't decide if that resemblance made it easier or more difficult for me to comprehend all of this.

About the time Alex was coherent enough for us to stand a chance of dipping our toes into more awkward subject matter, a nurse came in with his discharge papers.

"Stay on your back as much as you can today," she said. "Take it easy, relax, don't push yourself. Tomorrow, move around as much as you're comfortable, but don't overdo it."

"This will be fun to explain to my bosses." Alex scanned the paperwork she'd given him.

"There's a letter in there you can give to your employer," she said. "And don't worry, the details of your condition are kept to a minimum. You can just explain you had a minor surgical procedure, and that should be enough. Tell them you had a lumbar puncture."

Alex arched an eyebrow. "Which my boss would probably buy if I wasn't saying it in a male voice."

The nurse stiffened a little. "Oh. Well, yes I suppose that could be a problem."

Alex made a dismissive gesture. "I'll figure something out."

When we arrived at Alex's house, I parked in the same place I had when I'd come to check up on her last night. I tried not to dwell on how much my world had shifted—

Oh. Yeah. Nice choice of words. I resisted the urge to roll my eyes as I got out of the car and went around to the passenger side.

Alex opened the door and started to stand but faltered.

"Need a hand?" I asked.

"No, I'm good. Thanks." He stood gingerly, gripping the car door to steady himself. Once he was on his feet, he stopped, taking a few deep breaths before he closed the door and started toward the house.

"Is it the drugs or your head?" I asked.

"I think it's the drugs." He took another step and wavered slightly. "My head doesn't hurt. I'm just fucking dizzy."

"Here." I offered my elbow.

He met my eyes, probably weighing whether or not to accept. The need for balance evidently won over pride, because he put his hand on my elbow. "Thanks."

On the porch, I pulled my keys out of my pocket and found Alex's house key. He leaned against the railing while I unlocked the door, and once we were inside, he started toward the living room.

"Don't you want to lie down in the bedroom?" I asked. "Might be more comfortable."

"This is fine. And at least then you can watch TV if I fall asleep." He lay back on the couch and sighed. "Ah, much better."

"Need anything?"

"I think I'm okay." He paused. "I could go for something to eat, though."

"They didn't feed you at the hospital?"

"Not before I went into the OR, no."

"That's probably why you're so dizzy, then," I said. "I don't care what they say, an IV is not a substitute for the real thing."

"No, it isn't, but have you seen the shit they serve in hospitals?" He wrinkled his nose.

I laughed. "I'll give you that. I'd take airline food over hospital food any day."

"I don't know if I'd go that far, but right now, I could seriously go for some kind of food." He started to get up.

"Wait. Why don't you just relax for a minute, and I'll go make us something to eat. What are you in the mood for?"

He hesitated, then settled back onto the couch. "Anything that doesn't smell like a hospital."

"That narrows it down."

"I don't know." He shrugged. "Nothing too crazy. Just a sandwich or something."

"That's not too much for your stomach? After the drugs and not eating?"

"Only one way to find out."

I raised an eyebrow.

Alex laughed quietly. "I'm kidding. I'll be okay. My stomach's fine."

I chuckled and shook my head. Then I went into the kitchen. I knew my way around, so I got out everything I needed to make a couple of ham and cheese sandwiches.

While I made our food, I looked around the kitchen and dining room that had long ago become familiar, taking them in as if for the first time. If the situation had been reversed, if I'd known Alex as a man the first time I'd set foot here, nothing about the house would have tipped me off that a woman lived here. Not that women were required to have frilly, flowery decor while men were forbidden from anything without an NFL logo on it, but everything in Alex's house—from the furniture to the simple decorations—was as neutral as it could possibly be.

Every appliance in the kitchen was black or stainless steel, and there wasn't a single adornment except for a couple of newspaper comics under pizza delivery magnets on the refrigerator. In the living room where he was waiting for me, several large prints hung in simple black frames on the stark white walls. The images themselves were photos of wolves, something Alex loved and, as an added bonus, her mother hated. Besides the wolves, the walls were mostly bare.

There were few decorations on shelves or tables. It wasn't an aversion to clutter; God knew Alex and I were both the types who let old mail and "I'll get to it eventually" paperwork stack up on counters and desktops. I'd never paid a great deal of attention to the way she dressed, but now that I thought about it, most of her clothing was as neutral as her house. Jeans and T-shirts, slacks and polos. If there'd been any distinctly male clothing in her closet, either it blended in with her other clothes, or I'd simply never noticed.

Scrutinizing the whole picture, I realized there was very little on display to tip anyone off about Alex's personality.

Or, more to the point, gender. Genders.

It made me wonder what other lengths she'd gone to over the years to keep her identity a secret. She'd fooled me. I'd spent countless nights here over the last two years, and I'd never seen anything to hint that a man lived under this roof. I couldn't even begin to imagine what other details she'd thought of, what little tells she'd masked to keep them from giving herself away to me or anyone else.

And in the space of one weekend, all her efforts had been blown out of the water.

Sighing, I pulled two cans of Coke out of the refrigerator, then picked up our sandwiches and went back into the living room.

Alex sat up. "You're a lifesaver."

I handed him a plate and a soda. "Shouldn't you stay on your back?"

"I'll manage for a few minutes." He popped open the can. "No point in choking to death trying to eat lying down, right?"

I laughed. "I suppose not."

After he'd taken a few bites, he washed it down with some Coke. Then he closed his eyes and exhaled. "My God, I needed that. I didn't realize how hungry I was until now." He looked at me, a shy smile pulling at his lips. "Thanks, by the way. For everything."

"No problem."

Neither of us spoke for a moment. A million questions hung in the air. There was so much we needed to discuss, but we were both exhausted. He was still recovering physically. The doctor had told him to take it easy, and upsetting him wouldn't do any good. Best not to go there just yet. Not until he'd recovered and we'd both gotten some sleep.

Right, Damon. Just keep on rationalizing.

This was certainly nothing new. Alex and I were experts at avoiding conversations about difficult topics. The two of us could pretend a room wasn't on fire if discussing it was too uncomfortable.

I took a drink, then set the can on a coaster. "I'm kind of curious about what happened. Your folks just invited you over, drugged you, and blindsided you with this implant?"

Nodding, Alex scowled. "They asked me to come over to talk about some things like they always do." He rolled his eyes. "Because that always goes so well. Definitely should've known something was up when their asshole pastor showed up. Anyway, I guess they put something in my drink, and good night, Alex."

"Who put the implant in?"

Alex shrugged. "The pastor, maybe? I'm not really sure. He thinks he's a master faith healer, so God knows what else he thinks he can do."

"Unreal," I said. "I just can't believe a parent would force their adult child to get any kind of medical procedure like that."

"They've been after me to get this thing for the last few years. Ever since it's been available." He shook his head. "Thank God my sister's static. She'd have had an implant the day they hit the market." Alex shuddered.

"Are the implants . . . dangerous?"

"Don't know. I've never taken the time to read up on them. I don't want one—no shifter I know wants anything to do with them—so it didn't seem like something I needed to know about." Just before he took another bite of his sandwich, he added, "Famous last words, right?"

I shivered. "What I really don't get is how your folks think, regardless of how they feel about you being a shifter, that they can make this decision for you. You're an adult."

"They did, didn't they?"

"Well, yeah, but legally? And, my God, ethically?"

He gave a sniff of sarcastic laughter. "I'm an abomination, Damon. A freak. The law, what I want, all those things are irrelevant." He took another bite of his sandwich. After a moment, he sighed. "I guess I shouldn't have put this sort of thing past them. I figured they'd keep twisting my arm, but I never thought they'd take it this far."

"Why did you even go over there? You said yourself it never goes well." *And God knows I've seen the aftermath enough times.*

Alex sighed. "What can I say? Hope springs eternal. That, and they'd brought up possibly letting me see my sister. I haven't seen her in like three years, so . . ." He exhaled and ran a hand through his hair. "Don't know why I bother there, either. They've brainwashed her to hate what I am, so I have little doubt she hates *who* I am, too."

Both of us fell silent. I wasn't hungry, but I finished the sandwich anyway just to give myself something to do besides start the conversation we needed to have. When we'd both finished eating and my Coke was getting toward the bottom of the can, I sat back in the recliner.

"You going to press charges?" I asked quietly.

Alex tapped his finger on the edge of his plate for a moment. Then he met my eyes. "I don't know."

"Why not? That has to be assault and battery at the very least."

He gave a weak, one-shouldered shrug and absently played with the tab on his soda can. "But what would I gain? It's not like it would get this thing out of my back."

"Alex, they just forced a life-altering implant on you, not to mention—"

"Yes, I know," he snapped. Our eyes met—mine wide, his narrow—and I swallowed hard. Then he put up a hand and exhaled. "Sorry. I'm sorry; I didn't mean to bite your head off."

"Don't worry about it."

Our eyes briefly met again. Alex dropped his gaze. "I don't know if I should press charges or not. Like I said, what would I gain?"

"Well, they'd be in jail, for starters."

He twisted the tab on his Coke can around. "And my sister would, for all intents and purposes, be orphaned."

"Probably just as well, if they're as bad as they sound."

"The thing is, what's done is done." He snapped off the tab and dropped it into the can with a *clink*. "There's no reconciling with them now, so I'm not worried about severing ties. I don't care about getting revenge. Even if I was, they'd just consider themselves martyrs."

"Let them be martyrs, then."

"And what about Candace? She'd end up in foster care or something."

"Better than being raised in that house, I would think."

Alex sighed. "Yeah, I know. I'm torn about it. I know she's better off miles away from them and their bullshit, but I'm worried about shaking up her entire life like that. The kid's sixteen. She's got enough crap to deal with."

I leaned forward, resisting the urge to reach across the divide and put a reassuring hand on his knee. "Your parents should've thought of that before they committed a crime against their other child."

"True." He rubbed his forehead. At first I thought it was a frustrated gesture, but then his fingers moved to his temples, and he let out a low groan.

"You okay?"

"Yeah." He grimaced. "Still hurts a little."

"Why don't you lie down, then?" I stood and picked up the plates and cans. "I can take care of this stuff. You relax."

Alex didn't argue.

When I came back from putting our plates in the sink and the cans in the recycling, he had moved onto his back, resting his head on one hand.

"Better?" I asked.

"Much. And, hey, at least it isn't nearly as bad as it was before."

"There is that." As I took my seat again, I said, "Well, better or not, the doc says you're stuck with me for the next few hours."

"Can't promise much conversation."

"Don't worry about it." *Even if conversation is exactly what we need right now.* "Besides, I think the game's on."

"Is it? Crap, it *is* Sunday, isn't it?"

"Yep."

"What a way to spend the weekend," he muttered. "Want me to put it on?"

"If you want to watch it."

"Like you have to ask."

We both laughed. In the back of my mind, I wondered if Alex's love of football should have been a clue. Except of course, women liked sports, too, for God's sake. My Steelers-obsessed mother and Yankees-loving sister could attest to that.

Alex reached for the remote but paused and looked at me. "Thanks again for helping me out. And sticking around."

"No problem. I wasn't going to leave you high and dry."

We held eye contact for a few seconds, letting another opportunity to discuss the situation slip through our fingers. It was Alex who finally broke away, turning his attention back to getting the remote off the coffee table.

"What channel is the game on?" he asked.

"Four, I think."

He clicked on the TV and changed it to channel four.

The game had just started, so we watched it and let the room keep burning down around us.

CHAPTER 4

ALEX

My eyes fluttered open. I flinched in anticipation of sharp pain, but it didn't come. The headache had long since faded to a vague, annoying throb, and besides, the living room was dark. I smiled to myself, basking in relatively pain-free bliss. I actually felt almost human. *Almost.*

Without the painkillers in my system, my dreams hadn't been as weird, but they'd been clearer, more vivid, and the cold sweat dampening the back of my neck made me shiver. I was still exhausted. What the headache hadn't taken out of me, two solid days of sporadic, restless sleep had. It was going to take coffee and a miracle to make it through today.

But at least my head didn't hurt.

I glanced at the DVD player. The glowing turquoise numbers came into focus and announced that it was a little after five in the morning. Damon was out cold on the recliner. I'd fallen asleep on the sofa. How in the hell had we gotten here? After wracking my brain for a minute, I remembered watching bits and pieces of the game with Damon yesterday. I'd drifted off sometime during the second quarter, woke up during the third, fell asleep again, and just barely caught the end of the fourth.

Football. Sunday. Fuck, that meant today was Monday.

I groaned. Monday meant working both of my jobs.

At least my boss at the day job would let me email in sick. That was one of his few redeeming features, and it would let me skirt the issue of calling in with a male voice. If the implant was removed quickly, then I'd just burn some sick and vacation time before waltzing back into work like this whole debacle had never happened. If it took time to get this thing out, then I'd eventually have to go to work as a man. The thought of facing that unpleasant music turned my stomach, and I prayed for the millionth time that the implant came out *soon.*

Slowly, carefully, I got up off the sofa. I paused to stretch, working a few kinks out of my stiff neck and back before I went into the kitchen to start some much-needed coffee. While it brewed, I slipped off to the bathroom for a quick shower. Hot water and my first cup of coffee slowly tugged me out of the two-day-old haze, and while I sipped my second cup, I tried to make sense of everything.

Until this thing was out of my spine, I had to accept that I was a static male. One gender, one body. No changing from male to female even when my mind changed, which it did frequently. Some shifters only needed to shift once in a while, settling into one gender the majority of the time. There were others who may as well have been static; they had the ability to shift, but neither the desire nor the need to use it.

I was about fifty-fifty. Half the time, I was male in both mind and body. The other half, female. Choosing between the two would have been impossible.

Which was a moot point now, since I hadn't *gotten* the opportunity to choose. My skin crawled. A hazy image of restraint and panic flickered through my mind, but I quickly banished it. The memory of what my parents had done was blurry, and I hoped it stayed that way.

Speaking of staying that way . . .

I shuddered. I only wanted to shift because I couldn't. What happened when I *needed* to? When my mind was absolutely, one hundred percent female, and I couldn't get out of this male body? Oh, God . . .

A thought crossed my mind and almost made me drop my cup. The doctor in the ER had said implants given under circumstances such as mine were often black market. How likely was it that the one I'd been given was defective? In the three days or so since this had happened, I'd been so caught up in the pain, I hadn't actually *attempted* a shift.

Maybe it was just wishful thinking, but if the surgeon was sheisty enough to perform this procedure in my parents' living room against my will, there was always the chance he was swindling them, too. Injecting a dummy implant. Maybe one that was badly designed or shoddily constructed. Or in an ineffective place.

There was a possibility, however slim, that I could shift.

I checked to make sure Damon was still asleep. He was, so I ducked back into the kitchen.

I took a deep breath. Closed my eyes. A familiar, cool tingle started at the top of my neck, creeping downward, and my heart pounded. *Please, please, please.*

"Fuck!" White-hot electricity shot down my spine and through every nerve ending in my body, and I grabbed the counter for balance as my knees buckled beneath me. A shift always started with that tingle, but this was like a power surge. A spike on the grid that threatened to blow out every lightbulb in every house.

Jaw clenched, eyes screwed shut, I held my breath and silently begged the pain to pass.

When I could open my eyes, I glanced at my reflection in the kitchen window to make sure my back wasn't really on fire, and I felt like a bit of a jackass—a relieved jackass—when I confirmed that it wasn't. I leaned against the counter. My knees shook violently, as did my hand when I ran it through my hair.

Note to self: Next time, google this sort of thing before trying it.

My attempt at humor didn't help much. I gritted my teeth, refusing to acknowledge the lump that rose in my throat. Having the implant was one thing. Knowing for certain, confirming it for myself that I couldn't shift, was nothing short of devastating. Half of my identity had been severed. Amputated at someone else's whim. Kept from me by what may as well have been an internal shock collar.

This thing had to come out. Whatever it took, it had to come out.

"You need it, son," my stepfather Gary had said last year. "So you can live a normal life."

"By whose definition?" I'd said. "I can't live a normal life unless I can shift."

Gary had glared at me. "If you're shifting, it's not a normal life. We've discussed this, and I'm not going to argue about it anymore."

"So we're going to let this subject drop?" I said. "You're going to let me live—"

"We can get a court order," my mother said.

"What? I'm an adult."

"And if the court deems you mentally incompetent," Gary said with sociopathic calm, "then the decision will be ours to make."

I'd stared at them, stunned they'd even go there. "This is insane. You would actually try to convince a judge I'm mentally incompetent?"

"If that's what it takes to get you right with the Lord," my mother had said, "then yes, it's what we'll do."

Clinging to my coffee cup in the present day, I shuddered at the memory of that conversation and a dozen like it. They'd dropped the subject of a court order three or four months ago. Now I understood why. I thought they'd given up on trying to force it on me. *Evidently,* said the dull twinges still smoldering along the length of my spine, *I was mistaken.*

I was lost in thought and halfway through my third or fourth cup of coffee when Damon shuffled into the kitchen.

I forced a smile and injected some nonexistent good spirits into my voice. "Coffee?"

"Please." He rubbed his eyes. "God, what am I doing awake at this hour?"

"Couldn't tell you." I pulled another coffee cup down and poured him some. "But we did crash pretty early, so, it figures that we're awake now."

"Hmm, yeah, you're right." After he'd had some coffee, he looked at me. "How are you feeling?"

"Human."

"That's a good thing, isn't it?"

"Very."

"Are you going to call in to work?"

"Yeah. No way I can go in like this." I sipped my coffee. "Still going to the bar tonight, though."

"At . . . the bar? They know?"

I nodded. "Yeah."

He was quiet for a moment, then said into his coffee cup, "Oh."

"Half the people there are queer, Damon," I said, trying not to get defensive. "That's why I work there. So I can be out."

He lifted his gaze, and I braced myself for a tirade about trusting them over him, but he just said quietly, "You're supposed to be taking it easy."

"I'll be fine."

"Alex, 'tending bar' and 'taking it easy' are not the same thing."

I pursed my lips. "Tabby will understand. She'll let me slack a bit."

"You really think you should be bartending right now?"

I slammed my coffee cup down. "That club is one of the few places in the world where I can go in as a male or a female and *no one* cares. Fuck taking it easy, I *need* that right now."

Damon set his jaw. Then he let out a breath, but he didn't speak.

"I don't expect you to get it," I said quietly. "I need to go there. It's just about the only place where I don't have to be artificially static to keep people from being disgusted by me."

"I'm not disgusted by you, Alex."

"And would you have been if you'd known this in the beginning?"

"I . . . No! Come on. You know me better than that?"

I eyed him. "Is that why you haven't touched me since you found out?"

Damon looked away.

After a moment of telling silence, I rolled my eyes and growled, "You don't have to answer that."

He glared at me. "Hey, this has been a lot to take in. Cut me some slack, all right?"

"Oh, *do* forgive me," I snapped. "I've got a chip in my back forcing me to lead what the rest of the goddamned world thinks is a normal life, and you think *you* have a lot to take in?"

He put his hands up. "What do you want me to say? I'm not suggesting this is more difficult for me. Not by any means. But, Jesus Christ, it's been a bit of a shock, okay?"

"Oh, I can only imagine," I said with way too much sarcasm.

Softer now, he said, "Did you not trust me?"

"What would you have done?"

"Alex . . ."

"Look me in the eye, Damon. *Look at me.*" When he did, I gestured at myself and fought to keep my voice steady. "What would you have done if you knew about this when we first got together?"

"I . . . I don't know. I don't fucking know." His eyes narrowed slightly. "You didn't exactly give me the opportunity—"

"Oh, sorry. I should have mentioned that to my folks. 'You mind holding off on putting this thing in until I've had a chance to tell my boyfriend? Thanks.'"

"For crying out loud, Alex." Damon gestured sharply and rolled his eyes. "You can't honestly expect me to digest all of this overnight. What do you want me to say? Are you telling me you wouldn't have been shocked if you'd come by my place the other night and found out I was a shifter? If a woman answered the door when you were expecting me?"

"Look, if you can't deal with what I am—"

"I didn't say that. I'm just . . ." He avoided my eyes.

"What?"

"I don't know what to think about all of this, okay? Up until this point, my primary concern has been whether or not your life was in danger. Unless you wanted me to wait to take you to the ER until I'd decided how I felt about you being a man?"

I started to speak, but Damon put up his hand. "You know what? I should go."

"Damon, let's—"

"We'll discuss this later. I think we both need some time to cool off first."

He didn't give me a chance to protest before he turned and walked out of the kitchen.

I gritted my teeth. *Fine. Go. Last thing I need is someone else in my life who can't see past what I am.*

The front door closed. My heart dropped. His footsteps faded down the walk. When his car door shut and the engine turned over, I released a breath.

Great.

I knew full well this was a lot for him. It was quite possibly as difficult for him to accept that I was a shifter as it was for me to accept that I was now static. Guilt churned in my stomach. He'd taken this better than I ever could have expected him to, and what had I done? Kept him at arm's length. Of course he left. I'd all but shoved him out the door.

Good one, Alex. Alienate him before he alienates you. That method has served you so *well in the past.*

I sighed, then finished my coffee and put both our cups in the sink. We'd discuss this later, once we'd both had a chance to calm down. For now, there was the more immediate concern of my two jobs, particularly my day job.

Drumming my fingers on the kitchen counter, I debated whether I should call in sick or try to fake it as a female. If I could pull it off, maybe I could keep from outing myself. It was worth a try, anyway. And it was something to think about besides Damon and the conversation we still needed to have, which was a hell of a bonus.

I went into the bathroom and flicked on the light so I could scrutinize my appearance. Within seconds, my resolve had diminished. This was going to take some work.

Women could have short hair, of course, but the way mine was cut screamed "male" to me. Other people might not have noticed, but I would. That was why I'd had it cut like this in the first place, and why my female form had hair almost down to my waist.

I narrowed my eyes at my own reflection. *Guess that's what I get for giving in to society's conditioning when it comes to gender.*

I sighed. Masquerading as a biological female, I could condition myself to accept my appearance, to believe I was really passing myself off as a woman, but it would take time. It would certainly be a while before I was comfortable going out in public appearing as anything other than male.

Then my heart sank a little deeper. No matter what I did to my appearance, there was no masking my voice. I could adopt a female voice in male form, but it was noticeably different from my true female voice. Significantly lower, a little gravelly. Of course, I could always feign a severe cold. Laryngitis, even. No one would be the wiser if I could fake my appearance, too. It was only a temporary situation, after all. Once the implant was out, I'd go female again, and no one would ever know the difference.

Worth a try. I needed some hope that I could keep my secret between now and whenever the implant came out.

I dug around in a drawer for a new razor. The closer I could shave, the better. I was tempted to go over my face twice, but having my skin break out or bleed from every possible angle wouldn't help matters, so once would have to do.

When I was done, I raised my chin and inspected every last inch of my jaw. It was as smooth as it was going to get. I scowled. Hopefully I could hide the rest under some concealer.

From another drawer, I retrieved some eye makeup. A little eyeliner and some eye shadow would help draw attention away from the harder, more masculine lines that, to me, may as well have said "male" in red neon lights. Maybe some mascara would help, too, as much as I hated the shit.

I uncapped the eyeliner and leaned closer to the mirror.

It was a damned good thing I'd never done a lot of eyebrow-plucking as a woman. I was blessed with fairly thin eyebrows anyway, in both forms, and gaining that perfect skinny arch was just not worth the pain of yanking hairs out by the roots. I had my limits where vanity was concerned. That, and it would be one more gender-specific grooming ritual to remind me whenever I was in the wrong body. Shaving my legs when I felt male or my face when I felt female was bad enough. Feeling male while ripping out hairs to look female? No, thanks.

I smoothed the eyeliner with my finger so the line wouldn't be quite so sharp. The shifters in ancient Egypt had it easy in this department. All sexes had worn enough kohl to negate any leaning toward the feminine or masculine. Then again, shifters had also been drowned in the Nile with some regularity, so maybe the kohl wasn't such a hot trade-off after all.

While I tinkered with makeup, I did a quick run-through of every detail I'd have to gloss over. I had a few friends who could hook me up with a wig at a moment's notice. A turtleneck, much as I hated them, would mask my Adam's apple and keep any leering coworkers from noticing a stuffed bra. If I didn't wear any jewelry on my hands, there'd be nothing to draw attention to them. I had several pairs of plain dress shoes that could be worn with a pair of slacks and pass for something acceptably feminine.

Resting my hands on the counter, I stared at myself, and the sinking feeling in my gut made my teeth grind. Concealer and foundation gave my face a smoother appearance. When I leaned closer to the mirror, though, the hint of coarseness was there. Also, I was still freshly shaved. I'd be screwed when my five-o'clock shadow showed up well before quitting time unless I wanted to chance shaving again in the ladies' room. Wouldn't that be an awkward moment if someone walked in at the wrong time?

This was pointless. Even with makeup, even if I added a wig, there was no fooling anyone who knew me into believing I was my female form. A stranger might have bought that I was a woman, but anyone else would catch on in short order that something was amiss. I might have passed for a sister or some other relative. There were enough similar features: high cheekbones, blue eyes, more or less the same nose.

Too many differences, though. Differences that weren't easily concealed. I couldn't hide the fact that my shoulders were broader and my hips narrower now. As a female, my bone structure was finer. Not quite as angular. More feminine.

More. Fucking. *Feminine.*

I winced and looked away from the mirror.

I might be able to fool a few people, but it didn't matter how convincing I was to anyone else. I could make myself up, fake my voice or a cold, step out as a female, and people might not notice.

But I would know. Every time I heard myself speak, saw myself in a reflective surface, or simply moved, I'd know. I'd know I was nothing more than a man wearing makeup.

I sighed and picked up the bottle of makeup remover. There was no playing a woman today, which meant I'd better find a way out of my day job. Tabitha, my boss at the bar, would understand what was going on. She was one of the few who knew I was a shifter.

Now, I *needed* to go back to the club. I wasn't kidding when I'd told Damon it was one of the only places in this world where I could go as a male or a female and no one would care. It was the place where I could shake off that otherwise omnipresent certainty that someone would *know* what I was, that they'd *judge* me, that I'd repel and disgust and repulse them. It was an oasis from the steady stream of bullshit that had come my way since I first let it out that I could shift.

First things first, though.

Once every last trace of makeup was gone, I went into my office and turned on my laptop. I ignored the influx of emails in my inbox and opened a new message.

Paul,
Woke up this morning with a nasty migraine. Not going to make it in today. Probably out tomorrow too. Will let you know ASAP about Wednesday.
Alex N.

I attached a return receipt so I'd know when he'd read the email, then hit "send" before I could overanalyze the message. I always worried too much about the wording of these things. Paul liked messages short, sweet, and to the point, so that's what I gave him. With situations like this, I was glad to write them that way. Fewer words meant fewer lines to read between. Fewer red flags that might scream *Alex Nichols is a man, for Christ's sake. A goddamned* man.

With the email sent, I went into the living room to find my paperwork from the hospital. Dr. Erickson had written down the number for the neurosurgeon, and I needed to see that neurosurgeon *yesterday*.

Before I could make the call, though, my cell phone rang. I looked at the caller ID and groaned.

Mom.

☿ CHAPTER 5 ♀
DAMON

After I left Alex's place, I had just enough time to go home, grab a shower, change clothes, and head off to work. I was still fuming all the way to the office, but I also felt like an ass. With everything Alex had on his mind, should I really expect much sympathy for having a hard time with this? I'd just discovered that my girlfriend was now stuck as a male, but Alex was the one who was stuck in that male body.

Time to get some advice, and fortunately, I worked with someone who was just the ticket.

My good friend Jordan managed the purchasing department, and it wasn't unusual for us to meet in his office. As soon as I'd taken care of a mountain of invoices and phone messages, I slipped out of my office and went upstairs to his.

I knocked on the door.

"It's open," came the voice from inside. So she was in her female form today.

I pushed open the door.

She looked up from behind her screen. "Morning, D-man. What's up?"

I shut the door. "Do you have a few minutes? For something that's not work-related?"

A smirk tried to appear on her face, but she must have seen the lack of humor in my expression and responded accordingly. She sat back in her chair and gestured at the one on the other side of her desk.

"Sit down." She folded her hands in her lap. "What's on your mind?"

I took a seat, resting my elbow on the armrest and chewing my thumbnail. "It's about Alex."

Her eyebrows jumped. "She okay?"

"Sort of." I exhaled. "No, actually. She's not."

"What's wrong?"

"Well, I mean, she's not sick or hurt or anything, but she's—" I paused to collect my thoughts. "For starters, I just found out she's a shifter."

Jordan blinked. "*Alex?*"

I nodded.

"And she never told you?"

"No. I had no idea. And now . . ." I reached up to rub the back of my neck. *God, when did my muscles get this stiff?* "Her parents forced her to get some kind of implant, and now she's—"

"They *forced* it on her?"

"Yeah. Drugged her."

"Utter fucking jackasses," she snarled with more fury than I'd ever heard come out of her mouth before. "Just who the *fuck* do they think they are?"

I shook my head. "No idea."

"Is she all right? No side effects, complications, anything like that?"

"So far, so good. The spinal headache was pretty bad, but that's taken care of."

Jordan grimaced. "Ouch. Has she looked into getting it removed?"

"She's calling a neurosurgeon about it today." I winced. "I mean, *he's* calling a neurosurgeon."

Jordan raised an eyebrow. "He?"

"He."

"So, he's stuck in male form?"

I nodded.

"Oh." She unfolded, then refolded her hands. "I can imagine that's making things complicated."

"Just a little." I fidgeted in my chair. "How much do you know about these implants, anyway?"

"Next to nothing. Don't want one, haven't bothered to look into them." She shuddered. "Even if I wanted to be static, I wouldn't let them near me with one of those things."

Something chilled my veins. "Why not?"

"Think about it. Would you let someone stick something into your spine, that close to your damned spinal cord? Look, if I don't want to shift, I'll just . . . not shift. I don't need to risk my ability to walk, for heaven's sake."

"Are they dangerous? After they're in?"

"I've heard . . . stories."

"Are you going to tell me any of them?"

"No, because I can't be sure which ones are tall tales and which are true." She waved a hand. "No sense worrying yourself over things that might be urban legends."

"True," I murmured. "Why would anyone get one of these things, anyway? Voluntarily, I mean."

She shrugged. "They think it'll make life easier. And for some, maybe it does."

"Really?"

"Being a shifter in a static-friendly world sucks, Damon. We can't even get decent medical coverage."

"You can't?"

"Heavens, no. Not full coverage, anyway. It's all set up for statics." She snorted. "You statics don't know how good you've got it. You don't have to decide at the beginning of every enrollment if you want to have coverage for mammograms *or* prostate exams."

"I can only imagine."

"You can't even begin to imagine, sweetheart, and what Alex is going through now . . ." Jordan shook her head. "My God, it must be hell for him."

"I guess that's part of what I'm having trouble with. It's hard for me to imagine what she's going through. I only know what it's like to be static. I don't know what it's like to be able to shift between male and female, never mind wanting to."

"It's not about wanting to, hon. It's about needing to."

I made a frustrated gesture. "Either way, it's not something I understand."

"No one expects you to get it." She sat up and rested her forearms on the desk. "Most statics have no frame of reference. No way to understand what it's like putting on high heels when your mind wants to be male, or getting a hard-on when you're itching to be female. And don't even get me started on the body having a period while the brain is male." She tapped her thumb on the blotter a few times, then went on. "It's hard to explain, but . . . well, you know that feeling when you've been wearing a pair of dress shoes half the day, and they start getting uncomfortable? And then they get to the point where they're so fucking miserable, you can't think of anything except taking them off?"

I nodded.

"Now imagine that pair of shoes is your whole damned body, and now there's an implant that won't let you take off those shoes. If I had to guess, *that's* what this is like for Alex."

I exhaled. "So what can I do? I feel so . . . useless."

"Just be there. Let Alex know he still has you, even if things are complicated between the two of you." She tilted her head a little. "How *is* this affecting the two of you?"

I shook my head. "I don't know. I don't . . . that's why I came to you, actually. I think I'm still in shock, to be honest. And I . . . I don't know what to do."

"Well, he is still the same person," Jordan said.

"I know. But for the time being, he's a man." Heat rushed into my cheeks and shame twisted in my stomach. "The thing is, I don't want to lose Alex. I love her. Him. But I . . . how do I put this?"

"You're not gay."

"I'm not gay."

"Damon Bryce, don't you dare leave him because you're afraid people will think—"

"No, no, it's not that. I couldn't care less what anyone thinks." I chewed my lip. "It's how I feel. What I think." Forcing myself to look her in the eye in spite of the heat in my face and the guilt in my stomach, I said, "Can I make myself be attracted to another man?"

"No, but you're not talking about 'another man' here. You're talking about Alex."

"Who is now a man. And has been a woman all along, I thought."

"You know me as both a man and a woman."

"Yeah," I said with a shrug, "but we've never tried to have any kind of relationship."

"Well, no. Think about it this way, though. It isn't like you've just met him. You've been with Alex for a long time. He's no stranger. You know him."

"I know *her*."

"Same person, different skin."

"Except do I really know him? After he lied to me all this time?" I made another sharp, frustrated gesture. "What else don't I know?"

She grinned. "Well, somehow I doubt he's Jimmy Hoffa, and it's a safe bet he wasn't the second gunman on the grassy knoll."

I laughed. "Okay, you know what I mean."

"I do. And maybe what you two need to do right now is declare the physical relationship on hold until he can shift again."

Wincing, I said, "I feel like a jerk asking him to do that."

"Why?"

"Because I'm basically telling him I'm not attracted to him."

"*Are* you attracted to him? Physically?"

I dropped my gaze. Cheeks burning, I whispered, "No, I'm not."

"Well, it's a cold truth, but it is the truth. And I'm sure Alex understands that more than anyone." She regarded me silently for a moment. "Can you still be attracted to her as a female, knowing what you do now?"

I hesitated. "Would it make me a complete jerk to say I don't know?"

She shook her head. "No. Attraction isn't something that can be forced, and something like this is bound to throw you for a loop, at least for a little while."

"Exactly. And the thing is, once he gets the implant out, this will still have happened. Alex will always be both male and female, even if he's stuck in a static body. I just, I . . ." I threw up my hands. "I have no idea how to feel about that."

"Well, don't expect to figure everything out overnight. But D, listen to me. Even if you can't deal with a romantic relationship or a physical one with a man, he needs you right now."

"And I want to be there for . . ." I watched my hands wringing in my lap. "I'm just confused, I guess."

"Well, sit down and talk to him. Maybe spend some time talking about his past. If his parents did this to him, they've probably treated him like shit for being a shifter."

I nodded slowly. "They have a pretty bad relationship, that much I know."

"Doesn't surprise me, especially if they pulled this stunt. The more you understand about that, the more it'll make sense why Alex didn't tell you before that she was a shifter."

"You're probably right."

"When will you have a chance to talk to him again?"

"Don't know." I pursed my lips. "We got into it this morning, and I left."

"You *what*?"

I smoothed the air with both hands. "We'll work it out. It was just a spat. I left before it—"

"Damon." She shot me a pointed look. "Whatever it was, you need to settle it sooner rather than later so you can both deal with more important matters."

I avoided her understandably accusing eyes. "We'll talk tonight."

"Good."

"Well, thanks for the pep talk," I said with a weak smile. "I guess I should go pretend to be gainfully employed for a few hours."

Jordan laughed. "Yeah, me too. And anytime, baby. You need to talk about this, you know where to find me."

"Thanks." I got up and turned to go, but she stopped me.

"One more thing, D." When I turned back, she said, "It says a lot that Alex stayed with you this long even when she was afraid to tell you what she was."

"What do you mean?"

"Most of us can't be bothered to keep up that charade in a relationship for longer than a few months. Work and friends are one thing, but not in a relationship." She paused. "In this day and age, it's easier to find a mate who knows and understands instead of wasting months or years with someone who will quite possibly leave once they find out."

I furrowed my brow. "So, what are you saying?"

"I'm suggesting that you must mean a lot to Alex," she said softly. "She kept who she was quiet because who *you* were was worth it."

☿ CHAPTER 6 ♀
ALEX

1:17 p.m. Twenty-four hours and forty-three minutes until my appointment with the neurosurgeon. Twenty-four hours and forty-three minutes that couldn't go by fast enough.

I tapped my thumbs on the sides of my cup, watching the ripples disturb the surface of my untouched coffee. The only warmth left in the ceramic mug was from my hands; the coffee had long since cooled. I didn't even know why I'd ordered it except to justify sitting at this booth. Maybe I shouldn't have ordered it. Then the waitress might have thrown me out of the diner, and I'd have had an excuse not to be here.

On the other side of the gleaming white table, the bench was vacant. According to my watch, it wouldn't be that way for long.

I'd been here for almost an hour. It was much easier to persuade myself to go through with this if I was already here rather than at home, pacing back and forth with every reason not to drive halfway across town for coffee I didn't want with the last woman in the world I wanted to see.

Staying home also meant being close to my laptop. The temptation was nearly irresistible to google this implant, its potential side effects, and what it took to get it removed. Of course I believed in doing my homework before having any kind of surgery, but I wanted to hear it from the horse's mouth first. No horror stories, urban legends, or false hope.

So here I was.

The clang of sleigh bells turned my stomach, and the air pressure changed with the opening of the diner's front door. *Just one conversation. I can do this.*

Steeling myself, I looked over my shoulder.

My heart dropped.

As I expected, my mother had arrived. Her presence had my chest tightening with the expected mix of anger and nerves, but it was the person who walked in behind her that startled me.

When my mother and I had spoken earlier, I'd agreed to meet her on the condition that my stepfather didn't come with her. She knew it wasn't beneath me to walk out if that asshole showed up.

Neither of us had mentioned my younger sister.

Shuffling through the diner behind our mother, Candace was every inch the teenage punk, from her raggedy jeans and well-worn rock band T-shirt to her black and purple hair. Her clothes were just snug enough to make me envy how comfortable she was in her own skin. She dressed like she had nothing to hide. A little extra weight here and there? Oh, well.

Our mother must have *loved* Candace's hair: shaved on one side, the rest either spiked or flipped to the other side. How my sister had gotten away with hair like that in my parents' house, I had no idea, though knowing her, she might've threatened to get a tattoo if they didn't back down about her hair. Candace never had been one to take our parents' crap. I envied her for that.

She kept her eyes down as she slid into the booth ahead of our mother. Even the fringe of purple hair hanging in front of her face didn't hide her scowl. It was hard to tell if this was just a typical teenage attitude or contempt toward a brother she'd been taught to despise.

"Shouldn't you be in school?" I asked, forcing some playfulness into my voice.

Candace's lips tightened, and she just stared out the window.

Our mother folded her hands on the table. "I felt this was important enough that she could miss a day."

"This is between you and me," I said through clenched teeth.

"This is a family issue, and she's as much a part of this family as you are."

I laughed dryly. "Gary's tropical fish are more members of the family than I am. I hope Candace has a better position on that particular totem pole."

My mother glared at me. Then her expression relaxed a little, and she changed the subject. "How are you feeling?"

"Ever heard of a spinal headache?" I growled.

She winced. "Yes, I had one after I had Candace. From the epidural."

"Then I don't need to tell you how much they suck. Especially after two solid days." I gritted my teeth. "Fortunately, my boyfriend showed up and got me to the hospital so I could have it taken care of."

She stiffened slightly at the reference to Damon. "I'd have been there to take you to the hospital if you hadn't thrown me out."

"Then it was worth waiting for him." I held my coffee cup tighter. "And thanks for putting me in a position to have him find out like that."

She narrowed her eyes. "If you lied to him, don't blame me."

"It was my business what he knew and when he knew it," I snapped. "And now I might lose him over it."

"Then perhaps this implant has solved two problems."

"What? What are you talking about?"

Her expression was icy, and after a few seconds of eye contact, I read between the lines.

Sighing, I ran a hand through my hair. "Right, because God forbid I be gay, too. You do realize Damon only knew me as a woman, right? The only reason we're in this situation is—"

"And when would you have told him the truth?"

My cheeks burned. Over and over, I'd kicked myself for keeping it from Damon just a little too long. "In my own time. Right or wrong, it wasn't your decision to make." I clung to my coffee cup again. "And what about going back to work? How am I supposed to handle that?"

"Should've thought of that before you pretended to be something you're not."

I released a sharp breath. I desperately wanted to lash out and let my mother have it, but Candace was here. She'd witnessed far too much of the hostility between our parents and me, and having her here as a captive audience tempered my anger. Or at least my displays of anger.

Keeping my voice a hell of a lot calmer than I felt, I said, "I wasn't pretending anything. I am a man, I am a woman. End of story. It wasn't your place to force me to out myself to people I wasn't ready to tell."

"Your dad and I—"

"My *step*dad," I snarled. "Gary is not, and never will be, my father."

"Be that as it may, he is my husband, and as far as he's concerned, my children are his children. He cares about the two of you like you were his own flesh and blood."

"Now that I'm human in his eyes, you mean?"

"Stop it, Jason."

Rage boiled in my chest. "My name. Is. *Alex*."

"Not anymore." She glared at me the way she'd done when I'd misbehaved as a child. "You are a proper static now, so you need to let this nonsense go."

I pushed away my neglected coffee with both hands. "Forget it. I'm out of here." I started to get up.

"Wait." She reached for my arm but didn't grab on. "Please, don't go. Let's talk." She swallowed. "Alex, please."

I hesitated. Then I took my seat again.

"I understand this is hard," she said softly. "It's not something I ever thought would be easy, but I promise, I only wanted what's best for you."

I exhaled and stared into my cold coffee. That statement alone was why I'd agreed to see her, why I hadn't yet brought myself to file a police report. Why I couldn't bring myself to hate her.

Mom went on. "Do you really think we did this to hurt you?"

"No," I whispered. "I know you didn't." I forced myself to look her in the eye. "But I don't think you can quite fathom how much it did hurt me."

She dropped her gaze. "I'm sorry if you feel that way, but it *will* be better for you in the long run."

"How can you say that?" The anger didn't want to be contained now, but I bit it back anyway. "How can you possibly know?"

"Do you want to end up like your father?"

I stiffened. "An implant wouldn't have saved Dad."

Candace fidgeted, glaring at whatever held her gaze on the other side of the window. She batted the fringe of purple hair out of her eyes, but refused to look at either of us.

"It would have helped him," my mother said, oblivious to my sister's discomfort. "Being what you are and he was, it's not healthy."

"No, listening to everyone in the world tell me what a freak I am isn't healthy. An implant wouldn't have changed who he was any more than it's changed who I am." My voice tried to break when I added, "Being a shifter would never have killed me, and it didn't kill Dad."

"It wouldn't have killed you?" Her voice was suddenly unsteady and edged with anger. "Is that why I found my thirteen-year-old son on the bathroom floor with an empty pill bottle?"

I flinched. So did Candace.

Mom stabbed a finger in my direction. "Don't tell me you tried to kill yourself because Gary and I were trying to fix you." More fury crept into her voice. "We didn't even know what you were then."

"You didn't know, but I did," I threw back. "And I'd heard all the things you and Gary said about Dad. All of which were bullshit, and you *know* it."

She narrowed her eyes. "What your aunt told you about your father was a lie."

"Was it?" I met her glare. "So he made it into his forties as a shifter but suddenly decided it bothered him, and then offed himself over it? Coincidentally a year after he was forbidden to see his children?"

Candace folded her arms across her chest and focused harder on whatever was outside. God, it killed me to have her witness this conversation. They'd undoubtedly taught her to loathe the ground I walked on, so my presence probably repulsed her as much as it did my stepfather.

This was probably the last chance I'd have to have this conversation, though. I didn't think I could stomach another attempt at smoothing things out with my mother, so it was now or never.

I'm so sorry, Candy. Someday I hope you can forgive me for all of this.

I wrung my hands. "Mom, I don't know what I can do to convince you that Gary, your pastor, all these people, they're wrong about shifters. And you're all wrong about this implant."

"What do you mean? It made you static, as you should be."

I shook my head. "No. No, it didn't. My genders are up here." I tapped my temple with one finger. "Being a shifter just means I can adjust my body to match."

"That's nonsense. You were born a *boy*. You're a *man*."

"Sometimes, yes."

She sighed and pinched the bridge of her nose, but before she could speak, I said, "What is so wrong with shifting? There's nothing in your Bible about us. We're not hurting anyone."

"The Bible talks about men, and it talks about women." She gave an indignant sniff. "It does *not* discuss people who can switch back and forth like they're changing clothes."

"Then how can you be sure there's anything wrong with us?" I fought to keep my voice close to neutral. "You do know there's a theory that one of the Apostles was—"

"Watch yourself," she snarled. "That's blasphemy."

"Why? Because you don't want to hear it? It's not my theory, Mom."

Without turning her gaze away from the window, my sister spoke in a flat tone, "Jesus also hung out with a prostitute."

"Which is debatable in and of itself," I said. "But *if* Mary Magdalene was a prostitute, she wasn't born that way." I looked at my mother. "God didn't make her a prostitute."

"And sin made you what you were," she said. "But you're not anymore."

I exhaled. "Do you really think it's that simple? You have some crackpot doctor put a chip in my back, and suddenly I'm magically static? It doesn't change what's in my head."

"Which is why I think you need help." She was almost pleading now. "You need to see a therapist, and you need to do a lot of praying. What you were isn't *right.*"

I gritted my teeth. "Whether or not we can agree if shifting is right or wrong, it was my decision to make, not yours."

"You are ill, Jason. You have been for a long time." Her eyes darted toward my arms. Then she looked at me again and raised an eyebrow.

I self-consciously folded my arms on the edge of the table, hiding the silvery hash marks that scored the insides of my wrists and forearms. "What you did was illegal. Don't you realize you and Gary could go to prison for this?"

"What we did was right. If you want to press charges against us, go ahead, but we're right in God's eyes." She set her jaw. "Before you do, though, I hope you'll think about the consequences." Her eyes flicked toward Candace, then back to me.

My blood turned cold. So that was why my sister was here. Mom knew my weakness, my Achilles' heel. I'd been the protective older brother—or sister, at times—since Candace was born when I was nine. They'd forbidden me from seeing her for the last three years unless I agreed to get the implant, and more than once, it had almost worked.

If there was any leverage in the world that could persuade me for or against anything, it was my sister.

Go ahead, have us arrested, my mother said silently. *If you really want your sister to spend her last two years of high school bouncing around the foster system. We're all she has unless you take us away from her. Is that what you want, Jason?*

Mom, I swear to God, I will never forgive you for this.

When she spoke again, her voice had hardened. "I did what I had to do, and one day, you'll understand that. I'm your mother. I only want what's best for you."

And yet you'll use one of your children as a weapon against the other. "You're my mother, but you sure as hell haven't behaved like it since you found out what I am."

"I most certainly have. I've—"

"Have you? You stripped me down to nothing but a faulty, nonhuman *thing* that needs to be repaired."

"That isn't true. And if I have treated you that way, then I'm sorry. You're my son. I want us to be a family again." She rested an arm around Candace's shoulders. "All of us."

My sister's lips tightened, but she stayed silent.

"A family?" I forced back the lump that rose in my throat. "It's too late for that." I got up and pulled out my wallet.

"Jason—Alex, where are you going?"

"Hell, apparently." I threw a couple of dollar bills on the table to cover the coffee I'd never touched. "Good-bye, Candace."

For the first time since she'd arrived, my sister met my gaze. There was no expression in hers. No contempt, no sympathy. No anger, no sadness. Nothing. There was barely any recognition. My heart sank a little deeper. Three years and a lifetime of indoctrination, and I was a stranger to her now.

I turned to go.

"Alex, please, I only did what was best for you," Mom called after me. "I didn't want to see you tormented in this life or the next."

I stopped and looked over my shoulder. "Well, you know what they say about the road to hell."

And I walked out.

Instead of going home, I drove over to the bar where I worked nights. I was a couple hours early for my shift, but I didn't care. I needed to be here so bad I could taste it.

When I walked into the Welcome Mat, the familiar lights, sounds, and smells of the club shook some of the knots out of my shoulders. Any time life had me wound up—whether because of my parents, my day job, or being shoehorned into a static world—this place calmed me down. Today, more than ever, I needed that calming effect, and the club came through.

The Welcome Mat certainly lived up to its name. Everyone was welcome here. Gay. Straight. Bisexual. Asexual. Male. Female. Trans. Shifter. Static. Anyone and everyone, and Tabitha allowed staff members to eject patrons who were being assholes for *any* reason. The cops didn't help much, but we had some of the burliest bouncers on the planet with no patience for bigotry. Needless to say, people behaved here. Those who didn't were gone before they ruined anyone else's fun.

This place was my sanctuary.

Colin, one of the other bartenders, looked up from drying a glass. "Hey, Alex. You're early."

"I know; I needed to talk to Tabitha. She around?"

He nodded toward the back of the club. "In the office, last I checked."

"Thanks."

Tabby's office was open, so I didn't knock.

"Hey, you," she said when I walked in. She must have just gotten here herself. Her hair was pulled back into a messy ponytail and she was still dressed down in jeans and a T-shirt, though by the time the club opened for the evening, she'd be all cleavage and sequins.

"Hey," I said. "Can I talk to you for a few minutes?"

"Sure, sure."

"Sorry about the last few days." I closed the door behind me. "I hope I didn't leave you too far up Shit Creek."

"It's okay. I assumed something must have been going on." She leaned forward and folded her hands on the blotter. Her eyebrows rose. "Everything all right?"

Taking a seat in the chair opposite her desk, I chewed my thumbnail and avoided her eyes. "Not really, no."

"What's going on?"

I gritted my teeth, fighting to keep myself together. If anyone in the world wouldn't judge me for any of this, it was her, and with no reason to hold back, it was hard not to fall apart.

Concern widened her eyes. "Alex, baby, what's wrong?"

I forced back that stubborn lump in my throat, then took a deep breath. "Remember how I told you my folks were pressuring me to get the implant?"

Tabitha sat up straighter. "Alex, you didn't . . ."

"No, I didn't." I swallowed. "*They* did."

"What? What do you mean?"

"They drugged me. Forced me to—"

Her fist slammed onto the desk with such force I nearly jumped out of my chair. "Those cock-sucking, Bible-thumping, self-righteous *cunts*." Through clenched teeth, she said, "Tell me your folks are rotting in jail."

"No, I haven't filed a report yet. Against them or the surgeon."

"And just why the fuck not?"

"I should, I know." My mother's unspoken threat pushed down on my shoulders. "But I'm afraid of putting my sister through hell."

"Sounds like you'd be getting her *out* of hell."

"Doubt it," I muttered, recalling with a pang of sadness the way Candace wouldn't even look at me at the diner. "They've got her brainwashed."

"All the more reason to get her out. It'll be difficult for her, there's no doubt about that, but that doesn't mean it's a bad thing."

I raised an eyebrow. "It's for her own good?"

Tabby pursed her lips. "Yes, it really *is* for her own good. And, your parents aside, that surgeon needs to be in jail. That way he can't do this to anyone else."

"True."

"If your folks have to go down with him, so be it. This is on their heads, not yours." She leaned forward and gestured for me to put my hands on the desk. When I did, she clasped them between her own. "Alex, your sister may be upset with you for a while, and this will definitely be hard for her, but she'll understand. Maybe not now, but eventually, she will understand why you did what you did."

"And if she doesn't?"

"Doesn't change the fact that you'd be doing the right thing." She exhaled sharply. "I assume you're going to try to get the implant out?"

"As soon as humanly possible."

She grimaced. "I hear the removal isn't an easy procedure. And it's a pricey one, too."

"Great. And I have such a fantastic health plan when it *isn't* an elective, socially repulsive surgery."

"Well, maybe they'll make your parents pay for it."

"We'll see about that."

Tabby sighed and squeezed my hands. The fact that she didn't argue with me or push the issue, insisting the courts *would* make my folks pay for the removal, didn't make me feel much better.

"I have an appointment with the neurosurgeon tomorrow," I said quietly. "We'll see what he says."

"Yeah, keep me posted." She patted my hands, then let them go. "How are you feeling, by the way?"

"The first couple of days sucked." I fidgeted at the memory of my hellish weekend. "But I'm okay now. Physically."

"Do you need to take more time off?"

"I'm supposed to take it easy for a few nights, but I'd rather stay here."

"You sure?"

"I can't miss work. I need the money. That, and . . . I really need to be here right now, Tabby. And quite frankly, if I'm not working, I'll be drinking."

"You're welcome to stay, of course." A smile tugged at her lips. "Though I suppose you won't be dancing on the bar tonight?"

I laughed. "I'm afraid not."

"Well, damn," she said. "Colin and Dale will just have to handle it."

"Sorry," I said, chuckling.

"Oh, we'll manage."

I dropped my gaze and didn't speak.

"Something else on your mind?"

It was only when Tabby spoke that I realized how long it had been since the conversation had died. I chewed the inside of my cheek. "I don't know what to do about my other job. I have to go back eventually."

"Yes, I suppose that could be a challenge."

"To say the least." My shoulders dropped. "This morning I tried making myself up as a woman, just to see if I could pull it off."

She cocked her head. "And?"

"Didn't work so well. Made me feel worse, actually."

"In what way?" she asked. "Because you didn't look like yourself, or you couldn't make yourself feminine enough?"

"A little of both." I sighed. "It's just, no matter what I did, every time I looked in the fucking mirror, all I saw was a man wearing makeup."

"Oh?" Tabitha raised her chin slightly. She casually ran a scarlet nail up and down the front of her throat. When she paused emphatically on her Adam's apple, I cringed.

"Fuck. I'm sorry, Tab." I ran my hand through my too-short hair. "I'm sorry. That's . . . not what I meant."

"I know, baby. Just putting things in perspective."

"Yeah, but I didn't mean to insult you."

"You didn't. And I know the fact that I'm static doesn't make this any less frustrating for you." She grinned. "Besides, do you see a man wearing makeup when you look at me?"

"No, definitely not."

"Then I think we understand each other." She winked and sat back a little. "Maybe I can help you with tweaking your appearance if it's what you want."

"Nah, hopefully this thing will be out soon anyway, but I don't think any amount of makeup will make me look like my female self."

Her smile fell. "Probably not. Though you'd make a beautiful woman as you are now."

I laughed, heat rushing into my cheeks. "Thanks."

"I'm serious. You could do it, easily." She paused. "But I don't know if we could dress you up as *you*."

"How ironic," I muttered. "I could probably pose as a dozen different women, just not myself."

She grimaced. "Sorry, sweetie."

"It's okay. Hopefully it'll be a moot point soon anyway."

"True." She smiled, but it faded, and her forehead creased. "Does Damon know yet?"

"Yeah," I whispered. "He knows."

"He didn't take it well?"

"It could've been worse."

"That doesn't sound good."

I shrugged. "Well, we had a bit of a fight this morning, but..."

"But?"

I explained everything to her, from the moment he showed up at my door the other night to him walking out this morning.

"It was probably just, you know, stress and lack of sleep on both our parts," I said.

She tilted her head slightly. "I don't suppose there was a visit from the Alex who likes to shut people out when he thinks they're going to shut him out, was there?"

No point in lying. I was pretty sure the color in my cheeks gave me away anyway. "Yeah, maybe."

She reached for my arm and gave it a gentle squeeze. "Baby, that doesn't help matters. You know that, right?"

"Yeah, I do. And, I mean..." I paused, avoiding her eyes. "I'll call him after I'm off tonight. We probably just need to talk things over."

"Probably. And it does say a lot that he's still around. Plenty of other men would've been long gone."

"I know. Though I wonder if he just doesn't want to ditch me while I'm still recovering." Bitterness seeped into my tone. "Anyway, I'll talk to him. I don't know what'll happen, but we'll see."

"Yeah," she said without that note of optimism I so desperately needed to hear, "we'll see."

I cleared my throat. "You mind if I clock in early?"

"Not at all. Just take it easy, would you?"

"I will. Thanks, Tab."

"Anytime, sweetheart. Now come here." She stood and came around the desk, and when I stood, she hugged me. I closed my eyes, trying not to lose it. I never knew how much I needed human affection until I'd been at everyone's arm's length for a while, and now that she had her arms around me, it was all I could do not to break down and cry.

"This is going to be a bumpy ride," she said softly, stroking my hair. "But you will get through it, baby. And you know I'm always here if you need me."

"Thank you," I whispered.

She released me, but kept her hands on my shoulders. "Sure you want to work tonight?"

I sniffed, then smiled. "Yeah. Nothing like making you some money to take my mind off things."

"That's the spirit." She flashed a huge grin. "Now get out there and make me rich."

I saluted her, and she smacked my arm. In a somewhat better mood than before, I left her office and clocked in.

Even if I couldn't be comfortable in my own skin, at least I was comfortable in this crowd. It'd be better if it were busier, though. Late at night, I'd be shaking martinis, pouring tequila shots, opening beers, lighting Bacardi 151 and dropping it in Guinness for some Depth Charges, cleaning glasses and the bar top and more glasses. On the other hand, that was probably more than I should've been doing with the lingering twinge in my back. This early in the day, though, more chairs were empty than not.

When the door opened, sunlight poured in, backlighting the newcomer and making me squint. Once the door closed, severing the light and returning the bar to its usual dimness, the bottle of Triple Sec in my hand nearly tumbled to the bar.

Damon.

Our eyes met as he approached the bar. I focused on pouring my customer's drink. Once I was done, I moved to the barstool Damon had taken.

"Hey," he said.

I moistened my lips. "Hey."

He swallowed hard. "Listen, can we talk? About, um, about everything?"

"Yeah, I . . ." I glanced to one side and caught Tabby's eye. She nodded and gestured toward the door. I turned back to Damon. "I'll get my jacket."

☿ CHAPTER 7 ♀
DAMON

fter he'd clocked off and grabbed his jacket, Alex and I walked down the block to a restaurant we'd visited a million times in our past life. Neither of us spoke on the way down the sidewalk. The hostess was familiar with me, and she smiled when we came in. "Just one?"

I gestured at Alex. "No, two."

Her brow furrowed slightly, a hint of confusion registering in her expression as she looked at him, then me, then him again. It occurred to me that Alex and his coworkers came here a lot, too. We were both regulars, she knew our names, but she'd never seen us together. Well, not that she knew of, anyway.

But she didn't say anything about it.

"Right this way." She showed us to a booth by the window, took our drink orders, and left us to our silence. We both focused on perusing the menu, as if we hadn't memorized it eons ago, until she came back with our coffee.

Stirring some cream into mine, I finally spoke. "How are you feeling?"

He shrugged. "I've been better, but I'm not as bad off as I was the other night."

"That's good to hear." I stared into my coffee, unsure what else to say.

This time it was Alex who broke the silence. "Look, I know this is a lot to take in, and I'm sorry. About what I said this morning."

"It's okay. I should have been more patient. You have a lot to deal with."

"Okay, instead of arguing about who's sorrier like we always do," he said with a hint of a grin, "why don't we just agree to forget this morning happened?"

I laughed. "Deal." I had no idea how many squabbles we'd resolved this way. Squabbles were one thing, though. We still had plenty of other things to iron out, and hell if I knew where to start. "I'll be honest, Alex, I don't know how I feel. About any of this."

"I don't expect you to. It's . . . a lot." He rested an elbow on the table and rubbed his forehead with two fingers. "And if you're thinking you don't know how to handle a relationship, or you're barely keeping yourself from running for the hills, I understand that, too."

"I haven't run yet, have I?"

He looked at me. "You're a straight guy, Damon. As of two days ago, surprise! I'm a man. I'd be stupid to expect you to act like nothing's changed because of that."

I dropped my gaze. What could I say? After a moment, I met his eyes again. "So what do we do?"

Alex shook his head. "I don't know. I mean, presumably this isn't a permanent situation. Me being static, anyway. Once I get the implant out, I suppose we can play things by ear." He paused. "If you're . . . still okay with, you know, us."

"Playing by ear sounds good."

"And once the implant's out, at least I can be female again. Thank *God*."

"Is it . . ."

He raised his eyebrows. "Hmm?"

I took a deep breath. "Forgive my ignorance here, okay? I've talked to a few shifters, but I've never really . . . asked about it."

"Go ahead and ask. At this point, I think you're entitled to some answers."

Fidgeting a little, I searched for the words, hoping I could ask without sounding like the idiot I was. "So, do you just shift on a whim? Or, what?" Of course Jordan had answered that for me, but it was the only way I could think of to get the conversation rolling.

"Not on a whim, no." He folded his arms on the table. "Some days, I feel a hundred percent female. Through and through. Other days, male. And sometimes, I'm somewhere in the middle."

"What do you do then? When you're in the middle?"

Alex watched his finger trace a path around the rim of his coffee cup. "Sometimes I'll be in female form but dress kind of, I don't know, tomboyish. I don't usually go the man-dressed-feminine route."

"Why not?"

His cheeks colored slightly. "I'm more self-conscious that way. Feels more . . . conspicuous."

"How so?"

"Well, what stands out more to you? A woman in jeans and a baseball cap, or a man in a skirt?"

"Good point."

He sighed. "Social conditioning sucks, but . . . it is what it is. People are less willing to accept a feminine man than a masculine woman. It's hard to break that habit, I guess. Shoehorning myself into cultural standards."

"I never really thought about it, to be honest."

"Most statics don't. There's no reason to." He paused. "At least I can shift. Well, *could*. Tabitha, some of the other people at work, they'd chew off their own arm to be able to shift. They have to make do with whatever artificial alterations they can manage. Some get surgery, some don't. Tabitha won't get any of the surgeries until they're safer and more effective, not to mention less expensive. She has to make do with hormones and things like that." Alex looked out the window, but I doubted he focused on anything. "I feel like an ass complaining that I can't shift anymore when there are people who'd sell their souls to be a shifter even for a day."

"Yeah, but sometimes it's harder to deal with losing something than never having it."

"True." Our eyes met, and something tightened in my chest.

I cleared my throat. "Right now, since you can't shift, do you . . . I'm not sure how to word this. Do you feel more male or female?"

"I don't know." He absently wrapped both his hands around his coffee cup like she often did, clinging to it as if to ward off some chill I couldn't feel. "Part of me is itching for my female form. Part of me is okay with male." He let out a long breath. "On the one hand, I'm dying to be what I can't be right now. On the other, I'm just glad the implant didn't fuck me up. Quite honestly, I'd leave in the implant and cut off my own balls if it meant never having another headache like that."

I blinked.

Alex tilted his head. "What?"

Muffling a cough, I went for my coffee. "Sorry. What you said, it sort of..."

His brow furrowed. Then he chuckled. "The part about cutting off my balls?"

"Yes. That." I laughed, my cheeks as hot as my coffee. "Guess that's another part, so to speak, that I hadn't thought about. Never really thought about how much actually shifted."

He laughed. "It all shifts, Damon. It's seriously like having two different bodies. A friend of mine? She has twenty-twenty vision in female form, but wears contacts as a male."

"Seriously?"

He nodded.

"So what happens if you have, like, cancer or something?"

"That usually crosses over, too." He pursed his lips. "In fact, shifting seems to make tumors grow even faster. Something about the shift affects it on the cellular level, and ... Hell, I don't know how it works, but that's what I've heard. Pity it isn't the other way around, or they'd probably look to us for a possible cure, but since we're doubly fucked, we're of no use in that department." He sipped his coffee. "Injuries, though, they're pretty weird."

"How so?"

"Well, a fresh injury will carry over. Sometimes they even get worse. But scars? Check this out." He set his coffee cup down and turned his forearm up, then pointed just below his elbow. "Ever seen this?"

I looked closer. It wasn't like I had every inch of her body memorized, but I was sure I'd never seen that jagged scar.

"No, I don't think I have."

"You haven't. I don't have it as a female." He turned his arm again, but not before I noticed more unfamiliar scars. Thin, straight, irregularly spaced lines scored the inside of his wrist and forearm. I didn't ask. He didn't say. Instead, he leaned out of the booth and reached down to roll up his pant leg. "What about this one?"

I looked where he indicated, and damn if the two-inch, crescent-shaped scar on the inside of his ankle wasn't familiar. The sprinkle of dark hair around it and disappearing under his pant leg was new, but the scar, that I'd seen before.

I sat up. "Okay, that's trippy."

With a quiet laugh, he sat up, too. "Yeah, it's kind of strange."

"How the hell does that work, anyway?"

He shook his head. "Don't know. I've heard all kinds of theories about it, but no one's ever figured it out." Reaching for his coffee, he added, "Probably because no one bothers to do research on us unless it's to find out how to *fix* us."

"Go figure. And you can get the implant removed, right?"

"As far as I know. I have an appointment with that neurosurgeon tomorrow afternoon. From what I hear, though, the surgery is extremely expensive."

"You shouldn't have to pay for it. Under these circumstances, anyway."

"I shouldn't have to, but let's face it, I probably will. I highly doubt my insurance will cover something like that. Even if a judge orders my parents to pay, there's nothing that says they have the money to do it. The reality is, one way or another, at least some of this is probably coming out of my pocket. With the number of people having removals because of unwanted implantations, no one's exactly donating their services. Don't want to set a precedent."

"Money does make the world go round, doesn't it?" I muttered, recalling Jordan's comments about health care.

"Always has, always will."

"So what about—" I cut myself off. Was I being intrusive? Making him focus on something he didn't want to think about?

Alex traced the rim of his cup with his thumb. "Whatever it is, go ahead and ask. It's okay. I promise."

I hesitated, gnawing my lower lip. Then, "What about . . . kids?"

"What do you mean?"

"If you can shift from female to male, then . . ."

He watched me for a second. "Can I get pregnant?"

I nodded.

Alex focused on his coffee again. "No. We can get women pregnant, but can't have babies ourselves. It's . . . fuck if I know how or why, but there it is." Rolling his eyes, he muttered, "Would be nice if that meant no periods too, but being a shifter isn't exactly a genetic royal flush to begin with, so I shouldn't be surprised."

I wasn't sure what to say to that.

Alex swallowed. "So if you want kids, they won't be biologically mine."

"Or at least not biologically yours and mine." I drummed my fingers on the table. "One or the other."

He studied me for a moment. We'd never gotten this far in our discussions about the future—if marriage was taboo, then kids weren't on the table either. Quietly, he said, "Is that a deal breaker for you?"

"No," I said without hesitation. "Not at all."

Alex held my gaze, then lowered his. He picked up an empty sugar packet and absently started playing with it. Goose bumps prickled my skin as I watched his fingers roll the packet like a tiny cigarette.

Then he unrolled it.

Flipped it over.

Rolled it the other way.

Just like I'd seen her do countless times.

A subtle habit, something he probably didn't even think about, but it was like I was noticing all the things I didn't know I noticed about Alex.

His fingers stopped. I looked up and realized he was watching me. "What?" he said.

"Oh, uh, nothing." I gestured at the packet. "I guess I've seen you do that a few times."

He looked down at his fingers, turning the half-rolled packet back and forth as if he didn't even realize it was in his hand. Then he flicked it away. "Habit, I guess."

"Yeah." I picked up my coffee. "I noticed."

"I'm still me, you know. All the little habits and mannerisms, they carry over."

"So I'm gathering." I chewed my lip. "Okay, I've been wracking my brain about this. How exactly do we deal with us? With our . . . physical relationship?"

"Depends," he said softly. "Until the implant comes out, I'm a guy. If you want to rein it back until I can shift to female again, I'll understand."

"I feel like an ass for—"

"Damon." He leaned forward and lowered his voice a little. "I understand. I really do. It would be like me forcing myself to be with a woman."

"You're not into women? As a male, I mean?"

"No. I'm not bisexual."

"Huh. For some reason . . ." I shook my head and made a dismissive gesture. "Something else I hadn't thought about." *I'm not a gay man, but my girlfriend is. Weirder by the day.*

He sipped his coffee. "Most people don't seem to realize that bisexuality is no more common among shifters than statics."

"Really?"

"We shift genders, Damon. I'm the same person whether I'm male or female. Changing gender doesn't change who I'm attracted to. Naturally, I don't expect your attraction to change when my gender does."

"Except you're still the same person. I feel like I'm . . . rejecting you. And I feel like an ass for it."

"You're not. I understand." He took another sip and set the cup down. "Besides, this is only temporary. Once the implant is out, then I'll have my female form back."

"How does it work, then? In a relationship? Especially if a couple is living together?"

Alex shrugged. "Whatever's comfortable. Some couples sleep together without being intimate. Some have separate rooms. And, some have open relationships. That way, the shifter gets to satisfy the libido on both sides without making the static take one for the team."

"Seems like being with a bisexual static or another shifter would be ideal."

"In theory. But not all bisexuals are interested in shifters. Or attracted to both forms of one shifter." He ran his finger around the rim of his mug. "That, and who's to say he won't be in the mood for a woman on a night when his significant other wants to be male? Ditto with another shifter."

"Wow. Sounds complicated."

"You have no idea."

"I think I'm catching on." I folded my arms on the edge of the table. "Have you been with anyone who knew from the get-go you were a shifter?"

"A few. In one case, it was a mistake with a static, bisexual boyfriend. The only thing more aggravating than being rejected for it is being treated like a novelty sex toy."

I cocked my head. "A novelty sex toy?"

"Yeah. Some people are attracted to shifters in the same way they like bi women. They assume we're perfect for threesomes because we can please everyone." He rolled his eyes again. "My ex was like that. He was an ass anyway, which had nothing to do with being static, bisexual, or anything. He was just an ass."

"And what about others? Who thought you were static?"

He pursed his lips. "There've been a few. I've been a boyfriend, I've been a girlfriend, I've been both." He met my eyes and must have seen the question in them, because he added, "Yes, I've had sex as both a man and a woman."

"That was something else I was kind of curious about, actually."

"In what way?"

"You said something about living arrangements that some couples have, but if . . . if you were in a relationship with a static who wasn't bi, how would something like that work for you? Sexually?"

"You mean, can I be satisfied if my partner only wants to sleep with me in one form?" One eyebrow lifted slightly. *We're talking about you, aren't we?*

I cleared my throat. "Yeah. That."

His hands closed around his coffee cup again, another soft echo of the woman I knew. "I can be happy that way, yes. The desire's still there, but . . ." He shrugged with one shoulder. "I can manage."

"But ideally, you'd want it both ways."

His eyes locked on mine. "In a perfect world, yes."

I took a breath. "Listen, I do want to make this work, but it's a lot. Just give me some time to settle into it. Get it through my head."

He nodded. "I understand. I'm sorry you had to find out the way you did. That was never my intention."

I hesitated. "Answer me honestly. Why didn't you tell me?"

"Answer *me* honestly." He locked eyes with me. "What would you have done if I had?"

Shaking my head, I dropped my gaze. "I don't know."

Alex sat up a little, and in spite of my nerves, I looked at him again.

"The thing is, I didn't think this was going to go anywhere in the beginning. Neither of us did. So it didn't matter." He rubbed the back of his neck and sighed. "Then things started getting serious. The longer I went without telling you, the worse I felt about it, and the harder I thought you'd take it. I was scared of losing you, and I felt guilty for lying to you, and . . ." He made a frustrated gesture. "If I'd known this would happen, I'd have told you a long time ago."

"Is this why you didn't want me to touch you sometimes?"

Avoiding my eyes, Alex nodded. "It wasn't you." He chewed his lower lip. "Those were the times when I wanted to be in my male form so fucking badly, and the thought of having sex as a female . . ." He shuddered. "It wasn't that I didn't want you. I wanted you . . ." Drawing a deep breath, he looked at me. "I wanted you those nights, I swear it, but like this." He gestured at himself. "I was afraid to tell you, and I couldn't bring myself to pretend I felt anything close to female those nights." He wrapped his hands around his coffee cup again, and when he spoke again, I could *just* hear him over the restaurant noise. "There are times when the sound of my own voice makes me sick to my stomach."

"Which is why you always got quiet when you were depressed."

"Yeah. I'm sure you thought I was shutting you out. I wasn't."

"I understand now." More uncomfortable silence set in around and between us. Desperate for something to keep the conversation going, but in a different direction, I said, "I've noticed most shifters have fairly neutral names. Like yours. Was that just luck of the draw, or . . .?"

"Most of us choose our names. Something neutral so it doesn't tell people our birth gender. Otherwise, we start catching hell for not behaving *correctly*."

"What *is* your real name?"

Alex raised an eyebrow. "My real name, or the one my parents gave me?"

"Point taken. The one your parents gave you."

"Jason." His lips tightened like the word was sour on his tongue.

"So you were born a male?"

He nodded. "Yeah, and I haven't dared set foot in my parents' house as a female since I was a teenager, so I was male when I went over there to talk to them the other day." He raised his coffee cup in a sarcastic mock salute. "And now I get to stay that way."

"That must have been awful as a kid, having to hide half your identity from your parents."

"It sucked. Once my folks found out I was a shifter, it was pure hell." He clicked his tongue and laughed bitterly. "But then, I think that's par for the course for any shifter in this society. This world is designed for people whose brains match their bodies, and fuck anyone who not only can, but *needs* to change from day to day or hour to hour. I'm supposed to be whatever makes everyone else comfortable. When does someone give a damn what I need to be? Oh, yeah, we're all cool with shifters as long as they do it quietly, never talk about it, and God forbid they ever fucking change genders. You ever tried to live up to the expectations of two separate genders?"

"Can't say I have."

"You're lucky." Alex shuddered. "Do you have any idea what it's like to look in the mirror and see something that's *that* mismatched with what you feel? It's like seeing a stranger's reflection." He paused. "I mean, imagine if you woke up one morning, looked in the mirror, and saw a woman. Tell me that wouldn't fuck with your head."

Considering I'd shown up the other night, looked at my girlfriend, and seen a man, I was starting to understand better than he probably realized.

He went on, and I let him vent. "So now I'm what everyone thinks I should be, and that's hell, too. The problem with being static is I can't be comfortable in my own skin. Ever. Even when I actually feel like a male while I'm like this, it's always in the back of my mind that there will be times when I need to be a female. It was bad enough before, when there were times I couldn't shift, like at the office or—" His teeth snapped shut.

"Or around me."

Alex nodded, cheeks darkening. "Yeah. But at least I always knew I'd be able to eventually. Now . . . now, fuck, look at me." He gestured at himself again, more sharply this time. "I can't . . . I'm . . ." He tapped his fingers on his coffee cup and sighed. His shoulders dropped. "I'm sorry, Damon, I didn't mean to go off on a tirade like that. I'm just . . . frustrated."

"I don't blame you." Today had certainly been an education. I'd never realized how difficult things really were for shifters, never mind what losing that ability would do to someone. I'd never realized a lot of things, and I still had no idea how to feel about it. About any of it. "I don't blame you at all."

☿ CHAPTER 8 ♀
ALEX

My appointment with the neurosurgeon wasn't until the afternoon, and I'd taken today off from my day job, so I drove down to the police station in the morning. Might as well get as much done as I could while I was off work.

When I walked in, a bored officer greeted me from behind a high desk.

"What can I do for you?" he asked.

"I need to report a case of . . . assault and battery, I guess."

"You guess?" He furrowed his brow. "Who's the victim?"

"I am."

"What type of assault?"

"Um, well, I'm not sure. Is there a category for surgical?"

His eyebrows shot up. "Why don't you come with me?"

He took down my name, and then led me back to what looked like a small conference room. There, he handed me a legal pad, a couple of forms, and a ball-point pen. "Go ahead and fill those in the best you can, and write out exactly what happened. I'll send in another officer to speak with you as soon as someone's available."

He left, and I started on the form and statement. Rehashing everything that had happened that night was painful to say the least, and I supposed it was a blessing that I couldn't remember the worst of it. Couldn't remember *most* of it, anyway. The details were hazy, but the fear, the panic, the sense of being violated by people I was supposed to trust—that was all vivid and clear. I shuddered and kept writing.

There was something weird about writing my parents' names and address under "assailant(s)." Part of me wanted to telepathically beg my mother's forgiveness for doing this. The other part—the one that kept me filling everything out—just wanted to send her a telepathic "fuck you."

My sister, though, didn't deserve any of this. *I'm sorry, Candy,* I thought with every word I wrote. *I am so, so sorry.*

The door opened. A uniformed officer stepped in and closed the door.

"Mr. Nichols?" He extended his hand. "Officer Daly." After we'd shaken hands, he took a seat across the table from me. "So, what can I do for you?" Instead of waiting for an answer, he picked up the legal pad to read my statement. As he read, he didn't bother hiding his reactions to any of it—raised eyebrows, twisted lips, cocked head—and something told me it wasn't my parents' actions that had him recoiling.

Then he set the statement down and took a breath. "Okay. Well. Um, do you have any ID on you so I can take down some information?"

"Yeah, sure." I pulled both of my driver's licenses out of my wallet and slid them across the table.

He picked them up, then handed my female license back. "Just need the one, thanks. Now, how is your life negatively impacted by having this implant?"

I fidgeted as I put my license back into my wallet. "Does that matter? I didn't consent to it."

"Just trying to gather all the facts, sir."

Color me skeptical, but okay. "Fine. I can't shift."

His eyes flicked up from my driver's license, and an invisible question mark hovered above his head.

I rolled my eyes. "Oh, you said *negatively* impacted, didn't you?"

"Yes."

"Right." I cleared my throat. "I can't shift."

"Mm-hmm . . ."

"There's also the fact that it was, as far as I know, done under unsterile conditions outside of a medical facility."

"As far as you know?"

"Yes." I pointed at the report. "You did catch the part where I said I was drugged, right?"

"But you don't know if it was done in a nonmedical facility."

"No, because I didn't consent to the procedure and I wasn't fully conscious when it was performed."

"I see." Officer Daly handed me back my driver's license. For a moment, he chewed his pen and looked over my statement again. "Maybe the question should be, *why* were you resisting the implant?"

I gritted my teeth. "I fail to see how that matters."

"The more information I get, the better I'll be able to help you."

Oh, I'm sure. "Fine. I was resisting it because I didn't want it."

"You wanted to continue shifting?"

"Yes."

"Why?"

"Because I enjoy creating feelings of fear and revulsion in everyday people who are trying to mind their own static, heterosexual business. It amuses me." I inclined my head. "Would it help if I started laughing manically at this point, or would that be too much?"

He glared at me, then looked at my statement once again. "I'm curious, Mr. Nichols, why you wouldn't consent to something like that? Seems like it would make life easier for you."

"Oh, you know what? You're right." I folded my arms across my chest. "And I suppose when I was in my female form, I shouldn't have resisted if a man tried to rape me. After all, it might feel good, right?"

He eyed me. When he opened his mouth to speak, though, I cut him off.

"Is there someone else I can talk to?"

"Someone else?"

"Yeah. Maybe someone who has a clue? Or, you know, is interested in helping me file this report instead of asking inappropriate and irrelevant questions?"

He set his jaw and pushed his shoulders back slightly. "Are you telling me how to do my job, Mr. Nichols?"

"Well, you're implying rather heavily that I should accept this implant in spite of the fact that you obviously know jack fucking shit about shifters." I shrugged. "I'd say that makes us even, wouldn't you?"

He shot me another glare, and I expected some sort of snide comeback, but he stood. "I'll go see if one of the detectives is available. This is more their territory anyway."

"Thank you," I said through my teeth.

After he'd gone, I rested my elbows on the table and rubbed my temples. I should've known this would happen. In this city, which wasn't nearly as progressive as it liked to think it was, cops were notorious for blowing off shifters who'd been the victims of crimes. If we didn't want to be targeted, we shouldn't make ourselves targets.

Whatever the fuck that meant. I shuddered and thanked God I wasn't here to report a sexual assault.

Maybe this was a mistake.

No. No, of course it wasn't. Why should I let this slide? My parents hated what I was, and they'd spent the last decade or so making sure I felt like utter slime. I could *almost* believe my mother had acted with good, if misdirected, intentions. Gary, though? No way.

"Do you think I just woke up one day and decided to change genders?" I'd shouted at my stepfather in my youth. "This is who I am. It's what I am."

"It's unnatural," he'd said.

I'd narrowed my eyes. "Then take that up with your God, since He's the one who made me this way."

He'd glared at me with fire-and-brimstone eyes. "God will send you to hell for what you are."

Love you too, 'Dad.'

I sat back and scrubbed a hand over my face. Millennia of civilization, and shifters still weirded people out, terrified them, inspired murderous hatred. I could live a million years and never understand why. In some cultures, most of them centuries gone, we were revered as gods. In others, we'd been invaluable for espionage, especially during World Wars I and II. Sometimes no one cared about our existence, sometimes we were useful, sometimes people wanted us exterminated.

At least these days it wasn't as bad as during, say, the Inquisition. Still, it wasn't exactly sunshine and roses. We marched out of step with the accepted biological cadence, and people didn't know what to make of that. I still wasn't sure why it made anyone feel threatened. We weren't contagious. It wasn't like Officer Daly was suddenly going to sprout ovaries if he showed me a little compassion.

The conference room door opened and a man in a shirt and tie stepped in. He closed the door behind him and approached the table.

"I'm Detective Reilly." He extended his hand, but I didn't take it.

Glaring up at him, I said, "So are you going to tell me all the reasons I should be glad my parents did this?"

"No, I'm not." With that, his facial features softened, blurred, changed. In seconds, I was face-to-face with a blonde woman. Then, her features melted together again, and his male form returned. "Better?"

I relaxed and extended my hand. "Sorry about that," I said quietly as we shook hands.

"Don't worry about it." He took the seat the other cop had occupied. "I'm sorry about Officer Daly. I could have picked a dozen or so officers better suited for this than that cretin. The desk usually assigns me to any cases involving shifters, but . . ." He made a flippant gesture and muttered something under his breath. "Anyway." He picked up the forms I'd been discussing with the officer. "Now, I know this is difficult, but start at the beginning and tell me everything you told Officer Daly."

"It's all on the statement."

"Oh, you already filled it in." He read it over quickly. "All right, to make sure I have this straight . . ." He skimmed the statement again. "They slipped you a drug? Do you have any idea what it was?"

I shook my head. "Not a clue. I'm guessing it was something in my drink."

"And once you were mildly sedated from that, someone injected you with something else?"

"I think so." I wasn't even a hundred percent sure who'd given me the injection. I thought it was the pastor, but couldn't be certain. Shaking my head again, I added, "It's a little hazy."

"Do you remember anything between the drugs kicking in and when you fully awoke? Any periods of semiconsciousness?"

My mouth went dry. There were memories, albeit fragmented ones.

Moving. Or rather, being moved. Something cold on my back. Voices. Hands. Was someone chanting? Praying? I only caught the low, repetitive murmur, but couldn't make out the words. Opening my eyes, I couldn't focus on anything. Anyone. "Hold him absolutely still." *Pressure on the back of my neck. Someone pulling my head down and my knees up. Sharp pain in the middle of my spine. Burning. Numb.* "Candace, go in the other room." *Oh, God, no, don't let her see this. Disoriented. Lost. Can't breathe.* "Don't let him move at all."

"Mr. Nichols?"

Detective Reilly's voice startled me.

"Sorry." I moistened my dry lips. "It's all pretty vague. I don't remember much." What I did remember, though, I'd relived in all its terrifying, disoriented glory every time I'd tried to sleep.

"Were you forced to sign anything?" he asked. "A consent form, anything like that?"

"I don't know. Maybe."

His lips tightened. "If there's a consent form with your signature on it, that could give the defense some leverage, but they'd also have to show that it was performed in a proper medical environment." He absently ran his thumb back and forth along the edge of his jaw. "What I don't get is why they didn't make any effort to cover their tracks. Your parents have to know you're well aware that they were behind this. They had to know it would come back on them."

"They did. This will make them martyrs." I pursed my lips. "That's one reason I hesitated to even file the report. Nothing will make them think they're in the wrong on this. In fact, they'll see it as persecution, and it'll just make them feel more justified."

Reilly wrinkled his nose. "So there's no reasoning with them at all."

"None. And hopefully prosecuting them won't encourage other people to do the same thing."

"I think more would be encouraged if you let this slide and didn't press charges."

"Good point."

"I'll get on the phone with the district attorney as soon as we're done here. Obtaining an arrest warrant won't take much." He rested his elbow on top of the report and thumbed his chin. "We may need to have you undergo a psychiatric evaluation, just to cover our bases."

I pressed my lips together. "Any chance of getting someone who's sympathetic toward us?"

"Absolutely," he said with a nod. "The department has two shrinks on the payroll, and they're both fantastic. I've been to one in particular a few times myself."

"And what about the DA? Will he actually pursue this?"

"Yes, he's been an advocate for us for years." Detective Reilly shuffled some of the pages around. "There was another case like this a year or so ago, and he pushed to have everyone involved go down for the maximum charges."

"Speaking of which, how long would they . . . my parents . . . if they're convicted . . ."

"How long would they go to jail?"

I nodded, ignoring the prickle of the hairs on the back of my neck standing on end.

"Depends on the charges. When all's said and done, even if the judge hands down a long sentence, they'll serve a few years, at most. It's not murder, and unless they have criminal backgrounds . . ." He raised his eyebrows. I shook my head. He went on. "Then they won't be going away for life or anything."

"What will happen to my sister?"

"That's up to social services. How old?"

"Sixteen and a few months."

"Any relatives in the area?"

"Not in this state, no."

"What about your father?" He looked at his file. "You said your stepfather was involved in—"

"My father's dead."

Reilly acknowledged my answer with a subtle nod. "In that case, she'll most likely end up in foster care, at least temporarily."

I exhaled. "Fuck, I don't want to uproot her like that."

"Well, like I said, I'll talk to social services. If there are relatives who are willing and able to take her in, we might be able to keep her from spending much time in the foster system." He tilted his head slightly. "Legally, you can petition for custody as well."

Guilt burned in my gut. My sister already hated me thanks to our parents, and I couldn't imagine it would help matters if she was forced to live with me.

"I'll get you the numbers for some relatives in California," I whispered. "Please let me know what I can do to help. I don't want her staying in foster care, but I don't think I could take her in myself."

"I'll help you however I can." He paused. "You're doing the right thing here, Alex."

"I hope so."

After a little more paperwork, a promise to call when my parents were arrested, and a handshake, he showed me out of the station.

Outside, I paused on the steps. I couldn't believe I'd just gotten the ball rolling to have my own parents put in jail. I wanted nothing to do with them, but they'd instilled in me a deep-seated belief about parents as authority figures, even when I was an adult. They were masters at guilt and manipulation, and it was a wonder I'd resisted the implant this long. Having them arrested? That went against everything they'd ever tried to drill into my head.

But it was done. The gears were turning.

Please forgive me, Candy.

I took a deep breath. There was nothing more I could do here, so it was on to the neurosurgeon to see about removing this thing from my spine and getting my life back.

☿ CHAPTER 9 ♀
DAMON

All day at work, I was on pins and needles about Alex's appointment with the neurosurgeon. Words and numbers on reports, screens, and whiteboards ran together. I barely heard a word of marketing's presentation in the morning, and I was a fidgeting, pen-tapping wreck in the afternoon staff meeting. Whenever I could, I holed up in my office and obsessively refreshed my email in case he'd sent an update.

About an hour before quitting time, someone knocked on my office door.

"It's open." When the door opened, I looked up.

"Hey, hon." Jordan shut the door behind her. "How goes it?"

I leaned back in my chair and laced my fingers together behind my head. "It goes. What's up?"

"Nothing really. Just wanted to stop by and ask how things are going with Alex."

"It's better. We talked last night. I think we're on the same page now. As much as we can be, anyway."

"Well, good. Has he had any luck getting the implant taken out?"

"He had an appointment today."

"And?"

I shrugged. "Don't know yet. He hasn't called. But I'm on my way over there after work."

"Things going okay between you? As far as your relationship?"

"As good as they can be, I guess." I took a breath. "It's so weird. A few days ago, I was frustrated because she refused to discuss the idea of getting married, and now . . . now I have no idea what's going to happen. We're taking things a day at a time. This isn't going to be easy, that's for sure."

Jordan shook her head. "I don't think anyone expects it to be. It never is when a shifter has to come out to a partner."

I sighed. "It's so weird, this whole situation. I mean, last night, I kept looking at him and trying to see her. And once in a while, she was there. But other times, she wasn't. And most of the time, I don't know who I'm looking at."

"That's because you're not looking for Alex, you're looking for a woman." Jordan folded her arms across her chest. "When he's in that form, Damon, he's a man. He's not cross-dressing, he's not pretending, he is a *man*. But he's still Alex. What you need to do is stop looking for the woman you knew. Just look for the person."

"Yeah, I know." I stared at my desk instead of looking at her. "I'm still not sure how to feel about this."

"About this?" she asked. "Or about him?"

I forced myself to make eye contact with her. "Both, I guess. And as far as our relationship . . . the physical side . . . I . . ." Even after Alex had suggested putting that part on hold, I still felt guilty about it.

"I understand. We talked about this. You can't force attraction to anyone. Sexuality is what it is. But remember when you're talking to him, Damon, he is still the person you fell in love with. Male or female, static or shifter, Alex is still *Alex*."

I nodded. Deep down, I knew Alex was still the same person, but when I looked at him, I saw a stranger. A male stranger. How the hell did I reconcile this in my mind?

"Well," I said. "Hopefully he'll have the implant out soon, and this will be a moot point."

"Except Alex will still be a shifter."

"We'll deal with that when we get there. Maybe it'll be easier once she's . . ." I trailed off. There was no way to word it without sounding like a jackass. "Once he doesn't have to worry about the implant."

Jordan shot me a knowing look. "Maybe. Well, good luck. And don't forget what I said."

"I won't. Thanks."

As soon as I was off the clock, I hurried out of the office and went straight to Alex's place. Since he was expecting me, I keyed myself in as I often did, but the second I came through the front door, my heart dropped.

Two empty beer bottles sat on the coffee table. A third was in his hand, pressed against his forehead. His eyes were closed, his lips pressed tightly together. I knew that posture—and alcohol consumption—all too well.

Oh, shit. "What happened?"

Alex didn't look up and didn't answer.

My gut tied itself into knots as I sat on the couch beside him. "What did the surgeon say?"

"The short answer?" He stared at the floor, eyes red and distant. "I'm pretty well fucked."

The knots wound tighter. "In what way?"

"The surgery is extremely risky and invasive." His voice was slurred enough to make me suspect there were more empty bottles in the kitchen. "And there's a possibility the implant itself is a time bomb. Some of the ones on the black market aren't reliable. They can break down, and by the time any symptoms show, the damage is done."

"What kind of damage can they do?" My heart sped up and my stomach wound itself even tighter. "I mean, how bad?"

"Nerve damage. Paralysis." He paused. "Death." He pulled the bottle away from his forehead and took a long drink. "And if it doesn't interfere with nerves in the spinal cord, certain types of unapproved implants have this nasty habit of being extremely carcinogenic."

"Christ," was the only word I could get past my lips. The knot in my gut turned into a sick feeling. As worried as I'd been about the ramifications of all of this, it hadn't dawned on me that this could kill him.

God, please don't let me lose him . . .

Alex took another drink. "The good news is I dodged one bullet. Apparently the ER doc was right. When this procedure is done on the black market like mine was, it's not unusual for it to get infected, which is really bad when you're dealing with the spinal cord. Oh, and there's that whole paralysis thing. And death. Can't fucking forget death."

I gulped. "And you're . . . out of the woods for those?"

He nodded. "Most of it. Probably in the clear for an infection, and if the procedure itself was going to kill me or paralyze me, it would have happened before the drugs wore off." He clicked his tongue. "Oh, yeah, and without an experienced anesth—anesthesia . . . someone who knows how to knock me out. Without one of those on hand to make sure the dosages were correct and monitor vitals, I could have had a potentially lethal reaction to the drugs. I guess that isn't all that uncommon." Lifting the bottle to his lips again, he muttered, "Lucky me."

My mouth went dry. It was one thing to worry that our relationship might not survive this. It was another thing entirely to worry that *he* might not. "So, what now?"

"Now I go to a specialist who pretty much only deals with these implant things and see if he has better news." He gave a sharp, humorless laugh. "Not holding my breath, though."

"What *is* this thing, anyway? How does it work?"

"Interferes with the neuro . . . neuro—" He paused, the alcohol no doubt making the words difficult to enunciate. "The neurological impulse that triggers a shift. The electrical impulses, I guess." Some unspoken thought held his attention for a moment. Then he shuddered, rolling his shoulders. He gestured with his beer bottle again and as he brought it up to his lips, he said, "Something like that anyway. The doctor lost me when he got into some of the neurosurgeon-speak."

"We still don't have a cure for cancer, and they've developed an implant to keep people from changing genders. How the fuck does that make sense?"

"Fuck if I know," Alex said into his beer bottle. He took a drink, and for a long moment, didn't speak.

Staring off into space, he absently spun a bottle cap on the end table with his middle finger. It made a familiar, rhythmic scraping sound, bringing back a dozen or so memories of my girlfriend doing the exact same thing when she was nervous or upset. Another little tell that this was undeniably Alex.

Alex, whose life was in danger. Alex, who I could lose in so many ways in so little time. Fuck, I was going to be sick.

He rubbed a hand over his face. "Did I mention it's not a single implant?"

"It isn't?"

Shaking his head, he said, "No. It's three separate ones. They're all injected at the same time, but then they separate. Getting them out means finding all three, possibly cutting in three different places, and there's triple the risk of permanent damage." He tightened his jaw, and his Adam's apple bobbed slightly. "Turns out putting one of these fuckers in is child's play, but getting them out is an entirely different matter. It's major back surgery."

My heart sank a little deeper.

"It's just an injection to put it in. A needle between the vertebra, in go the implants, and they float around until they find a place to settle in." He gestured with his free hand, the movement as slurred as his words. "Getting them out is seriously invasive, especially if any of the implants have fused to the nerves or bone."

The beer in his hand suddenly looked really, really tempting.

"On top of all of that," he went on, bitterness saturating his tone, "it's considered an elective surgery, especially since it's a reversal of another elective surgery. It'll take months of letters, red tape, and God only knows what else to prove it was given to me against my will." He drained his beer.

"How much does it run?"

"Depending on the surgeon and the procedure . . ." He coughed against the back of his hand, and when he spoke again, his voice wavered. "It can be anywhere from sixty to a hundred grand. Or more. So assuming I don't go bankrupt trying to prove I never consented to have them put in, and assuming I can figure out how to pay to get them removed, there's also the fact that the longer they're in, the more dangerous the surgery is."

"Scarring?"

He nodded. "They embed themselves, and the longer they're embedded . . ." He cleared his throat. Again. "So, to recap . . . Leaving it in could kill me, taking it out could kill me, and living with it for the rest of my life will make me wish I was dead. How the fuck was *your* day?"

Before I could reply, he stood, grabbed the beer bottles off the coffee table, and started toward the kitchen. I sighed and followed him. His gait wasn't completely steady, and he stumbled a little, brushing the doorway with one shoulder. He wasn't fall-down drunk yet, but I had a feeling he had every intention of getting there as quickly as possible.

He set the three empty bottles on the counter beside two others. When he pulled an unopened one from the refrigerator, I raised an eyebrow.

"Alex, are you sure you should—"

"What the hell do you want me to do?"

I jumped. "Just slow down. It's not going to help."

"*Nothing* is going to help," he snapped. "Is it all right with you if I find something in this goddamned world that doesn't make me feel worse?"

"You'll feel like hell in the morning."

"I feel like hell now." He slammed the bottle down on the counter so hard I was surprised it didn't shatter. "What do you want me to do, Damon? Tomorrow, I have to go back to my day job and face a boss who thinks shifters are disgusting, not to mention coworkers who only know me as a woman. For now and into the foreseeable future, I have three implants in my spine that are making my life hell and might even kill me. I just went through the motions to put my folks in jail and my baby sister in foster care. My boyfriend is stuck with a man in place of his girlfriend, and no matter how much he doesn't want me to see it, it's clearly bothering him." He put up his hands, and as he spoke again, his voice cracked. "And you want to begrudge me a fucking drink?"

"Alex, I'm sorry," I said softly. "I'm not downplaying how this is affecting you. I just . . ." What could I say?

"Then let me have a drink," he whispered, and picked up the bottle again. I didn't object when he opened it. Didn't say a word when he took a long drink. Didn't hold his gaze when he looked at me with a "go ahead and stop me" challenge in his eyes.

"I'm sorry," I murmured. "I'm not . . . I'm just worried about you. I'm . . . I'm scared, to be honest."

Alex ran a shaking hand through his hair. "I'm sorry, Damon."

"Don't be." I stepped a little closer. "This isn't your fault."

He kept his gaze down. "You know, this is one of the parts of being static that is absolute hell. Society says men and women have to behave certain ways. Usually, if I want to act a certain way, I can switch to the gender where it's more acceptable." He sniffed sharply. He set his shoulders back but couldn't hide the way his hands still shook.

"But now . . . I can't. Society says a woman can get emotional, break down, lose it even for a few minutes, but a guy has to be fucking stoic."

I put my hands on his shoulders. "Fuck society, Alex. It's just us here right now, and even if it wasn't, fuck everyone else."

He rubbed his forehead. "I'm fine. I'm fine. Just . . ." He shrugged out of my grasp. "I'm fine."

We both knew he was as far from "fine" as he was from sober. What the hell was I supposed to say, though?

He leaned against the counter, his shoulders dropping under some unseen weight. "I swear to God, getting this thing out might kill me, but if I leave it in, I might end up killing myself."

I stared at him. I'd never realized how deeply this affected any shifter. Guilt burned deep in my chest. How much had I unknowingly contributed to this? Forcing him, without even realizing it, to be a woman when he desperately needed to be male?

"Alex, you could . . ." My voice trembled. "You could have told me."

"We've been through this, Damon." His eyes met mine. His exhausted, pained eyes. "My family knew, and it disgusted them. So much so that they're willing to go to prison for *correcting* me." He dropped his gaze. "You were the first person I ever loved like this, and I was so fucking scared of losing you." He pulled in a ragged breath. "I still am."

"I'm still here, aren't I?"

"Yeah." He looked at me through his lashes. "But for how long?"

"Alex, I'm not going anywhere."

He searched my eyes. Then he turned around and rested his hands on the counter like he just needed something to hold him upright. "There's one other thing."

I was afraid to ask, but I whispered, "What?"

Over his shoulder, he said, "Sometimes the implants do permanent damage. Even if they're removed quickly."

"You mentioned that," I said. "Nerve damage, things like that?"

"Well, that, but . . ." He let his head fall forward. After a moment, he faced me, and when he met my eyes, the hint of an extra shine in his sent a chill right through me. "There's a chance I won't be able to shift again. Ever."

My heart dropped into my feet. "Never?"

He nodded. His cheek rippled as he set his jaw. "So, if you do stay . . ." He gestured at himself, and his voice faltered. "This might be all there is."

"When will you know?"

"If I can shift?"

"Yeah."

"My appointment with the specialist is in two weeks. After that, it just depends on how long before they can schedule the surgery, and how long it takes to recover afterward."

I was numb. Stunned. Completely at a loss. Finally, I said the only thing I could trust myself to articulate: "I guess we'll see what happens then."

Yeah, we'd see what happened. With the implant. With Alex.

With us.

☿ CHAPTER 10 ♀
ALEX

After Damon left for the night, I drank more than I should have. Way more. I just couldn't bring myself to give a fuck how I'd feel in the morning. All I wanted was to be numb for a few hours. Numb and preferably unconscious.

On the bright side, it helped me sleep.

On the not-so-bright side, it meant waking up to the blistering shriek of my alarm and crawling out of bed with a massive hangover.

As I poured my coffee, a prickly ball of nerves settled in my stomach. I had to go back to work today. There was no getting out of it. I couldn't afford to burn any more sick time, I couldn't afford to take any unpaid leave, and I sure as shit couldn't afford to lose this job. Even if I increased my hours at the Welcome Mat, I quite possibly had a hundred-thousand-dollar medical bill looming. So, that meant I had to go in today and face the music and let the chips fall where they would.

It also meant I had to watch my every step at work from now on. Showing up at least ten or fifteen minutes early to avoid being even one or two minutes late. Making sure I came back precisely on time from every break. Being damned careful to keep all of my call logs filled out and my customers happy. I didn't dare accidentally walk off with so much as a pen.

It wasn't that I was a slacker or the type to cut corners. Quite the opposite. I was an honest, hardworking employee, and I had the reviews to prove it. The thing was, my boss was a master at finding legal grounds to fire people he wanted gone for illegal reasons. The pagan guy down in engineering? Came in late a few too many times. Pregnant receptionist? Fired two months before her due date for stealing office supplies. A customer service rep who went to HR because the boss was flirting and behaving inappropriately? Terminated after her customer complaints tripled over the course of three months.

All of those were legitimate grounds, of course, but everyone knew better. The pagan engineer was late because of childcare issues that weren't a problem until the day someone saw his pentagram pendant. The receptionist walked off with a few pens, whereas the boss in question made no effort to hide the occasional ream of paper that left with him. And yes, the customer service rep's complaints had tripled. They went from two to six, while all the other reps were consistently well into the teens.

My boss was notoriously anti-gay, anti-trans, anti-shifter, anti-anything-off-the-accepted-definition-of-normal. He was careful how he articulated that around the workplace, but it was no great mystery. If I knew him as well as I thought I did, he'd be sniffing around for a reason to cross me off the payroll. I wasn't going to hand him a reason to fire me. He'd have to work for it.

With enough coffee in my system to tide me over and keep me from falling asleep at the wheel, I drove in to work. All the way there, I berated myself for ignoring a buddy's advice a few years ago when I applied for this job.

"Alex, men are treated better and paid better in this industry. It's a fact, kid. You're just setting yourself up to have to work harder for less."

As a feisty college grad, hell-bent on changing the world's view of those who didn't fit perfectly into socially accepted gender categories, I'd blown off his advice and applied for the job as a female. I knew I was setting myself up for some discrimination. A smaller paycheck. Callers asking to speak to men. Colleagues looking down my blouse and not taking me seriously. But damn it, they would *learn* to take me seriously.

Oh, silly me. Crusading for gender equality while trying to earn a living was more exhausting than I'd expected.

Having to show up at work in my male form after all this time? Fuck. Now, instead of being "that chick down in tech support, how cute," I could be the subject of "holy shit, one of *those* people works here?" The occasional leer was annoying. Now my coworkers could all try to sneak a peek at the freak on the fourth floor.

On the way into the office, I kept my eyes down. It wasn't unusual for vendors and customers to walk through the building, but I felt conspicuous. My badge was clipped to my belt, and I kept a hand over it, afraid someone would see my name and make the connection. Or see that I was an employee, not a visitor, and try to figure out why they didn't recognize me. Or worse, introduce themselves to "the new guy."

Fortunately, no one approached. Maybe they didn't notice. It would be a different story when I got to my own floor.

Steeling myself, I knocked on my boss's door.

"Come in," came the voice from the other side, and I closed my eyes as nausea rose in my throat. If I had to make a list of the people in my world who I didn't want knowing what I was, he was easily in the top five.

I pushed the door open.

No recognition registered on his face. "Can I help you?"

"Yeah." I pulled a folded piece of paper out of my pocket and watched my hands unfold it. "I would have done it over the phone, but I wanted to make sure you got a copy of this." I handed it to him and managed to look him in the eye.

He peered at the letter. "What's this?"

"A medical waiver."

Furrowing his brow, he started reading it over. "But I've never seen you in my— *Oh, my God.*" He dropped the letter like it had bitten him, and stared at me with wide eyes. "*Alex?*"

I nodded. "Yes."

"Have a seat," he said flatly. I sat in one of the chairs in front of his desk while he read over the rest of the letter. His lips twisted and the furrow in his brow deepened. Not much different than Officer Asshole Daly's response, if decidedly less subtle. I didn't think I'd ever seen the man looking so squeamish and uncomfortable. I did find a tiny bit of satisfaction in the fact that he probably felt ill thinking about all those times he'd hit on me or looked down my shirt. Well. Now he got to feel as uncomfortable as I had whenever he'd leered at me.

He set the letter down and cleared his throat. "So, you need a few more days off, then?"

"No, I can work." I tapped my fingers on the armrest. "I'm actually looking into getting the procedure reversed, so I may need to burn some sick leave for that."

"Reversed?" He chuckled. "They stick you in the wrong body or something? I'd be pissed about that, too."

I gritted my teeth. "Something like that. Anyway, I just wanted to update you on what's going on. I guess I should get to work."

"Right. Thank you." His gaze darted toward me but quickly flicked to something on his desk. "Do you, um, need me to send around a memo or anything? Let people know what's . . . going on?"

Yeah, right. I could only imagine how that nice little memo would be worded.

"No," I said. "I'll deal with it."

"Are you sure? Might be better to just nip these things in the bud. Keep people from speculating and gossiping."

Oh, there was no nipping that in the bud. People would notice. They'd gossip, speculate, gawk. All I could do was go to my desk, get to work, and act like nothing had changed.

"I'll manage. If I change my mind, I'll let you know."

"You know where to find me," he said with a superficial smile.

"Thanks."

Stomach still churning, I got the fuck out of his office. His discomfort made my skin crawl, and God knew how the conversation would've gone if Human Resources hadn't been a phone call away, but at least it was over.

Now to go deal with everyone else.

The walk back to the elevators wasn't bad. This was a big company, there were bound to be unfamiliar faces in the halls, especially here on the lower floors where bigwigs met with clients, field representatives came and went, and prospective employees were interviewed. Should've known on my way in that I wouldn't be noticed, but no one ever said paranoia and rationality were close friends.

The third, fourth, and fifth floors were badge-access only, though. If someone was there, they were supposed to be, otherwise they were promptly escorted elsewhere. I wouldn't turn any heads on the lower floors, but once I stepped off an elevator, people would notice. Unfamiliar faces attracted attention from office drones like shit drew flies. It broke up the monotony. Gave everyone something to talk about besides work.

I took the elevator up to my floor, and when it stopped, I swiped my badge through the reader. The red LED went dark. The green one came on. Then the doors opened, and with my heart pounding in my chest, I stepped out into the lion's den.

Eyes focused straight ahead, paying no attention to the buzz of "Hey, who's that guy?" coming from the occasional cubicle, I walked to my own cube. When I reached my desk and took a seat, the whispering began in earnest.

"... you don't think ..."

"... come on, no way ..."

"... okay, you explain it, then ..."

"... could be a temp ..."

I put on my headset and tried to ignore everyone. It's amazing how gossip was amplified when it was about you. On a normal day, people could stand right outside my cubicle and loudly dish juicy tales about the CFO and his secretary's ongoing affair, and I had no trouble tuning it out enough to help a caller troubleshoot a malfunctioning monitor. Today? Every whisper made it to my ears like people were shouting in my face.

"... no one's heard from Alex in days ..."

"... that doesn't mean ..."

"... well, it's possible ..."

"... the last person I expected to be one of them ..."

One of them? Really? I rolled my eyes and tried not to groan aloud. *Just eight hours, Nichols. You can do this.*

The phone queue showed seven calls waiting, which meant it would ring as soon as I logged on. Blissful distraction, yes, but the second I answered that phone ...

Get it together, Alex. Just jump in with both feet and get it over with.

I took a quick drink of water, cleared my throat, and logged on.

It rang. I closed my eyes. And I answered.

"Technical support, Alex Nichols speaking."

That stopped every conversation within a three-cube radius. Well, for a few seconds.

"... No. Fucking. Way ..."

"... dude, I so told you ..."

"... wait, you mean you knew about ..."

"... come on, don't tell me you didn't ..."

I covered one ear with my hand, blocking out the whispers so I could focus on the customer speaking into my other ear. It helped, and I made it through without too much difficulty. It was a relatively easy call anyway, which was always welcome first thing in the morning. Just a faulty power supply that could be easily swapped out. And it was always nice when the person didn't ask to speak to one of the "other"—translation: male—technicians.

Oh, right. Because I am one of the "other" technicians.

As soon as I hung up, the phone rang again. Calls usually came in waves like that. For an hour or so, it would be one after another, every rep glued to his or her headset. Then, nothing for twenty minutes, forty minutes, an hour. Those lulls were the periods when we'd take care of emails, reports, and whatever other tasks the powers that be thought tech support should be saddled with. That was also when the gossip mill worked double time. When conversations didn't have to be rushed and condensed into those brief periods when customers were on hold. Today, with every passing call, I dreaded that lull.

It came, though.

I'd barely taken off my headset before Glenn, one of the techs from a few desks over, materialized in the entrance to my cubicle. A phony smile was plastered across his face.

"Hey, um, Alex?" He cocked his head and furrowed his brow a little.

"Yes?"

His eyebrows jumped and his jaw dropped. Always a subtle one, Glenn.

Yes, it's me, asshole.

He quickly cleared his throat. "Uh, so where've you been? We've all been worried about you the last few days."

I'm sure. Something tells me you just drew the short straw to come over here and confirm it's really me. "Been out sick."

He watched me for a moment, probably wondering if I'd elaborate. When I didn't, he fidgeted, resting a hand on the corner of my cubicle in a pathetic attempt to look casual. "Well, glad to have you back."

"Thanks."

He made a quick escape, and I tried to get back to work.

"Alex?" A voice turned my head. Rick Soliday from engineering stood right where Glenn had just minutes before.

"What's up, Rick?" I asked.

His eyes widened slightly, as if he'd tried to contain his reaction but didn't *quite* succeed. More subtle than Glenn, though, I'd give him that.

Rick cleared his throat. "I, um, I just came down to give you the updated troubleshooting procedure for the six hundred series." He handed me a few copies of the manual.

"Thanks," I said. "By the way, you can just send this stuff through inter-office mail. You don't have to walk it all the way down here."

"Oh, no, it's okay." A hint of a smirk tugged at his mouth. "I was wandering this way anyway, so . . ."

Sure he was. Apparently word was getting around, via email or phone most likely.

"As long as you didn't have to make a special trip," I muttered, trying not to let my irritation show. He finally left, and I had no doubt the next spectator would be along soon. I was right. For the better part of the morning, a steady stream of people found bullshit reasons to drop by my desk. Of course there were plenty who were fine with it, acknowledging the "situation" with little more than a fleeting look of surprise or a startled pause on the phone before returning to business as usual. All it took to cancel out a dozen of those, though, was one of the not-so-subtle jackasses like Rick or Glenn. The only thing missing was a damned carnival barker.

"Step right up, see the fourth-floor freak show! What once was a woman is now a man, have a peek, have a look!"

I shuddered.

My phone rang, and I could tell by the ringtone it was an internal call. I cringed, wondering if it was someone else who already knew or someone who was about to find out. One glance at the caller ID eased the tension in my stomach, though. Ken Randall and I had been friends since I started here, and he was the only one who, prior to today, knew what I was.

I pushed the button to answer the call. "Hey, Ken."

"Oh, crap, so people weren't kidding."

I scowled at no one in particular. "Already worked its way up to your floor?"

"Ya think? The rumor mill is on fire with this one." He paused. "So what's going on?"

"Long story. By the way, sorry I had to bail on you and Luann tonight."

"Oh, don't worry about it. Sounds like you have a lot going on. Lu's sister said she'll watch the kids, so we're covered."

"That's good. I didn't want to leave you high and dry."

"You're fine. So, are you . . ." He hesitated. "Are you permanently male?"

I lowered my voice. "Possibly. I don't know yet."

"Did you get that implant thing?"

"Unfortunately."

"Shit."

"Tell me about it. Listen, I've got to get back to my calls. I'll fill you in on everything later."

"All right. Luann and I are praying for you."

"Thanks, man." I hung up, feeling a lot better after hearing from Ken. I rarely found comfort in someone as religious as him, but like my aunt in California, he was compassionate and nonjudgmental, especially when it came to shifters. His beliefs were about as different as could be from the fucked-up cult my parents belonged to, and religious or not, it always helped to have an ally or two in situations like this. Maybe I'd get through the day after all, just knowing someone had my back.

One of the prerequisites to working in technical support was a heroin-like caffeine addiction. We may as well have had coffee IVs hooked right into our aortas for all we as a department consumed. Throw in my hangover from last night, and I was sucking the stuff down so fast, it was no surprise when it finally caught up with me.

I logged off the phones, took off my headset, and left my cubicle. Nerves coiled in the pit of my stomach as I walked down the hall. In most public places, it was a habit to pause and make sure I was going into the right restroom, that my body matched the stick figure on the door. I'd worked here long enough that I'd stopped thinking about it, so one of my nagging fears now that I was here in my male form was that I'd forget. Go left instead of right. Walk past the wrong stick figure.

The other nagging fear was the very act of going into the right one. My coworkers weren't the most progressive group of people on the planet. It still bothered some of the guys that Lane from shipping used the men's room like they did. God forbid a gay guy had to take a piss.

With that in mind, I deliberately made the trek to the opposite side of my floor. This particular department had been eradicated in the last round of layoffs, and all that remained was a ghost town of cubicles. That and a couple of restrooms few people bothered using. Rumor had it they served the same purpose as out of the way supply closets, empty offices, and, if a pair was particularly daring, unoccupied conference rooms. At least if I ran into a couple in here, they'd be as likely to pretend they hadn't seen me as I was them.

Thank God, the men's room was deserted. It stayed that way right up until I went to the sink to wash my hands.

The door opened. I looked in the mirror, and my blood turned to ice water.

In walked Joe Gorton and Zach Holloway, the last two coworkers with whom I'd wanted to cross paths anytime soon. If my boss was in the top five people I didn't want knowing about me, these two were in the top three.

Every company had a Joe and a Zach. They were the guys every female coworker avoided at company parties, and I'd have bet money the freaks, geeks, and queers at their respective high schools had spent a great deal of time looking over their shoulders in the halls. They were a pair of schoolyard bullies who'd never grown up, plain and simple. The two of them were sleaze in neckties, and they had just enough charm to repeatedly persuade an HR director of their innocence.

Being stuck in an elevator with Zach a few months ago had been bad enough. Having Joe corner me at the bar at the Christmas party was irritating and a little unnerving.

Having the two of them between me and the men's room door? Being outnumbered and male in their presence?

Fuck.

I pretended not to notice them.

"That is some crazy shit, man," Zach said to Joe.

"I know, isn't it?"

They stopped in front of the door, and they were either oblivious to me or pretending to be. Considering they'd conveniently shown up in the most out of the way restroom in the building while I was in here and were casually blocking my only escape, I'd have put money on the latter.

"I'm telling you," Joe said. "This year's Christmas party? Any chick is getting a package check before she comes home with me."

"Don't want any *Crying Game* action?"

"Oh, fuck, are you kidding?" Joe made a gagging sound.

Zach laughed. "I don't know if a package check would do much good, though. I heard when they switch, it all switches. Junk and all."

"Yeah, that's what I've heard, too." Joe shuddered. "Well, let's put it this way. I better not fuck a woman and wake up next to a dude, or I'm not going to be happy."

I refused to look at their reflections or my own as I turned off the faucet and reached for a paper towel. I felt like a deer standing too close to a couple of wolves, moving as slowly and quietly as possible. No sudden movements, no drawing attention to myself.

They were well aware of me, though. They had to be. Why else would they be blocking the door while they carried on their passive-aggressive conversation?

I gritted my teeth, debating whether to just wait until they got out of the way or engage them and ask them to move.

"Fucking disgusting, though," Joe went on. "Can't believe someone would pass themselves off as a chick, then turn around and be one of those. What the fuck?"

"Well, like you said." Zach clapped him on the shoulder. "Package checks, just to be safe."

"No shit." Joe stepped away from the door and started toward one of the urinals. "And God help a bitch if she turns out to be a guy."

Zach laughed, and I made the mistake of looking in the mirror just in time to meet his eyes before he followed Joe. We held eye contact for a couple of seconds, and I swore he couldn't have looked more menacing if he'd been smacking his palm with a baseball bat.

As soon as I had a clear path for the door, I got the hell out of there. The door didn't shut in time to mask the roar of laughter, and I shivered as I started down the hall.

God help a bitch if she turns out to be a guy.

I shivered again. Fucker was probably just embarrassed to figure out he'd been hitting on a shifter at the Christmas party. He'd been laying it on thick all night long, thinking I was single because Damon, who'd been down with the flu, wasn't there with me. Everyone saw it, everyone knew what he'd been doing, and now everyone knew the woman who'd been in his sights was a shifter.

Needless to say, Joe wasn't happy.

I told myself he'd never do anything dangerous. This wouldn't go any further than passive-aggressive swipes, dirty looks, and his brand of obnoxious, if subtle, hostility. Anything to make sure, at every available opportunity, that I knew he found me repulsive.

And people wondered why so few shifters came out.

I kept my eyes down and walked back to my desk as fast as I could, willing my skin not to turn inside out. In theory, I should have run straight to HR, but there was no point. No one had ever gotten an accusation of sexual harassment to stick to one of those assholes. Though retaliation was illegal as all hell, there were ways, and Zach and Joe always found them. I didn't know if one of them was banging the HR director, or if they'd just mastered the art of sweet-talking their way out of things, but every woman who'd ever gone toe-to-toe with one or both of them eventually regretted it.

It was their word against mine. I didn't stand a chance.

So, I returned to my desk, put on my headset, and pretended I wasn't in a cubicle-littered circle of hell.

After another rush of calls, my direct extension rang.

"Technical support, Alex Nichols speaking."

"Alex, this is Detective Reilly."

I sat up straighter, keeping an eye out for eavesdroppers. "Yes?"

"I just wanted to let you know your parents and the pastor-slash-surgeon are now in custody. They'll be arraigned first thing in the morning."

Relief and guilt swept through me. "Do I need to be there tomorrow?"

"No, but the DA will be in touch with you to discuss the psych eval and your testimony."

I swallowed hard. Jesus. Testifying against my parents. No matter what they'd done to me over the years, they were my parents. Well, my mother was. Gary could rot in hell.

"What about my sister?" I asked. "She wasn't there, was she?"

"No, she was in school when the officers picked up your mother, and your stepfather was arrested at his office."

"Does she know yet?"

"A social worker is on her way to the school," Detective Reilly said. "She'll be informed of the arrest and taken into foster care."

I still didn't know how to feel. Candace probably loathed my very name right now. Our parents were in jail. Her entire life had been upended. So had mine.

And there would be a trial. *That* I was not looking forward to.

☿ CHAPTER 11 ♀

DAMON

I t was only eight thirty, and Alex was originally supposed to tend bar until eleven. He'd gone into work tonight to make up for one of the nights he'd missed over the weekend, but then he called to say he was cutting out early. When he walked into the diner up the street from the Welcome Mat, I didn't have to ask how he'd gotten out of his shift.

Shuffling through the door, eyes down and shoulders sagging, he didn't look like he could last another hour, never mind another three. He dropped into the booth across from me, acknowledging me with a quiet "hello" and a weak smile. When the waitress came up to the table, he just ordered a cup of coffee.

"Not hungry?" I asked.

"Not really, no."

Shit. I recognized that look, that body language, even if it was in a different body. Normally, he was famished after working both jobs. When he looked like this and wasn't hungry, it wasn't a good sign.

"Long day?" I asked.

He groaned. "I don't think I have ever felt dirtier in my life."

"Really?"

He nodded and avoided my eyes. "Nothing quite like being parked right in the middle of a grapevine that's got your name all over it."

"Ouch."

"Yeah."

"Anything you can do about it? Go to HR? Something like that?"

He laughed humorlessly. "What good would that do? There's nothing that says someone can't be uncomfortable with something. Even if that 'something' happens to be another coworker."

"I seem to recall there are rules against making your coworkers uncomfortable."

"If it were that black and white, I'd be fired for making the entire department uncomfortable." He sighed. "The thing is, it's not like I can prove anything. I mean, a guy from engineering comes down to hand me something he could have just emailed me. Can I prove he just wanted an excuse to rubberneck for a minute?"

"I guess you can't."

"Or when a couple of sleazebags in the men's room are talking about making sure they do package checks on women at the company Christmas party so they don't—" His voice cracked, and he paused to take a deep breath. Then he cleared his throat and said, "So they don't get any *Crying Game* surprises in bed?"

"You're kidding."

"Nope. They weren't talking to me, but come on. One of the guys was the one who was hitting on me at the company party, so it's not too hard to put two and two together. Except it's not like I can make a big deal out of something I just overheard, you know? They weren't saying anything to me, and I can't prove it was about me."

"I don't know," I said. "There was a big to-do at my office a few months ago after a woman overheard a couple of guys comparing notes about some actress's breasts. She nailed them for sexual harassment, and they were in some hot water over it. Wasn't about her, but it made her uncomfortable, so . . ."

Alex shrugged, his shoulder moving like that subtle gesture took every bit of energy he had left. "But what would it solve? Short of having everyone in the building fired who knew me as a woman, there's no way I can just sweep what I am under the rug. People know. The cat's out of the bag. And whether I like it or not, there are people who can't stand shifters."

"You still have to work in that environment, though."

"I'll get used to it," he said. "It'll settle down around the office, people will get over it, and it won't be as big a deal."

I wasn't sure which of us he was trying to convince.

The waitress brought his coffee, and after she'd gone, he wrapped his hands around it. Without looking at me, without really looking at anything, he said, "The detective called. They arrested my parents today."

"That's—that's a good thing, right?"

"I don't know." His eyes were distant, his tone flat. "I really can't decide if it is or not."

"Any word on your sister?"

He shook his head and dropped his blank gaze. "She's probably in a foster home by now, and I gave social services the names and numbers of some relatives in California."

"Think they'll get custody?"

"Don't know. They haven't been in contact with her in years, but besides me, they're her only relatives who are of legal age to be her guardian. It's either them or foster care." He picked up his coffee, staring at it for a long moment as if the decision to take a sip required significant internal debate. Then he set the cup back down with a quiet clink. "I'm just worried about her. The poor kid does not need this shit."

"Neither do you. Alex, someone committed a crime against you. I know you want to protect your sister and keep this as far from her as possible, but you're doing the right thing."

He finally met my eyes and whispered, "I hope so."

"Your sister will get through it. Yeah, she might be upset now, and she might even resent you, but there will come a time when she'll understand why you had to do this. Or rather, why your parents have to take the consequences of what they did."

He rubbed his hand over his face. "Depends on how brainwashed she is."

"In which case, the way she feels is on them, not you."

Alex nodded, but said nothing.

"Any idea how long before your parents go to trial?"

"Not long. Arraignment is tomorrow, and they want me in for a psych eval on Friday. The DA is pushing it hard, and he said this afternoon it probably won't be more than a week before the trial starts. Isn't like they need much evidence, you know?"

"I suppose they don't. You going to go?"

"I have to. I'm testifying. And there's that whole 'facing your accuser' thing."

"Oh, right."

"My boss will *love* that. 'Guess what, I need to take a week or so off to testify while my parents stand trial.'" Alex groaned and shook his head.

I searched his expression for a second. "Do you want me to be there?"

"It's up to you." He looked into his coffee cup. "I can't ask you to take that much time off work."

"I have vacation time. Don't worry about it. I don't think . . ."

He lifted his gaze. Then his eyebrows.

I cleared my throat. "I don't think you should have to go through that alone."

We locked eyes for a moment. Some unspoken thought lurked behind his. All at once he took a breath, his lips parting slightly as if about to bring the thought to life, but then he let the breath go and looked into his coffee again.

"Something on your mind?" I asked.

Alex chewed his lip. His hands—first the left, then the right—slipped around his coffee cup and held it for dear life. He might have shuddered, but I couldn't say for sure. He swallowed hard.

"Listen, during the trial," he said without looking up, "you're probably going to hear a lot of things. About me, my past, my parents. Stuff I'd really rather not talk about right now, but . . ." He trailed off. Finally, his eyes met mine again. "I wanted to let you know up front. It isn't going to be pretty."

"It's a criminal trial, Alex. I don't expect it to be pleasant."

"I know. But there's a lot of things I haven't told you. And from talking to the DA, it's going to come out during the trial." He let go of his coffee cup and laid one arm over the other on the edge of the table, strategically placing them so the faint scars on his forearms weren't visible. "All of it."

"Wouldn't it be better for me to hear it from you, then?" I asked. "Rather than with whatever spin the lawyers try to put on it?"

He definitely shuddered that time. "Probably. But I'd . . ." He fidgeted, dropping his gaze, and something tightened in my chest when I noticed the hint of white in his knuckles as he dug his fingers into his arm.

"Is it the kind of thing you're not comfortable with me knowing about at all? I mean, are you trying to tell me you'd rather I wasn't there, or—"

"No, it's not that," he said quickly. "In fact, I—" He paused, swallowing hard. "I want you to be there." With some effort, he looked at me, and his eyes said nothing if not *I need you to be there.* "If you're really okay with it, I mean."

"Of course I am. If you need me to be there, I will."

A faint smile pulled up the corners of his mouth. "Thanks." The smile faded as quickly as it had begun. "I just wanted to make sure you knew what to expect ahead of time."

I leaned forward. "Alex, if you're worried about what I'll—"

"I'm not." He looked at me through his lashes. "It's just, a lot of stuff I really don't want to discuss. Not that I don't want you to know about, but . . ." Another shudder.

My stomach tried to fold in on itself. I wanted to ask. I wanted to know. I wanted to hear it straight from him, but I knew this low, depressed state well enough not to push. Alex could clam up and shut down like nobody's business, and he was already close to that point. No sense throwing gas on the fire.

Alex unfolded his arms and picked up his coffee cup. I looked into my own drink, avoiding any chance of the scars on his forearm catching my eye and making him more uncomfortable.

His coffee cup clicked on the saucer, the sound echoing in the taut silence between us. Neither of us said anything more. We finished our respective drinks, paid our checks, and went out into the chilly evening air. The silence followed us, and it stayed as we stood outside the door. Hands in pockets. Eyes down. No words.

It was Alex who finally spoke.

"How are you doing with all of this?" he asked.

"What?"

"This whole situation. With me. Us. Everything. How are you doing with it?"

I shrugged. "Okay, I guess."

"You guess?"

"I don't know, to be honest. Still . . . processing it all."

Our eyes met. He was the first to break eye contact, looking out at the street. Then his eyes flicked back to me again. Beat. It was my turn to look away.

Muffling a cough, he looked at his watch. "Man, it's late. I guess I should get home."

Something sank in my chest, and I pretended not to recognize it as an opportunity slipping away.

"Will you be okay tonight?" I asked.

"Yeah. I think I just need some sleep." He didn't look at me when he said it, which meant "sleep" could be loosely translated to "I'm going to drink until I pass out."

"Alex, are you—"

"Don't." He looked me in the eye, and the determination was as palpable as the fatigue. "Just, don't. Please. I'll be fine."

I want to believe that. From the back of my mind came another thought that promised to keep me up tonight. *Even if you'll be fine, what about us?*

Alex shifted his weight and glanced up the street toward the Mat and, presumably, his car. "Guess I should get going. Seven o'clock comes early."

"Yeah." I swallowed. "It does."

We made, broke, and made eye contact. Neither of us moved.

Talk to me, Alex.

Goes both ways, his eyes said.

I don't know where to start.

Neither do I.

Alex cleared his throat and made another gesture toward the Mat. "I'd better go. I'll, um, call you?"

"Sure. Yeah." I rocked from my heels to the balls of my feet. "Have a good night."

"You, too."

So, without touching and with far too much left unsaid, we went our separate ways.

I wondered if Alex slept that night. I sure as hell didn't.

☿ CHAPTER 12 ♀
ALEX & DAMON

How are you feeling? Worried about you.

D

The email stared back at me from my too-fucking-bright-when-
I'm-this-hungover screen.

I should have known better than to drink that much on a
work night. In fact, I *did* know better, having learned it the hard way a
few too many times, but I did it anyway. Again. At least that meant I'd
gotten some sleep. Restless sleep, maybe, but also blissfully dreamless.
Booze or no booze, I was guaranteed to feel like shit this morning, so
I didn't suppose it made much of a difference.

I hadn't looked at anyone on the way into the office, but the
whispers started as soon as I stepped off the elevator. Seconds into
what promised to be a long day, and the disgusting, dirty feeling
already clung to my skin like a spiderweb, refusing to go away, refusing
to be ignored. This would be the day from hell. As would tomorrow.
And the next day. And the one after that.

Muttering a string of profanity to myself, I'd put on my headset
and logged onto the phones, hoping for a call to come in and bring a
few minutes of blessed distraction.

Nothing.

I'd busied myself with emails, reports, and all the other things I
was required to do in between calls. Unfortunately, if I wasn't getting
calls, no one else was either, which meant they were free to gossip
incessantly or come by my desk for no reason.

Then Damon's email had appeared in my inbox, and for a moment,
the spiderweb lifted off my skin.

How are you feeling? Worried about you.

He may as well have written, *I know you drank yourself blind last
night. At least let me know you're still alive.*

My cheeks burned, and the throbbing in my head didn't help the guilt any. Damon rarely gave me crap about my drinking, but he knew about it. I sucked at hiding it, just like he sucked at hiding how much it bothered him.

Pity I'm not as good at hiding my drinking as I was hiding the fact that I'm a shifter.

I winced and rubbed my eyes. *Christ, just tell him you're alive so he can relax.*

I sent him a quick email.

I'll live. Just need some coffee.
Me

Drumming my fingers on my desk, I read and reread Alex's email. I wasn't sure if he was being terse, or just short and to the point. The presence of the message was a relief, though. He'd dragged himself into work and could form a coherent, if brief, message. That meant I could stop worrying quite so much.

His email did nothing to help me concentrate, though. A few words, and my already preoccupied mind was inching even farther away from all things work-related. Like I needed an email to distract me. There was a photo of Alex and me pinned to the corkboard beside my desk, and today, that picture was driving me crazy.

It was one of those slightly crooked camera-held-at-arm's-length self-portrait snapshots, taken a few months after we'd started dating. Not something that would win any photography awards, but I liked it. I had one arm around Alex and the camera in my other hand, and she had both arms around my waist. Her hair was up in a messy ponytail as it often was, and she had a smile that still made my heart skip. Looking at the photo now, I kind of wished we'd left our sunglasses off so I could see her eyes.

I sighed and turned my attention to the computer screen and the work I'd neglected all morning. There wasn't much point. It wasn't like I could concentrate. Even when I'd looked away from the picture, I couldn't stop myself from seeing it.

After a while, I gave up and stared at the picture.

I still had no idea what to do about us. I didn't know what Alex expected me to do. Elbows on my desk, I clasped my hands together under my chin.

In theory, I could leave because she'd lied to me. She'd deceived me into believing she was a static woman, and it was only when the issue was forced that I'd learned the truth. No trust, no relationship. Or I could say I refused to deal with Alex's drinking anymore.

Hell, maybe I could sell myself some oceanfront property in Arizona while I was at it. It would be nothing but a cop-out. Total bullshit.

It was no lie that I had a tough time with Alex's drinking. It had bothered me throughout our relationship, but I knew why she drank, and if I were in her position, I'd have probably drunk a hell of a lot more. It wasn't healthy, but it was understandable. That, and if it was a deal breaker, it should have been a deal breaker six months, a year, two years ago.

"You're going through hell right now," I could say, "but I've just conveniently decided that I've had enough of your boozing. G'bye."

As for her dishonesty, the truth was I knew why she'd lied. I just regretted not making her feel like she could tell me.

The even deeper truth was that I didn't want to leave. I just didn't know how to stay. Did we go on as friends? A celibate couple? No, we were both far too sexual to be happy living celibate lives. An open relationship? That thought made me fidget. I wasn't wired for that kind of relationship. Monogamy had always suited me. That was why I'd wanted to get married in the first place.

My heart sank a little farther.

I didn't want to leave, but I couldn't manufacture a physical attraction to this man who lived in Alex's house, had all of Alex's quirks and mannerisms, and knew mine the way only Alex did. That wasn't the Alex I'd thought about in the shower before work this morning. Or the Alex I was terrified of losing. The Alex I refused to believe I'd already lost.

I winced. *Of course he's Alex. But he's not. But he is.* Leaning forward, I rested my forehead on my tightly clasped hands.

Fuck it. We needed to discuss this or I'd never be able to concentrate on anything.

I unfolded my fingers and ignored the tingle of blood rushing back into them. I pulled up the email he'd sent earlier and clicked *reply*. My fingers hovered over the keyboard, but the words didn't come.

Why don't we stay in tonight so we can talk things over?

Backspace. Backspace. Backspace.

I really think we should spend some time discussing—

What? Us? Our relationship? This whole insane situation that still didn't fit into my head?

Backspace. Backspace. Backspace.

I kept drumming my fingers on the desk while I stared at the blank email, at the empty white space, silently demanding an answer for how to fill it. I wanted to keep the line of communication open until I figured out what to say and how to say it. Finally, I settled on throwing the ball back in his court.

How's work going? Feel like doing anything tonight?
D

I scowled at Damon's email. The only thing I felt like doing tonight was very similar to what I'd done last night. On the other hand, I needed to see him. We needed to talk about . . . Christ, what *didn't* we need to talk about?

I muttered a few obscenities and rubbed my aching temples. Then I sat back and, without thinking about it, let my gaze drift to the picture beside my monitor. My chest tightened, with emotion, frustration, maybe a mix of the two, and I caught myself seriously considering taking the picture down. More than ever before, that framed five-by-seven of Damon and me was pure, aggravating distraction.

It was a shot of us at his brother's wedding last year. Damon in a tux, me in a blue dress I'd damn near starved myself to fit into. God, we looked so happy. We *were* happy. Chuckling to myself, I remembered the look on his face when he saw that dress. Come to think of it, I never did get around to sewing it back together after we'd ripped it that night in our hotel room.

My mind wandered back to a three-day weekend a few months before that picture was taken. We'd been casually dating for a while, but decided to go out to the coast together. Everything had lined up perfectly. Tabby gave me the entire weekend off. Damon and I snagged a reservation in a hotel right on the beach. My mind and body matched without the need to shift into something he didn't know I was.

And the weather? The weather had been awful. It was warm, being mid-summer and all, but it poured almost the entire time, giving us every reason to spend the whole weekend wrapped up in blankets and each other. Not that we'd needed a reason, but I couldn't remember ever having so much sex in so little time.

It hadn't been just sex, though. We spent as much time lying in bed and talking as we did making love. The rest of the world didn't matter, and for a few days, it was just us, a bottle or two of wine, and a California king bed.

The rain had stopped on Saturday afternoon, so we took advantage of the break and walked down the beach. The blanket under his arm and the glances we kept exchanging said it all: we weren't out there looking for seashells or sunsets.

He'd barely gotten the condom on when the skies opened up again.

"Damn it," he'd muttered, glaring up at the clouds. "So much for sex on the beach."

"Says who?" I'd grabbed the front of his unbuttoned shirt and pulled him down to me.

A file drawer slammed, startling me back into the present. I fidgeted in my chair, resisting the urge to crawl out of my skin. Letting myself daydream about a hot, intimate moment in my other form was hellishly masochistic when I couldn't *be* in that form.

I took a long drink, wondering when my coffee had turned cold, and tried to focus on the email I was supposed to be answering.

I wondered what Damon thought of the situation now that there was the possibility this implant wasn't coming out. Or, surgery or not, that my female form might never come back.

And if it didn't, what would happen to us? Losing half of my identity was bad enough. Losing Damon? I wasn't sure I could handle that much salt in this wound.

We needed to talk. Badly.

I looked at my computer screen. We had a line of communication open, albeit one made of brief, noncommittal emails. Still, it was a start. As good a place as any.

I put my fingers on the keyboard. What the hell could I suggest for tonight? Talking, that was what. We needed to do a lot of talking, and we needed to do it sooner than later. I didn't particularly want to, mostly because I was afraid of the conclusions we—*he*—would come to about our situation.

I scowled at his email again.

Last night wasn't a good time for a binge. Not just because of the headache and the redness that no amount of Visine would take out of my eyes, but because it gave Damon one more reason to step back. I'd practically handed him another excuse to walk away from me.

Hey, Damon, I lied through my teeth for two years, and you know what? I think instead of spending more of this evening with you, I'm going to go home and drink myself stupid, and we both know it.

I rubbed my eyes and sighed. I needed help. With everything. The drinking, the depression, everything.

And no matter how much I wanted to convince myself I could handle it if he left, the fact was, I needed Damon. I needed him, and I wanted him, and fuck if I wasn't stuck in a body I couldn't ask him to want.

If you want him to stick around, quit pushing him away, idiot.

I pulled up his email and typed a reply.

Yeah, we can get together. I think we might want to sit down and do some talking about things.

Me

I read it a few times over, my nerves prickling at the two simple sentences. Maybe it would be better to feel him out first. Gauge his mood, what he wanted out of this evening.

I deleted what I'd written, wrote another message, and hit send before I could think twice.

Got anything in mind for tonight?
Me

What did I have in mind? Oh, now there was a loaded question. What I wanted was for Alex and me to go out like we had hundreds of times before. As a couple. As two people in love.

Or just stay home, talk—not about anything serious or earth-shattering, just whatever came to mind—while I gave Alex a foot massage.

God, I missed that. Alex was almost always game for a foot massage. I used that to gauge how serious a depressive phase was. If she wouldn't even let me rub her feet, then she was in bad shape. If she just didn't want to talk, wasn't interested in sex, but was okay with the massage, then I could breathe a little easier.

It was a way for us to physically connect without making her uncomfortable. It didn't solve everything, but it closed some of the distance between us. On those nights, I'd take what I could get.

And now I was the one who wouldn't touch Alex.

But what was I supposed to do? I loved Alex. I loved the Alex I knew before the night I learned she was a shifter. How did I feel now? Part of me wanted to be angry and betrayed that she'd kept it from me for so long. I understood her reluctance to trust anyone with that information, but I couldn't deny it hurt that she hadn't been able to trust *me* with it.

Even if I could get past all of that, then what?

I wanted to make things work with Alex. If he regained the ability to shift, and we could regain the intimacy we'd had before, then maybe we could do this. But what if he didn't? What if we didn't? What if I couldn't?

And how would I have felt if Alex had accepted my proposal a few months ago? If this came out after we were married? Instead of now, when it was—and the thought made me sick with self-loathing—still socially acceptable for me to walk away?

I loved Alex and always would, but I didn't know *how* to love him now. What would happen when we got tired of not touching?

Even if I was physically attracted to him as a male, then what? He was the same person, just in a man's body, but I'd never been with a man before. I didn't have the first clue what to do. I mean, I knew what *I* liked. I knew what women liked. Things like anal were nothing new to us, though I wondered how the hell I'd react if Alex wanted to switch roles. That could be—

Damon. Slow down.

No two ways about it, we needed to talk. Badly. This was driving me to distraction. I looked up at our picture on the corkboard and sighed.

After a moment, I reached up and pulled the picture down. I gave it one last look, then slid it into the top drawer of my desk.

On my computer screen, his email was still waiting for a response, the cursor blinking like an impatiently tapping foot. Gut churning with guilt, mind going a thousand miles an hour, I typed a bland, benign response.

We could go out or stay in. Your call.
D

My call. I sighed. We could keep this up all damned day, knowing us. Why did it have to be so fucking hard for us to talk? That had never been easy for us, and today, we couldn't even get past a volley of noncommittal emails.

That wasn't to say that we never talked or couldn't talk. In our past life, there were nights we'd sit on the sofa for hours, just talking. And of course, Damon always ended up rubbing my feet, which was pure bliss. I was sure the man had sacrificed a virgin or twelve to the Patron Saint of Foot Massages. His touch was magic. And he didn't just soothe the pain from standing behind the bar all night; he could almost put me in a trance. A foot massage from him relaxed me like a full body massage from anyone else.

Right about now, I could have gone for one of those foot massages. *Yeah, right. I'm sure he gives those to his male friends all the time.* My heart sank.

There was no way I could express to Damon how thankful I was that he was still around. But what if the implants left me unable to shift into my female form even after they were removed? Damon had been a godsend, but I'd already leaned on him so heavily before this happened. He'd been a rock for me even when I'd rejected his touch and refused to tell him why, and he'd never hesitated for a second whenever I finally relaxed enough to lean on him.

There was a night maybe six months ago when I was so depressed, I could barely get off the sofa. Damon's concern was written all over him, from the upraised eyebrows to the gentle hand on my shoulder and his soft voice, but I couldn't explain it. How could I tell him about the conversation I'd had with my parents earlier that day? If I'd told him my stepfather had said it'd be better for me to risk dying under anesthesia than to voluntarily live another day as the creature I was, then I'd have had to explain what I was. Damon couldn't begin to understand that my parents hated me unless he understood *why*.

And I hadn't been able to speak then, anyway. The sound of my own voice had turned my stomach. I'd needed to be male so badly that night, but I'd needed Damon more, so I'd hidden in my female body instead of being alone.

We hadn't talked, but he hadn't left either.

I looked at the picture beside my monitor again. Seeing his face hurt more than seeing my own, and I couldn't stand it any longer. I grabbed the frame off my desk and shoved it into a drawer.

Then I faced his email again. My fingers rested on the keys, and I begged the words to come to me. *Come on, just get it out. Quit putting it off, and maybe we can both get some sleep.*

Taking a deep breath, I started typing.

Maybe we could stay in tonight. Talk about—

Backspace. Backspace. Backspace.

I stared at the blinking cursor and the vast expanse of nothing in front of it.

Damon, we really need to discuss things. I know this is difficult for you. Believe me, I under—

Ctrl+A. Delete.

Discussing it via email wasn't going to get us anywhere. We needed to discuss it face-to-face. Besides, anything could be misinterpreted in an emotionless message. Better to wait until we were in the same room.

Let me know what you want to do.

Me

When I got back from a staff meeting, Alex's email was waiting, and I supposed it shouldn't have surprised me that we were no closer to a consensus about tonight. All through the meeting, I hadn't been able to stop thinking about him or our situation. I'd hoped he'd be the one to stop the staring contest and just out and say it, but no luck.

Did this conversation have to be in an email, though? I could always bring it up tonight at dinner.

Nerves coiled in the pit of my stomach. Bringing this up wouldn't be easy.

"Listen, I'm not sure what we're doing . . ."

"Any thoughts about . . ."

"So, Alex, about our sex life . . ."

I sighed. Maybe I was rushing this. Alex had enough on his mind without listening to all the reasons—none of which I could articulate without sounding like a jerk—why I wasn't sure how things would pan out between us. We couldn't ignore the subject forever, but did we have to address it tonight? It had been less than twenty-four hours since his parents were arrested. He was stuck in a static body that was probably still hurting from however much he drank last night.

When did things get so fucking complicated? I knew every relationship would have its ups and downs, but thinking back to the beginning, I never could have imagined any of this. Not the way I'd fall in love with her, and not the way things would be now.

The night we met, she'd caught my eye from across the room, and that was it. One way or another, I'd *had* to talk to her. Of course, that almost backfired. I was so nervous about approaching her, I'd had one too many shots of liquid courage. I was lucky I could remember and articulate my own name, never mind ask for hers, but somehow, the words came out.

To my drunk and shy surprise, she'd said yes.

One dance had turned into two. Two turned into three. Three turned into finding a booth in the corner of the room and talking over the music until we got tired of shouting and went outside. Going outside turned into a long conversation, a long look, and a long, knee-shaking kiss.

And the rest was history.

Looking at the empty space the picture had occupied beside my desk, I wondered if the rest *was* history. In spite of her emotional ups and downs, not to mention her drinking, we'd had something really special. I loved her like I'd never loved anyone before.

I missed feeling that way about Alex. He was more of a stranger to me now than she'd been that night I drank up the courage to ask her for a dance.

I wanted that feeling back. Could we get it back? Was there a point of no return we'd crossed when I wasn't looking?

And for the millionth time, I asked myself, *was* Alex's gender really that important? It mattered to him, but should it matter to me?

Exhaling, I let my head fall back against the chair. Maybe we both just needed some time to deal with everything. No decision needed to be made tonight. We'd invested two years into our relationship. Two of the best years of my life. We were less than a week into this, so maybe it was too soon for do-or-die.

I took a breath and sent a message back.

I could go for Mexican tonight. Bolero's?
D

Maybe I was overanalyzing everything. Damon needed time to process all of this, and I didn't blame him. Cornering him into a conversation he wasn't ready for would probably be counterproductive.

He was still here. Whether or not our relationship ultimately wilted, he was still here. Friend, boyfriend, either way, I hadn't lost him yet. There was no sense beating him over the head with all of this and pushing him away, especially not days before a trial during which I was sure I'd need his shoulder *badly*.

We'd get to it. For now, Damon still seemed to enjoy my company. For now, that was enough. Why make it more difficult than it was?

There was time. Tonight, I just needed to be with him. Everything else could wait.

Meet me at my place after work?
Me

One thing at a time. One day at a time. Even if Alex and I did call it quits and go our separate ways over this, it wouldn't be this evening. There was too much chaos that went beyond us, and it didn't feel right to hash it all out tonight.

See you then.
D

⚦ CHAPTER 13 ♀
ALEX

Some god-awful country band blared over the speakers at the Welcome Mat. It wasn't the usual sound for this place, just whatever CD someone had put in while we prepped the bar, cleaned the tables, and got the club ready to open.

The music annoyed me, but at this point, my favorite album by my favorite band would have annoyed me. Everyone and everything was on my last nerve today. It was a Saturday, so at least I hadn't had to go to my day job. I probably would have strangled someone. How I was going to get through a busy night dealing with people in various states of inebriation, I had no idea. One hour at a time, I supposed.

For now, things were quiet aside from the shitty music. Colin and Dale shot the breeze while they checked the bottles in the wells, filled ice bins, and cleaned soda dispensers. Tabby was in the back doing paperwork. Sadie and Haley, two of the cocktail waitresses, chatted as they pulled down chairs and arranged tables in the lounge.

I busied myself with anything that kept me as far from everyone else as possible.

Everything was . . . off. I hadn't felt like eating. I'd managed half a cup of coffee in the time it usually took me to down three.

Maybe coffee isn't what I need to be drinking right now.

I pushed that thought away. No drinking on the job. That was nonnegotiable when working for Tabby. State law or not, she'd have had my head on a pike if I ever clocked in with booze on my breath.

It sure was tempting, though. Even being here at the Mat, in my sanctuary from a judgmental world, I couldn't relax. I couldn't take a step without feeling like my feet were encased in cement.

Damn it, what the fuck is wrong with me?

Maybe it was just nerves. My parents' trial was due to start on Monday.

This was something else, though. Something all too familiar.

The explanation for my mood was in the back of my mind, just beyond my awareness, like a person standing around a corner. I knew exactly who and where they were, but as long as I didn't acknowledge them, they didn't exist. The song on the CD player ended, and another began. It had just enough steel guitar to grate on my nerves, so I decided I'd make myself useful in the back room instead of up here. We needed a few more containers of margarita salt anyway. Right. That was it.

I went into the storeroom and found the box with margarita salt in it. After I'd pulled out a couple of containers, I paused to do a quick mental inventory and figure out if we needed anything else up front. Toothpicks? Napkins? Bitters? No, pretty sure we were well stocked.

I scanned the stacks of various supplies in case anything jogged my memory. As I did, my gaze drifted across the one window in the room, and when I caught a glimpse of myself in the glass, I almost dropped the margarita salt. I froze, staring at my own transparent, barely visible reflection.

Of course it shouldn't have surprised me, seeing my male face looking back at me. I supposed it wasn't a surprise as much as it was a cold slap of reality. I knew I was male right now, but seeing meant believing.

I forced myself to turn away from my reflection. Closing my eyes, I took a deep breath. *Get it together.* I could get through this. I had to. I was stuck as a male. No matter how badly I needed to be in a female body right now, it wasn't going to happen. Obsessing over it and wishing it weren't so wasn't going to help matters.

But knowing that didn't stop me from doing so. I set the margarita salt on a shelf and rubbed my temples. This whole situation was going to drive me insane. No two ways about it.

Usually, if I was truly desperate to shift, such as while I was with my family or at my day job, I could hold out until I got home. Once I was alone behind locked doors, I could shift. If I was staying with Damon, I could grab a shower and, for a few minutes, be what I needed to be.

For now and the foreseeable future, there was no "when I get home tonight." No sneaking off to the shower, no spending a few minutes alone in the restroom at my day job. There was no getting away from myself. From the need to be something I couldn't be. None. For the first time, in this place where I'd always been safe and okay, I wasn't.

Cold sweat beaded on the back of my neck and electric panic snaked up the length of my spine. It was like having a terrible itch, but being unable to scratch it. *Ever.* I shuddered. *Don't think like that. This is not permanent.*

"Tabby, are we out of Grand Marnier?" James called down the hall.

"There's an unopened case in the back," she replied. "I'll order another, but there should be plenty in there for tonight."

I sighed and rubbed my eyes, the sound of Tabby's voice tossing guilt into the mix of emotions. She'd have sold her soul for the ability to shift *once*. I could only imagine what it was like to be permanently trapped in the wrong body from day one. Even if I remained static, my body would sometimes match my mind. Tabitha would always be a woman trying to make do with whatever modifications she could manage on a biologically male body.

I took another deep breath, promised I'd quit feeling sorry for myself and get through the night, and went back to figuring out if there was anything else we needed for this evening.

I carefully avoided the window and its damning reflection, but hell if I could forget seeing my own male face in it.

Fuck it. If we needed anything else, one of the other bartenders could come back and find it. I needed to get out of this room and away from its window before I lost my mind.

I grabbed the margarita salt and went back up front.

Tabby was behind the bar when I stepped out, and she looked up as I set the salt beside the well.

"You get lost back here?" she asked with a grin.

I gave a quiet laugh that was as forced as it sounded. "Something like that."

Her forehead creased with concern. "You okay, hon?"

"I'm fine."

Her eyes said "I don't believe you," but she didn't argue.

While I continued stocking the well and cleaning the bar, I glanced at my watch. Four fifteen. Forty-five minutes until we opened.

Probably two or three hours before the rush started, and almost eight before I could clock off, go home, and have a few drinks myself.

I rolled my shoulders to get rid of the tension. It was absolutely alien to be this wound up here at the Mat.

Deal with it, Alex. Just deal with it.

Forty-five minutes later, the neon sign lit up, the door was unlocked, and the first customers strolled in.

Here we go. A few hours. I can get through it.

Oh, but there was one thing about this job I'd conveniently forgotten. I'd kept it tucked away in the back of my mind along with all the other unpleasantness I hadn't wanted to deal with, but it shoved its way to the front right about the time one of the regulars took a seat at the bar.

Kim. He'd been coming here forever, and he flirted with all the male bartenders.

Including me.

"Hey, gorgeous," he said with a grin, folding his hands on top of the bar.

I smiled in spite of the queasiness in the pit of my stomach. "Hey, Kim. The usual?"

"The usual." He winked. "Easy on the vermouth, though. One of your other boys went a little overboard on it the other night."

"Duly noted." I avoided his flirty gaze and went about pouring his drink.

"Ooh, good-looking crew tonight." Kim craned his neck and checked out the other guys behind the bar. "I may have to ask the DJ to put on one of your dancing songs."

I laughed, injecting more enthusiasm than I felt. "I'm sitting out for a few nights, I'm afraid."

He frowned. "Oh, but I like watching you dance."

I shrugged apologetically. "Back's giving me some grief. Doc says no dancing on the bar for a while." A little white lie, but less painful than the truth, which was that I just didn't have the physical or emotional energy to get up on the bar and dance.

"Well, when you're feeling better, I fully expect you to make up for lost time," Kim said.

"I'll do what I can." I slid his drink across the bar. He handed me a ten.

"Keep the change," he said with a wink.

I smiled, but my heart wasn't in it. Not even close. When patrons flirted—and everyone at the Mat flirted with everyone—it was fun. It didn't put me off. It never bothered me. Some of them knew I had a boyfriend, some didn't. We all flirted anyway because, hell, why not?

Tonight, I didn't have it in me. Mixing drinks was the most anyone was getting out of me this evening. Dancing on the bar? No. Flirting? *Hell* no.

The flirting was the worst part, if I was honest with myself. Because tonight, they were flirting with an apparition. An illusion. Someone who was the polar opposite of me. Every time someone grinned, or winked, or batted their eyes, I wanted to scream, "You're seeing something that isn't real!"

Joe's voice crept into my head. *"Can't believe someone would pass themselves off as a chick, then turn around and be one of those. What the fuck?"*

My head spun. *I'm not faking what I am. Can't you see? Can't anyone here see? I want to be . . . I need to . . . I fucking can't . . .*

"Well, like you said," Zach had replied. *"Package checks, just to be safe."*

"No shit. And God help a bitch if she turns out to be a guy."

Cold panic flooded my veins. My knees tried to buckle. I grabbed the edge of the bar for support, forcing myself to take slow, deep breaths.

Fuck, I'm losing it.

A hand on my shoulder made me jump.

"You all right?" Colin asked.

"Yeah." I ran a hand through my hair—short, short, too fucking short—and tried to hide how badly that hand shook.

"Alex, are—"

"I'm fine," I snapped. As soon as the words were out, I cringed. "Sorry. I'm sorry. I didn't mean to bite your head off."

"It's okay." He withdrew his hand. "But, seriously, you don't look so good."

"I think I'm going to take a break."

"Good idea." He raised his eyebrows. "You *sure* you're all right?"

No. No, I'm not. I nodded. "I'm fine."

"Okay, well, if you need to take a longer break, we've got it under control out here." He gestured at the sparse early evening crowd. "Take your time if you need it."

"Thanks."

I went back into the tiny room that passed for a break room. My knees stayed under me just long enough to pull one of the plastic chairs out from the table, and I sank into it. Elbows on the table, hands rubbing the back of my neck, I screwed my eyes shut and tried to just breathe. I hadn't thought it was possible to be so uncomfortable in my own skin at the Mat, but I was this close to losing it. God, I was going to fall to pieces.

Don't think, don't freak out, just breathe.

Heavy, high-heeled footsteps approached in the hallway, and I couldn't decide if I wanted Tabby to come in here or just keep going and leave me alone. I didn't want to talk to anyone or see anyone, but hers was a shoulder I could always lean on.

"Hey, kiddo."

I looked up to see her standing in the doorway, arms folded across her ample chest.

She cocked her head. "Having a rough day?"

The chair squeaked as I sat back in it. "You could say that."

"Anything you want to talk about?"

I shook my head. "Not really, no."

The slight lift of her eyebrow screamed skepticism. "Sure about that?"

Dropping my gaze, I nodded. "I'll be fine."

"Okay." She paused. "If you need to talk, just say so."

"Will do."

She turned to go.

Just before she disappeared around the corner, I said, "How do you deal with it, Tab?"

She stopped and looked at me. "Deal with what?"

"Not being able to . . ." I paused. "Being in a male body when your mind needs to be female?"

She folded her arms again and leaned against the doorframe. "I made my body as female as I can with what's available to me. Beyond that, until they come up with a safer and more effective gender reassignment surgery, I don't have much choice, do I?"

"Yeah, but what keeps you getting out of bed in the morning?"

"Hope. That I might be able to afford the surgery someday and change completely. As far as I'm concerned, though, I am a woman. There's only so much remodeling I can do, but . . ."

"What if that remodeling wasn't available?" My voice was little more than a whisper, but still too damned male. "If you were . . . stuck?"

She shrugged. "Make do, I guess."

I sighed. "I don't know how you do it."

"That's because you haven't had to do it for the last forty-seven years." Tabby sat in the chair beside mine. "If I'd ever been able to shift, and then suddenly couldn't, I'd be falling apart, too. You know what they say, sweetie. You don't know what you've got until it's gone."

Damon's face flickered through my mind, and I struggled to keep my emotions in check. "Or until you're about to lose it, I guess."

"What do you mean?"

I don't know what's going to happen with Damon. If I can't accept me, how can he? I'm just sitting on go, waiting for him to walk out.

I shook my head and cleared my throat. "Nothing." I leaned forward, rested my elbows on the table again, and resumed rubbing the back of my neck with both hands. "I guess this is just hitting me harder today."

She squeezed my arm. "You can take the night off, you know."

"No, I need the money. And I can either dwell about it here or dwell about it at home." I laughed dryly. "At least I'm not drinking when I'm here." I moved my hands from my neck to my temples, like I could manually remove all of this from my brain. "I feel like I'm making this bigger than it is."

"Bigger than it is? Baby, this isn't a minor thing."

"Yeah, but it's not like I have cancer or anything. I mean, assuming the implant doesn't *give* me cancer."

"Yeah, yeah, yeah, it could be worse." She stroked my hair. "There's always something that could be worse. That doesn't mean you're overreacting if you buckle under something like this."

I didn't say anything.

"It affects every part of your life, hon. Not everyone understands that, but you know I do, and I don't think you're making this into something it's not." She rested her hand on my shoulder. "And if you need support, by all means, ask for it."

"I definitely need it," I whispered.

"How much do you have?"

I exhaled. "Not much. I'm the subject of gossip at my other job. I've got one friend there who's got my back, but otherwise, I'm a one-man freak show." My voice shook. "Damon still can't make heads or tails of the situation, and I don't know how to discuss it with him."

"He's still around, isn't he?"

"For now."

"That says a lot, baby. A lot of guys would be long gone by now."

"I know. I just, I don't know how much of that is because he wants to stay, or because he feels guilty about leaving."

"I doubt he's staying because he feels guilty, sweetie. This is a lot for someone, especially a static, to take in, but he's standing by you."

I rubbed my forehead. "I should have told him sooner. It would have been so much easier for both of us to deal with if I'd just gotten it over with early on."

"Maybe he wasn't ready to hear it. If you'd told him in the beginning, it might have been too much for him, but maybe now . . ."

"I think it'll just make it harder for both of us when he ultimately leaves."

"You never know." She paused. "Did I ever tell you what happened when I came out to my family?"

I chewed the inside of my cheek and shook my head.

She sat up a little straighter and looked me in the eye. "I was sure my parents would throw me out. One hundred percent sure, no doubt in my mind, I'd be out on my ass if I opened my mouth about it. So I waited until college. Made sure I had all my ducks in a row, and that way, when they cut me off financially, I could finish my degree and still eat."

"That must have been hard," I said.

She nodded. "Keeping who you are a secret is always hard. But I had to."

This revelation surprised me. As long as I'd known her, Tabby had had an enviable—and unusual, for someone who was transgendered—relationship with both of her parents.

"So what happened when you told them?"

"Well, I was home for Christmas during my sophomore year. That visit was agony, Alex. I was there for two weeks, and it wasn't until the very last night that I got up the nerve to tell them." Her eyes lost focus. "I've never seen my folks that shocked before in my life."

"What did they say?"

"Not much at the time. My dad was pretty upset, but he didn't throw me out. They let me stay that last night. When I got up the next morning, my dad was in the kitchen. He said he'd been up all night thinking about the whole situation and, my God, he looked the part. He got real quiet there for a few minutes, but he finally said it was going to take some time, but he'd get used to the idea."

I blinked. "Really?"

"Really. About knocked me over with that. And it was still a little awkward that day and when they took me to the airport, but it wasn't as bad as I thought it would be. So then I regretted waiting so long. I mean, I'd had that weight on my shoulders for years, and I could have gotten rid of it a long time ago. But"—she held up one emphatic finger—"there's more, and this is the important part."

"Okay . . ."

"When I was home on summer break, we sat down and had a good, long talk about it. And you know what he told me?"

I shook my head.

"He said he kind of had a feeling something was different about me. Ever since I was a kid, he knew. And all through my teenage years, he was sure I was going to tell him I was gay, and he was just waiting for me to say it so he could fly off the handle. No son of his was gay. Or a cross-dresser. Anything. No way. But around the time I hit my late teens and headed off to college, he started thinking about it more, and it occurred to him that whatever was different about me hadn't changed in all that time, so maybe it was more than just a phase. And maybe, just maybe, it was okay." She put a hand over mine. "So, by the time I told him, he'd already done some soul-searching of his own, and he was ready to hear it. If I'd broached the subject a few years earlier,

Daddy and I wouldn't be nearly as close as we've been for the last three decades or so."

I'd envied her relationship with her parents for a long, long time, and now even more so.

"Maybe Damon wasn't ready to hear that you were a shifter when he first met you," she said. "But maybe he's still around because he *is* ready to deal with it now."

"Damon didn't have a clue, though. Your dad suspected it. Damon...he..."

"Damon knows *you*." Tabby squeezed my hand. "That, and the night he found out, did he act like you repulsed him?"

In my mind, I replayed as much of that night as I could, what pieces weren't blurred by blinding pain and nausea. He'd been surprised, of that there was no doubt. Hostile at first, and I couldn't blame him for that, since his immediate thought was that I was his girlfriend's lover. But after he knew the truth, he'd stayed. Even after I was discharged from the hospital and had practically shoved him out my door, he'd come back. And he kept coming back.

"No," I said quietly. "He's never acted that way."

"Then have some faith in him and quit beating yourself up for not telling him. You both have two years invested in this relationship. Don't let a week or two of indecision make or break it."

"Good point."

She put her arm around me and let me rest my head on her shoulder as she stroked my hair. "Listen to me, sweetheart. You'll make it through this. You're a strong, strong person, and even though it's tough, you'll get through it."

"And what if I can't get this thing out?"

"Then you find a way to live with it."

"God, I hope that doesn't happen."

"Me, too. But if it does, you'll be okay." Still stroking my hair, she whispered, "Think about those times when you were a teenager and you didn't think you could live another day."

I shivered. She was one of the few outside my family who knew how many times I'd considered killing myself. One of even fewer who knew how many times I'd *tried* to kill myself. Even Damon didn't know about any of that.

"You thought you couldn't make it, but you did," Tabby said. "And things got better. They've been bad and worse, but you've had a lot of good times since then, haven't you?"

I nodded.

"And right now is one of those really shitty times. Most people would have crumbled under it by now." She squeezed my shoulder. "You haven't crumbled, and you know from experience that even the worst of times do, eventually, get better."

"I'm just not sure how this one will." I raised my head and looked at her. "Unless I win the lottery and find someone who can get the implants out without killing or crippling me in the process."

"Well, if you're stuck with the implants—"

"Assuming they don't kill me."

"Right," she said. "And you'll have bad days as a static, but you'll make it through them, and there will be good times again, too." She went quiet for a moment, then went on. "I mean, look at it this way. Your parents have made you miserable over this whole thing. They've driven you to almost killing yourself a few times, and now they've forced you to be static. Haven't they had *enough* control over your life without making you miserable every waking moment for the rest of it?"

"I hadn't thought about it that way."

"And I'm not saying that's easy by any means, baby." She put a gentle hand between my shoulder blades. "There are going to be days when you just do not want to get out of bed in the morning. Believe me, I know. But you have to look at yourself in the mirror, even when you hate what you see, and tell yourself you're going to get through the day."

That prospect made me shudder.

"You've heard all the crap I've been through," she went on. "Statics don't understand transgendered people any more than they understand shifters. Sometimes, when it's really bad, I think the only reason I make it from one end of the day to the other is because it's a 'fuck you' to all the people who wish I was dead."

"Seriously?"

She smiled. "Hey, whatever works, right?"

I grinned. "Okay, true."

"So, moral to the story is, if you can't get through the day for yourself, get through it because you know it pisses other people the fuck off."

"I'll remember that," I said with a quiet laugh. "Damn it, why couldn't I have had a mom like you instead of the one I got?"

She snorted. "Oh, honey, I'd be a horrifying parent."

"I don't know. You do a pretty good job of filling in where mine fucked up."

"Alex, darling, Cinderella's stepbitch was a better mother than your mom."

Chuckling, I said, "Okay, you're right. But you know what I mean."

"Yes, I do." She hugged me again.

I closed my eyes and held onto her. "Thank you, Tab."

"Anytime."

She let me go, and we both stood. Before we left to return to the front of the club, Tabby took my hand. Clasping it between both of hers, she looked me in the eye. "There's one more thing I want you to keep in mind."

I inclined my head.

"Everyone here, both the employees and the customers, adore you," she said. "We've all got your back, and even when your brain and body don't match, you're still Alex to us. I know that doesn't fix everything, or even scratch the surface, but I wanted you to know."

I smiled, biting back a flood of emotion. "Thanks."

"Anytime, hon." She nodded toward the front of the club. "Think you can make it through the rest of the night?"

"Yeah. I think I'll be okay."

"Good. Now get out there and make me some money."

☿ CHAPTER 14 ♀
DAMON

The trial was brief, wrapping up in less than a week, but it was hell for Alex. The defense attorney tried to win the jury's sympathy by portraying Alex as an unstable alcoholic who'd resisted therapy for severe depression. His father's suicide, as well as Alex's own attempts as a teenager, were paraded in front of God and everyone. One side pointed to the self-destructive behavior pattern as a manifestation of the emotional toll of trying to function as a shifter in a society designed for and accepting of statics alone. The other side used it as another example of mental instability, both in shifters and in Alex himself. His parents had acted illegally, and they acknowledged that, but their attorney insisted they'd acted with Alex's spiritual, mental, and emotional well-being in mind.

The defense even made a feeble argument, complete with a so-called expert witness, that Alex's resistance to the implant was a symptom of his incompetence to make the decision at all.

"Shifters who refuse the implant are in dire need of extensive therapy," the alleged expert had said. "Forced treatment of a shifter is no different than forced treatment of a patient with a severe form of schizophrenia. When a patient's illness clouds his judgment, it's necessary for others to step in and take action for his own good."

The prosecution, of course, eviscerated her. He brought out the psychiatrist who'd evaluated Alex, and while she acknowledged his depression and drinking problem, she declared him fully competent to make his own decision regarding the implant. Plus, Alex's parents and the pastor—who'd also been the "surgeon"—were nowhere near qualified to declare Alex competent or not. Still, Alex and I both worried the other expert's comments may have planted seeds of doubt into the heads of some of the jurors.

Next up on the stand was a neurosurgeon specializing in these implants. He testified for the prosecution, and calmly rattled the jury with grim facts about the devices, potential side effects, invasiveness of the surgery, risk after risk after risk. By the end of that testimony, sweat curled the ends of Alex's hair.

The worst part of the trial was when Alex took the stand. The defense attorney ripped him to shreds, questioning him so mercilessly that just thinking about it made my stomach turn. She made a point of using his given name, sneering every time it found its mark, until the judge ordered her to use "Mr. Nichols" instead. Even then, she emphasized "Mr." just to get under his skin, and it worked. Alex never lost his cool, fortunately, but when he got home that night, he killed better than half of a bottle of tequila.

At long last, both sides rested, and after the closing arguments, the jury was dismissed to hash it out. I'd go to my grave wondering what went down in the deliberation room. The case was as cut and dry as any I'd ever seen. Alex was an adult. Neither his parents nor the surgeon were qualified to deem him unable to make his own medical decisions, and a qualified psychiatrist had deemed him fully competent. The surgery was performed without his consent, in unsterile conditions, using an implant that wasn't FDA approved. Even the most bigoted shifter hater had to have seen that Alex's parents and the surgeon acted illegally.

Cut and dry or not, it took six hours for the jury to reach a guilty verdict.

One of the most heartbreaking moments came not during the testimonies, but after the verdicts were read and his parents were taken from the courtroom in handcuffs. Sitting with a social worker and her foster parents on the other side of the room, Alex's younger sister collapsed into sobs. He took one look at her, then turned away, grimacing with more pain than when he'd had the spinal headache. If there was a moment when I was certain he'd regretted pressing charges, that was it.

As soon as court was adjourned, we made a quick exit with the DA, carefully dodging both family and media. After slipping out through a back door, I drove Alex to my place, where we hid his car in my garage. Cell phones stayed off. So did the television. We shut ourselves in and shut the world out.

The trial was over. His parents—and most likely the pastor who thought he was a surgeon—were going to jail.

Still, Alex was in no mood to celebrate.

He'd said next to nothing on the drive home. I suspected part of that had to do with the conversation he'd had with the DA before we left. Though it was highly likely the defendants would be ordered to pay for the surgery, the DA agreed with Alex's pessimistic prediction that getting the money would be like getting blood from a stone.

"The pastor's assets have been seized pending an investigation," the DA had said. "And from the sound of it, he was as broke as your parents. Getting close to a hundred thousand dollars out of any of them probably isn't going to happen."

I appreciated his honesty. I was sure Alex did, too. Still, he might've held off on that little tidbit for a day or two. Alex had enough on his mind.

One elbow on the armrest of my couch, Alex chewed his thumbnail and stared into nothing with blank eyes. His foot tapped rapidly, and his fingers drummed on his knee. He looked simultaneously restless and exhausted.

"How are you holding up?" I asked.

Alex sighed. "I just put my parents in prison. My sister's world is flipped on its ass. I still have this thing in my spine. I . . . really don't know."

"Want a drink?"

"Several, actually."

I laughed quietly. "How about starting with one?"

He managed something in the ballpark of a laugh, and I went into the kitchen to get us a couple of drinks. When I came back, we both sat on the couch, beers in hand and alone with our thoughts.

Out of nowhere, Alex broke the silence. "Ever wonder what kind of a backlash there would be if someone came up with an implant that could change a static into a shifter?"

"Somehow I doubt that would make it very far. The world wants to make more shifters static, not the other way around."

"And they wonder why so many shifters commit suicide," he muttered.

"The suicide rate is really that much higher?"

He nodded. "Surprised?"

"Yes and no." I played at the label on my beer bottle with my thumbnail. "Just seems like, as a society, we'd be over this sort of thing by now."

"You would think." He took a long drink. "Things *are* better now. Health care's catching up. Discrimination is illegal, even if it's not enforced as much as it should be. Being a shifter isn't grounds for automatic child removal or requiring supervised visits. We can get the same custody arrangements as statics. Some judges are still asses about it, but the tide is turning very, very slowly."

"Something tells me today might help turn that tide."

He stared at the coffee table with unfocused eyes. "I'll believe that when I see it."

"A jury ruled in your favor," I said. "Yeah, it took them a while to reach the verdict, but it *did* ultimately come out in your favor."

Alex shrugged. "The law was on my side. They didn't have much choice."

"Which is why it took them six hours to deliberate?" I resisted the urge to put a hand on his arm. I'd seen Alex depressed too many times before, and I couldn't be sure if even the most platonic contact would be welcome now. "Maybe this means people are catching on that being a shifter and wanting to *stay* a shifter isn't a bad thing."

He didn't respond.

"Let's face it," I said. "Ten years ago, the prosecutor would have been hard-pressed to persuade a jury that you were mentally capable of refusing the implant, even with the psychiatrist's testimony. The burden of proof wouldn't have been on the defense, let's put it that way." I paused. "Twenty years ago, I doubt this would have ever gone to court. Another ten before that, you would have been institutionalized long before this ever happened."

Alex shuddered.

"Society's getting there," I said. "You said so yourself. Every case like this, everyone who's willing to stand up like you did, is one step closer."

"Always glad to be the sacrificial lamb."

I swallowed hard, but didn't know what to say. Seeing him like this killed me, just like it had every time she'd fallen into a depression over the last couple of years. For a fleeting moment, my mind went back to that weekend we'd spent at the coast. Her demons hadn't followed her then. Whatever was waiting for her back home seemed forgotten. For those three days, it was only us. That was the one and only time I'd ever seen her truly happy, and ever since then, I'd *ached* to see that again.

It was there. I'd tasted it once. I just didn't know how to bring it back, and it sure as hell wasn't coming back on a day like today. He certainly deserved to feel that way after what he'd been through. There had to be a karmic scale out there that had long ago reached the point of "okay, enough bad shit, let's send this guy some happiness."

The urge to reach for him and put an arm around him was, more than it had been since all this had started, almost irresistible. We hadn't touched in weeks, and tonight, I wanted to be close to him, if only to provide comfort. Even before things had gotten so complicated, we'd had moments like this, and when they'd happened, I was completely helpless. I couldn't find the words to encourage him, make him feel better, anything.

So this time, I settled for the next best thing. "Another drink?"

"Please."

With fresh beers in hand, the silence hung between us once again. I finally spoke. "Mind if I ask a personal question?"

"I've been answering them for the last week," he said into his drink. "One more won't make much difference."

"Is it true what they all said during the trial? About attempting suicide when you were a teenager?"

He looked at me, his expression blank. "You think I lied under oath?"

"No, no, I'm just curious about it. You don't have to answer. I know you've probably talked about it more in the last week than you ever wanted to."

Alex didn't respond right away. He took a long drink, rolled it around in his mouth, and all the while, his eyes were focused on something in the distance. A few times, I thought he was letting the subject die, but then he spoke.

"My parents think I tried to kill myself twice," he whispered. "They don't know about the third time."

The hairs on the back of my neck stood on end. "What happened?"

"The first time was when I was thirteen." He rubbed his forehead. "After my stepdad told me what really happened to my father. He said my dad had been so ashamed of what he was, and so haunted by it, he'd killed himself. And I thought, hell, if Dad couldn't handle this, then neither could I. But later, I talked to my aunt, and she said that was bull. He didn't kill himself because he was a shifter."

I moistened my parched lips. "Why did he do it?"

Alex swallowed. "Because after my mom took us from him, he had nothing left." He focused on peeling the label off his beer bottle. "She refused to let him see us because he was a shifter, and back then, the courts were on her side."

"Did she think it was contagious or something?"

"She was still afraid we'd both turn out to be shifters, and she was sure he'd encourage us to try shifting. Like he'd egg us on or something." Alex sighed and set the bottle on the end table. "Anyway, then when I was fifteen, my folks sent me to this summer camp. I didn't realize 'til I got there that it was just a month-long seminar of trying to browbeat me into realizing there was something wrong with me. I mean, what did they want? It wasn't like I could stop being a shifter. Even if I didn't shift, the gene was still there. The need to shift was still there."

"So you tried to kill yourself after that?"

He shook his head. "If I'd done it after, I might have succeeded. I did it at the camp, and someone found me in time."

"Is that what happened to your wrists?" I asked softly.

He pulled his forearm against himself, turning the other wrist downward to hide the scars.

"You don't have to—"

"These weren't suicide attempts." After a moment's hesitation, he held out his arm. The lines were hair-thin and perfectly straight, though not parallel to each other, scoring his skin all the way from his wrist to just below his elbow. "I really don't know if it was a cry for help, a way to get attention, or just a way to have control over *some* pain, but . . . there it is."

"Did it work as a cry for help?"

He snorted. "Hardly. I spent my teenage years wearing long-sleeve shirts for a reason." He glared at the scars. "I don't know what I was thinking, honestly. I was so fucked up in the head back then."

"How long did that go on?"

"Couple of years. I stopped when I was sixteen or so, I think."

"What changed?"

He laughed humorlessly. "Started drinking." He lifted his beer bottle to his lips. "Didn't hurt as much." After he took a drink, he watched his fingers playing with the bottle cap on the end table. "I almost succeeded when I was seventeen. Killing myself, I mean."

My blood turned cold. "You did?"

Cheeks coloring slightly, he nodded. "That's the time my parents don't know about. I had my stepdad's pistol. Out, loaded, ready to go."

I swallowed. "What stopped you?"

"It occurred to me that he'd probably get some sick satisfaction out of knowing I'd taken care of 'the problem' using his own gun. He always made a point of making sure I knew where the gun and ammo were, so . . ." Alex trailed off, shrugging with one shoulder. "That, and I was only a few months away from eighteen. I just needed to get through a few more months, and then I could get out."

"Damn," I whispered.

"Yeah." He stared at nothing for another long moment. "You know, sometimes I wonder if my dad would have stayed around if he'd known I was a shifter."

I cocked my head.

"I mean, you think he'd have offed himself if he knew he was leaving me—a shifter—behind with my mother and stepfather?"

"If he was a shifter, wouldn't he have known you were, though?"

"Not necessarily. It's genetic, but I don't know, I guess it's recessive or something. My sister's static, so . . ." He shrugged. "Dad probably didn't know I was, too. I knew before he died, but I had no way of reaching him. And I guess even if I could have, I was afraid he'd tell my mom. Don't know why, but . . . I was a kid. I was scared."

"But you eventually told your mother?"

"She figured it out." He gave a dry laugh as he lifted his beer bottle to his lips again. "There's only so long you can hide that there's a female in the house who's going through puberty. I kept it a secret until I was fourteen, and suddenly they understood—they thought—why I'd tried to do myself in the year before. And it was pretty much downhill from there until I moved out."

"Wow," I whispered. "I honestly never realized how much something like this could rule your life."

"It shouldn't, but when you constantly hear how horrible you are, what a freak you are, how there's something wrong with you . . ." His voice caught. He looked away, then quickly went for his drink.

"What's wrong?" I asked.

Alex cleared his throat. "That was one of the reasons I was afraid to tell you."

"What do you mean?"

Looking into his nearly empty beer bottle, he said, "With you, I finally felt like there wasn't anything wrong with me. When I took you to the Mat, you didn't freak about the people there. Shifters, trans, anyone. And I guess I got hooked on that. On being around someone who made me feel . . ."

I leaned forward, inclining my head slightly. "What?"

"You made me feel human." He looked at me. "I didn't want to lose that."

"But you just said you knew I was cool with shifters."

"Being cool with it and sleeping with it are two different things. As we're both finding out the hard way now. Thanks for sticking by me, though. This can't be easy for you."

"Sticking by you is the easy part," I said softly. "Watching you go through this? Not so much."

"You say that now," he said, his voice shaking a little. He dropped his gaze. "We'll see what happens if I'm stuck as a man for the rest of my life."

"I don't care if you are." I reached across the void and finally made contact, putting a hand over his. His breath caught. Mine did too. His hand twitched under mine, and I thought for a moment he'd pull it away, but he didn't.

"Alex, I want you to be able to shift because that's what you need to be happy. But . . ." I swallowed hard. "Even if you can't, I'm not going anywhere."

He avoided my eyes. "Listen, I don't want sympathy, Damon. I don't want you to stay with me because leaving would make you feel guilty. I hope you'll at least stay around as a friend, because I really do need the support right now, but as far as our relationship . . ." He looked at me again. "We've already kicked the physical side of it, and I know you want that—with someone—as much as I do. It's your call, continuing this or not, but I won't hold it against you if you can't do it."

What could I say to that? Alex didn't disgust or repel me, but at least for now, he was male. I was heterosexual. Yeah, I'd made him feel human, but the fact remained we were *both* human. Only human. I couldn't make myself feel something that wasn't there. I couldn't force chemistry, I couldn't fake it, and he deserved someone who didn't have to.

For lack of anything else to say, I asked, "Another drink?"

"I haven't passed out yet." He set the empty bottle on the coffee table. "So, yes. Please."

He wanted to drink himself numb. Drown everything in a brown bottle. Escape, if only for a few hours.

Just this once, I didn't try to stop him.

☿ CHAPTER 15 ♀
ALEX

I called in sick the next day. Let them fire me. So what if I'd already been out the whole week because of the trial? I was hungover, depressed, demoralized, and I couldn't afford the fucking surgery anyway, so what did I care if I burned more sick time? Wasn't like I could go anywhere. I'd taken a cab home from Damon's last night since we were both too shitfaced to drive. My car was still at his place, and there was no way in hell I was coughing up the money to go to my shit job so I could be gawked at while my head pounded and my boss accumulated reasons to can me.

I spent the day doing as close to nothing as I could. Video games when my head didn't hurt too much, television when it did. My phone was still off, and I logged into my email just long enough to exchange a few messages with Damon about getting together tonight. Besides him, the world outside these walls could go to hell.

A little after four, though, the doorbell rang.

I groaned aloud. Some of the local media had been hounding me since my parents went to trial, and ever since the verdict was read yesterday, I'd left my phone turned off specifically to avoid them. *Tell me they haven't found my damned house.*

Expecting to see a reporter peering back, I looked through the peephole. My heart jumped into my throat.

With trembling fingers, I turned the dead bolt and opened the door. It took a second, but I finally found enough breath to whisper, "Candace."

"Hey," she said quietly.

"How did . . . how did you find me?" *And why are you here?*

She avoided my eyes. "Your address is on some of the papers from the court. They were in my case file."

"Oh."

For a moment, we stood in silence, just looking at each other.

"Can, um, can I come in?"

"Yeah. Yeah, sure." I stood aside. My heart pounded as she walked past me. I shut the door, then faced her. "This is a surprise."

"I know." She tucked a strand of bright purple hair behind her ear. "I tried calling, but you weren't answering."

"Yeah, sorry. I've had my phone turned off. To avoid . . ." The media. Who wanted to talk to me. About putting our parents in jail. I gestured down the hall. "Can I get you something to drink?"

"No, I'm good. Thanks."

"I could go for a cup of coffee, though. Come on." I led her into the kitchen. The truth was, I didn't need coffee. Now that she was here, I was too jittery for caffeine, but my hands were going to start shaking if I didn't keep them busy.

"I'm not catching you at a bad time, am I?" she asked.

"No, of course not." Back to her, unable to look her in the eye, I pulled a cup down and set it on the counter. "How are you holding up? With . . . Mom and Gary . . ."

"I'm okay. That's actually why I'm here."

I gulped. That was what I was afraid of, and the memory of her breaking down in the courtroom gave me chills. *Jesus, she must hate me.* Without turning around, focusing as much as I could on keeping my voice even and pouring the coffee without spilling it, I said, "I'm sorry, Candace. I really am. I . . . had to. Trust me, it was—"

"I came here to thank you."

The coffeepot almost crashed to the counter.

It wasn't the words, though. It was the voice.

No, I was imagining it.

I set the coffeepot down so I wouldn't drop it, but I still didn't face Candace. "What did you say?"

"I said, I came here to thank you."

The voice. The *male* voice.

Slowly, I turned around. My lips parted and my breath froze in my lungs. With a shaking hand, I grabbed the counter for support.

Long, unruly hair fell in ink-black tendrils over his shoulders, which filled out his rock band T-shirt a little more than before. His features shared a youthful roundness with his female form, but with a dusting of stubble along his jaw and a slightly heavier bone structure.

His eyes were the same blue, and his eyebrows were raised as he waited for my reaction.

"I thought . . ." I coughed, trying to get my lungs and mouth to function. "I thought you were static."

He chuckled. "So did Mom and Gary. And now I'm not under their thumbs anymore."

"But . . . in the courtroom . . ." I shook my head. "You . . ."

"Dude, that was relief. You have no fucking idea."

"I . . ." Disbelief kept me tongue-tied for a moment. I finally managed to whisper, "How long have you known?"

"Since I was nine."

"And you hid it from them? All these years?"

He nodded. "I told them I couldn't shift. And I made them think I was drinking the Kool-Aid at that crazy church, so they believed me and left me alone." He grimaced. "I went to a bunch of those stupid protests, too. You don't hate me, do you?"

"What? No. God, no, I don't hate you." I crossed the kitchen and put my arms around him. As he hugged me back, I closed my eyes. "I thought *you* hated *me*."

"Mom and Gary wanted me to."

I laughed softly. "And since when have you ever done what you're told?"

"Exactly." He laughed, too, but then fell silent. After a moment, he sniffed sharply. "I'm sorry, Alex."

The sound of my brother saying my real name was overwhelming, and I fought to keep my composure. When I was sure my voice wouldn't crack, I said, "You have no reason to be sorry. You were smart to hide what you were from them."

"I know, but I—"

"What's your name?"

He was quiet for a few seconds. "Sam."

I smiled. Our father's name.

"Not very original, is it?" he asked.

"It doesn't have to be." I pulled back and grinned at him. "I think Dad would be proud."

"And Mom would be pissed."

I laughed. "That she would. Come on, have a seat." I gestured toward the living room. "Let's talk."

Once we'd gotten situated on the sofa, I said, "This is definitely a surprise. I was sure you were static."

"Kind of nice not to have to hide it anymore," he said.

"I'm sure. So, do you go male or female most of the time?"

"Male. I kind of go whichever way, but I like being a guy. I don't know if it's because I had to be a girl around Mom and Gary all the time or what."

"That could be. When you get shoehorned into one form, it makes you want to be the other." I rolled my eyes. "Believe me, I understand."

"Yeah, I'll bet. I guess I'll figure it out. Most of the time, when Mom and Gary weren't around, I dressed so people couldn't tell one way or the other anyway. Is that weird?"

"No, it's not weird." I paused. "Does anyone else know?"

"Well, my girlfriend knows."

I blinked. "You . . . have a girlfriend?"

Sam nodded. "Yeah. She's great. She's totally cool with me being a shifter." He laughed quietly. "Kind of funny, actually. We were friends as girls for a long time, and when I came out to her as a shifter, I started spending more time around her as a boy. Then it just . . ." He shrugged. "Just happened, I guess."

"Wow." I envied him. I'd struggled so hard with depression and the desire to kill myself, I didn't even get around to dating until college. "Okay, this is probably way too personal, but being the responsible older brother, I have to ask." I raised an eyebrow. "You and your girlfriend, you're . . . being careful, right?"

"Are you insane?" He smirked. "Can you imagine if Mom and Gary found out their daughter had knocked up some chick?"

I laughed. "Jesus, they'd shit kitten-shaped bricks. They freaked out enough when they found out I have a boyfriend."

"You do? Oh, that's right. I remember you mentioning that when we were in the diner with Mom."

I nodded, my humor fading a little. Watching my fingers tap on the armrest, I said, "Yeah, I've been seeing someone the last couple of years. We're kind of sorting things out right now. With me being a shifter and all. And . . . male."

"He didn't know?"

"No." I sighed. "I was afraid to tell him, kept putting it off, and . . ." I gestured at myself. "As it always does, the truth came out on its own." I looked at Sam for a moment. "How did you keep it from Mom and Gary?"

"I don't even know. I probably wouldn't have been as careful if I hadn't seen what you went through . . ."

"Well, at least it helped someone. Does anyone else know?"

"A few friends at school. The whole group is pretty cool with shifters, and the ones who know about me keep it on the down low."

"Wow. That's—that's great."

"Yeah." He grinned. "It's funny, there's another guy in the group who's known he was a shifter since first grade. Totally out, doesn't give a shit what anyone thinks. You should've seen the way people flipped out when he got the male lead in the school play last semester, and then got the female lead this semester."

"You're kidding."

"No, everyone thought shifting gave him an unfair advantage." Sam shrugged. "The drama teacher said if he was good enough for the female lead and good enough for the male lead, then tough shit."

"I need to meet this teacher. He sounds awesome. Do your foster parents know?"

"Tammy does. I haven't told Bill yet, but he's pretty chill, so . . ."

"And she's okay with it?"

Sam nodded. "Yeah, she's cool with it."

"How is it, the whole foster care thing?"

He played with a tear in his jeans. "I don't know; it's okay. At least I can keep going to my high school for now."

I chewed the inside of my cheek. "Any idea how long you'll be there?"

"Don't know. The social worker said they're making arrangements or something with Aunt Beverly and Uncle Ray."

"How do you feel about living with them?"

He focused a little harder on tugging the fringe at the edge of the tear. "They're nice and all, but I really don't want to go to California." He looked at me. "All my friends are here. Lisa's here. My girlfriend, I mean."

I stared at the cushion between us for a long moment. "You know, there's no guarantee it would work, but legally, I can petition for custody."

His eyes widened. "You can?"

I nodded. "I don't know if they'll grant it. History of 'issues' and all. But . . ." I hesitated. "But I can petition for it. Would you be okay with living with me?"

"Yeah, definitely. I'd rather live with you than go to California."

I smiled. "Well, I can give it a try. We'll see what happens."

"Awesome." Sam snickered. "God, Mom will be pissed if she finds out."

I laughed. "Yeah, that she will."

We both fell quiet for a minute or two. I ran through a mental list of all the things I'd need to do in order to get custody of Sam. Who knew if I could even afford to, but all of that could be dealt with later.

"So, are you going to get the implant thing out?" he asked out of the blue.

I exhaled. "I'd like to. I don't know how the hell I'll pay for it, though."

"I thought the judge was going to have Mom and Gary or the pastor pay for it."

"Yeah, and that looks great on paper, but getting the money out of them?" I shook my head. "Not so much."

"That sucks," he said. "Oh, and Gary tried to make me get it, too."

My blood ran cold. "I thought they didn't know you were a shifter."

"They didn't." He fidgeted, probably masking a shudder. "But since I had the gene, Gary tried to convince Mom I should get the implant anyway. In case I just hadn't figured out how to shift or something."

"I'm surprised she didn't go along with it."

"She thought it was too dangerous to do just in case."

I gritted my teeth. "Nice to know she was aware of the risks, then."

"She was." Sam exhaled hard. "You should have heard them fighting about it. He finally convinced her God would take care of you, and if it killed you, at least you'd die static."

My stomach turned. I'd known Gary felt that way, but I never realized my mother believed it. "Are you serious?"

He nodded. "They really buy this stuff. They think they're doing God's work." He rolled his eyes. "I would've thought if God wanted us all to be static, He'd have made us that way."

"Oh, but why do that when there's someone like Gary to take care of it?"

"Ugh. It is *so* nice to be away from that shit."

"I know the feeling, believe me."

"And at least Tammy and Bill's church isn't crazy."

"How is it?"

"Different." Sam shrugged. "It's kind of weird to get through a sermon without breaking out in a sweat and wanting to kill myself."

My breath caught. "Sam, you haven't actually wanted to kill yourself, have you?"

"Not in church," he said with a completely straight face. "I was too afraid I'd survive and have to face Mom and Gary after making a scene." We locked eyes, then both snorted with laughter.

"Okay, come on, seriously," I said finally. "You haven't, have you?"

He shrugged again. "I've gotten depressed a few times, but no."

"Well, you're going to catch hell for this in your life. It's just part of being a shifter. So if you *ever* need to talk, about this or anything else, call me."

"Assuming your phone is on, right?"

"Yes, assuming it's on. In fact . . ." I picked my phone up off the end table and pressed the power button. "There. Now it's on. Don't you dare leave without giving me your number."

"I won't."

"Okay, enough about all that depressing shit," I said. "I haven't talked to you in three years. Tell me what else you've been up to."

As Sam told me about the interests and hobbies he'd taken up over the last few years, this whole situation played out in the back of my mind. There was a possibility I would be static for the rest of my life. The implant could still kill me or cripple me. But at least my sister was out from under my parents' roof and no longer at risk of getting the same procedure that had turned my world on its ass.

In its own perverse way, maybe this was all worth it.

♂ CHAPTER 16 ♀
DAMON

When I got to Alex's that night, he wasn't alone, but his mood was brighter than I'd expected. He was sitting on the couch with a teenager I didn't recognize, the remains of a pizza on the coffee table, and a Coke in his hand.

"Hey." He grinned when I walked into the living room. "I've got someone I want you to meet."

"So I see."

"Damon, this is Sam." Alex beamed. "My brother."

My eyes flicked back and forth between them. "Your . . ."

"Formerly known as Candace," Alex said.

I looked at Sam, and the penny dropped. "You're a shifter, too?"

"Yep, I am." He extended his hand. "Nice to meet you."

"Likewise," I said as we shook hands.

"We've just been doing some catching up," Alex said. "Amazing how much you miss when you don't see someone for three years." The comment didn't sound nearly as bitter or melancholy as I would have expected. In fact, as he smiled at his brother, I couldn't help thinking that Alex looked and sounded more relaxed than I'd seen him in a long time. More than I'd ever seen him in his male form, for that matter.

"You off work early or something?" He pulled up his sleeve and looked at his watch. "Oh, holy crap, it's almost seven already? When did that happen?"

Sam's eyes widened. "Damn, it is? I should get home." He stood.

"Do you need a lift?" I asked.

"No, no, it's okay. There's a bus that picks up a block or so from here."

"A bus?" I said. "Come on, kid, we can drive you. It's not a big deal."

Sam glanced at Alex, then at me. "Are you sure?"

"You don't mind?" Alex asked me.

"No, not at all."

Sam smiled. "Cool, thanks."

Alex put what was left of the pizza in the refrigerator. Then the three of us got in my car, and I drove over to Sam's foster home. It wasn't far from Alex's place. Maybe ten minutes, if that. That was encouraging; maybe the two of them could spend more time together since they didn't live so far apart.

Sam invited us in to meet his foster mother. As soon as we walked into the kitchen, I recognized her from the trial. The memory of Sam collapsing in tears against her still made me shiver, especially recalling how visibly it had affected Alex, but we both must have misread Sam's emotions.

Sam's foster mother extended her hand to Alex. "I'm Tammy. You must be Alex?"

He nodded as he shook her hand. "Nice to meet you."

"You too," she said. "I've heard so much about you."

"All good things, I hope?" There was a note of caution in the joke.

"From Sam? Are you kidding?" She laughed. "I think you're the only one in the family he doesn't speak ill of."

Alex laughed halfheartedly. "If you knew the family, you'd understand."

"So I've heard." She looked at me. "And you are . . .?"

"Damon." I look at Alex, unsure of how to elaborate about who exactly I was.

"My partner," Alex said.

"Oh, right." She shook my hand. "Well, it's a pleasure to meet both of you."

After a bit of small talk, Sam needed to get to his homework, so Alex and I again shook hands with Tammy. Then Alex hugged Sam before making doubly sure they both had each other's phone numbers.

Alex and I took off, and we swung into a fast-food place on the way home. He'd had pizza with Sam earlier, but I was ready to chew off my own arm. Once I'd eaten, we went back to his place, grabbed a couple of beers, and lounged on the couch.

"You going to be able to see Sam now?" I asked. "More regularly, at least?"

"I hope so. His foster parents obviously don't have a problem with me, and he said he wants to see me more." Alex smiled. "And it's not like they have to worry about keeping him out of trouble. You know the kid's in Honors Society *and* three AP classes?"

"Really?"

Alex nodded. "Guess being a bookworm runs in the family."

"Apparently it does."

"He's a good kid. Has his head screwed on pretty straight. I'm proud of him."

"As well you should be." I paused. "Okay, so, that brings up another question. When I'm talking about someone who's a shifter, in general, how do I know whether to call them *he* or *she*?"

"I usually go by whatever form they're in. Sam said he gravitates more toward being male, so I'd err on the side of *he*. If it's someone like me who is pretty much fifty-fifty, either way is probably okay. With anyone, though, you can't go wrong by asking."

"Seems like an awkward question."

"Not really. It shows you actually give a shit about their feelings, which kind of negates any awkwardness."

"You'd think we'd have another set of pronouns for shifters."

"People have tried, but it's hard to get something like that to stick when people are already used to one set of pronouns." In a low growl, he added, "And besides, a good portion of the population is pretty sure we already have one."

"Oh?"

"'It.'"

I rolled my eyes. "Classy."

"Yeah, really. I'm just glad I didn't have to put up with that crap today, and now I'm *really* glad I called in sick. No work bullshit, and I got to spend an afternoon with my brother. Even if it does get me fired."

"Fired? For calling in sick?"

"Knowing my boss, yeah." He swore under his breath. "You know, I'll probably end up getting fired for abusing my sick time before those assholes ever get nailed for harassing me." He paused, then shook his head. "Ah, well. Such is life. I just don't feel like letting it under my skin tonight. I'm in a good mood for once, damn it, so the rest of the world can fuck off."

"I'll drink to that." I held out my beer bottle, and Alex clinked the neck of his against mine.

He swallowed the last of his beer. "Tonight? I'm just going to relax for once."

"Good. You deserve it." I paused. "Do you . . . do you want me to rub your feet?"

His eyebrows shot up. "You serious?"

I grinned. "Why not?"

"Like I'm going to turn that away." He stood. "Let me get us each another beer first." He took the two empty bottles and disappeared into the kitchen.

He came back and set two fresh, opened bottles on the table. Then he lay back on the couch with his head on the armrest, and I sat on the opposite end, facing him, with his feet in my lap.

He laced his fingers behind his head and watched my hands. "You sure you don't mind doing— Oh, holy shit."

"Should I stop?" I ran my thumb back and forth along the arch of his foot.

"No. Definitely don't."

For a while, we were both silent. I watched my hands, occasionally glancing up at his peaceful expression. I'd expected this to feel strange and uncomfortable, but it wasn't. Even when my fingertips drifted up into the thin hair on his lower leg, or slid over bones that had more substance than I was used to, it didn't feel weird. Though the terrain beneath my hands was unfamiliar, the contact wasn't. We'd finally bridged this gap and were skin to skin for the first time in too long, and no amount of leg hair or thicker bones was going to temper my relief. He was a man, but he was Alex, and I was touching him. This was perfect.

As I traced his arch with my thumb again, Alex groaned. "Jesus, Damon, I still want to know who bought your soul in exchange for teaching you how to do this."

I laughed. "Just Damon's magic touch, you know that."

"I'm telling you, you could make a killing doing this for everyone who works at the Mat."

"You think?"

"Uh, yeah. But then, I don't know. I kind of like having it all to myself."

I chuckled. "I could always start charging you for it."

He opened one eye for a second. "You would, too."

"Hey, if I can make money, why not?"

Alex just laughed.

I smiled. "You know, it's really good to see you back in better spirits."

"Good to be this way again, let me tell you. Sorry I've been such a downer lately."

"A downer?" I said with a cough of startled laughter. "My God, Alex, with everything you've been through, I wasn't exactly expecting you to be giddy."

A faint laugh pulled up the corners of his lips. "I suppose not. Just, I hate dragging other people down, you know?"

I ran my fingers up the back of his ankle, along his Achilles' tendon, just grazing some of the fine hair of his lower leg. "Under the circumstances, I think you can be forgiven."

"Well, thank God for that." He picked up his beer and sat up just enough to take a sip. Then he set the bottle back on the coffee table and relaxed onto the couch again. It was his second beer, but he sipped it like soda. Just something to drink, not an express ticket to numbness and distraction. I wondered if he knew how much of a relief that was for me.

I continued rubbing his feet, which worked out tension I hadn't even noticed in my own neck and shoulders. When my hands started to ache a little, I kept going, even if I was just gently running my fingers up and down his not-ticklish-at-all skin. The physical contact was a relief in and of itself. It didn't have to be firm pressure, just a touch. A connection, something to relax us both while we shot the breeze. For all I'd been worried about making physical contact with a man, I didn't want it to be over, and he didn't object, so I didn't stop.

Alex told me about Sam, and the discussion they'd had about Alex petitioning for custody. I told him about my day, which was just the usual office bullshit. We mused about our predictions for the upcoming season of a cop drama we'd been hooked on for a while. Anything and everything except all the important, stressful, and depressing shit going on. It was like we'd locked it all outside when we closed the front door. It would all be there tomorrow, and we'd deal with it then, but for tonight, it didn't matter. It didn't even exist.

This was a glimpse of the way we were before, relaxing with a couple of beers and talking about whatever we felt like with no dark clouds hanging over us. No one was drunk, just pleasantly buzzed. My God, I'd missed this side of Alex, and this side of us. Talking, touching, even if we didn't talk about the big stuff, and even if that touch was something I could tell myself was purely platonic.

For once, we just enjoyed each other's company.

And as always when things were this enjoyable, the evening flew by. Before I knew it, the clock on Alex's DVD player was creeping up on eleven thirty.

"Damn, it's getting late."

"Is it?" He looked at his watch. "Wow, time just keeps getting away from me today."

"Time flies when you're having fun, I guess."

His smile bordered on shy. "Yeah, I guess it does."

We held eye contact for a moment. Then I cleared my throat. "I should probably get home."

"Yeah, I need to get some sleep myself." Alex swung his legs off my lap and onto the floor, and we both got up. He glanced at the beer bottles on the table. "You okay to drive home?"

I hadn't had much to drink, but my head was still light. "Probably not, no. I guess I should call a cab."

"Or . . ." He caught himself.

"Or, what?"

"You're, um, welcome to stay here," he said. "If you want to."

My heart beat faster. "You sure?"

"Yeah." Alex smiled cautiously. "Did you think I'd throw you out?"

"No, I suppose you wouldn't."

We both laughed, but it was forced. Halfhearted.

He pursed his lips. "Um, where do you want to sleep?"

Our eyes met.

"I, uh . . ." I cleared my throat. "I can just, you know, crash out here."

He didn't *quite* turn away in time to hide the flinch before he started toward the hall closet. "Sure. I'll see if I have a spare blanket."

"Great. Thanks."

He glanced back at me, and our eyes met again for an awkward, silent couple of seconds. I wondered if I should have opted for that cab after all. Maybe we weren't ready to go down this road yet.

Down what *road? Idiot, you're just crashing on the couch. Quit overthinking everything.*

I *was* overthinking it. If anything, sleeping under the same roof had to be a step in the right direction. Didn't it?

Alex handed me a pillow and blanket. "I guess I don't have to tell you where the bathroom is or anything like that." He gestured over his shoulder. "Your toothbrush is still in the master bathroom, and you still have some clothes here."

"Convenient," I said with a soft laugh.

He smiled, though it didn't reach his eyes. "Yeah, I guess it is."

"That'll save me a trip home in the morning."

Another forced smile. Without speaking, we went into the master bedroom so I could get what I needed. It was weird walking into this room under these circumstances. I focused on just getting a change of clothes and everything else I'd come for, trying not to notice all the landmarks of our relationship in this room. Trying not to think about the damage we'd done to some of the furniture in here, or the times staying here on a weeknight meant being exhausted as hell at work the next day.

With clean clothes tucked under my arm, I paused on my way out of the room. "Well, I'll see you in the morning, I guess."

"Yeah." He swallowed. "Good night."

"Good night."

We looked at each other, and I couldn't quite convince myself I was overthinking the emotion in his eyes.

We exchanged murmured "good nights" again, as if a second attempt might get our feet to move us in the right directions. In opposite directions. Fortunately—I supposed—it worked. I headed down the hall, and he went into the master bathroom.

Going through the motions of getting ready for bed was weirder than venturing into his bedroom had been. I was so used to brushing my teeth in the master bathroom and sleeping in the bedroom, being at the other end of the hall tonight was . . . strange. Isolated. Like there was more distance between us than if I'd gone back to my own house for the night.

A faucet turned on. I caught myself thinking of all the times I'd driven her nuts while she'd tried to get ready for bed. There was nothing I loved more than putting my arms around her waist and kissing her neck while she tried to brush her teeth or take off her makeup.

"You are such a pest," she'd say, trying to sound stern in between laughing.

"Want me to stop?" I'd murmur against her neck.

"I'm going to make you sleep on the sofa if you don't."

"No you won't."

"Prove it."

A hand under her shirt. A lingering kiss behind her ear. A whisper of what I planned to do to her if she'd please let me join her in bed.

A soft whimper from her lips.

And I would be safe from the couch for another night.

At the other end of the house, the faucet shut off. I sighed and went back into the living room to try to get some sleep.

I stared up at the ceiling from the couch, fingers laced behind my head on the pillow he'd given me. No sound came from the bedroom. The whole place was dark now, and the occasional creak of the settling house emphasized the stillness.

Over and over, my mind's eye replayed that flinch when I told him I'd sleep out here.

Gender aside, the person in there was the woman—man, shifter, whoever—I'd been trying to persuade to marry me. I'd wanted Alex for better or worse, in sickness and in health, and what did I do when things went to shit? Kept him at arm's length. Slept a safe distance from him, because God forbid I get too close to another man.

Couldn't imagine why she'd hesitated to discuss getting married. This must have been what she was afraid of. That once I knew, I'd push her away.

How right she was.

I loved him. There was no doubt about that. I still loved Alex in male or female form. But how far would that carry us in the bedroom? Sex had been no small part of our relationship before. Alex had a hell of a sex drive. So did I. I wanted to continue that intimacy, but . . . how?

It wasn't a matter of pride or shame, worrying I'd be labeled "gay." I didn't care about that. But the fact was, I'd never been physically attracted to men. I couldn't force it, and if I tried, he'd catch on. He wanted something genuine, not a patronizing charade.

Still, being this far apart wasn't going to bring us any closer together, physically or otherwise.

I doubted he was asleep now. He was probably staring at his bedroom ceiling in the darkness like I was staring at the living room ceiling.

And why?

I couldn't think of a reason. I couldn't justify why I was out here and he was in there. Physical attraction aside, there was no way to reconcile this separation with my love for him. He wasn't asking me to have sex with him. There was nothing that said we couldn't sleep together in the literal sense.

Nothing except my own hang-ups, anyway.

"Remember when you're talking to him, Damon," Jordan's words echoed through my mind, *"he is still the person you fell in love with. Male or female, static or shifter, Alex is still Alex."*

Then what the fuck was I doing out here?

Taking a deep breath and steeling myself, I threw off the blanket he'd given me and got up off the couch. Every step down the hall made my heart beat faster, but I kept going.

The bedroom door was ajar. Holding my breath, I pushed the door open.

What little light came in through the window just barely illuminated him. He was on his side, his back to me. I couldn't tell if he was asleep. If I knew Alex as well as I thought I did, he was awake. Still, listening, wide awake.

Heart pounding, I sat on the edge of the bed. The whisper of the sheets and mattress revealed subtle movement. He didn't sit up or roll over, but he'd moved enough to acknowledge my presence and make my breath catch. No turning back now.

I slipped under the covers. Paused. Waited. No eviction came, so I silently begged him not to reject me as I moved closer to him. He didn't move. Didn't speak.

Certain he'd shove me away at any moment, I reached for him.

The warmth of his skin met my fingertips. Muscles twitched beneath my touch. Stilled. Surprise, then, not revulsion, and when he didn't pull away, I rested my whole hand on his arm. My heart thundered so hard he *had* to have heard it.

His fingers found mine. For a split second, I was sure he'd lift my hand off him and push it away, but instead, he gently drew my arm around him. I slid closer. Molded my body against his. He slipped his fingers between mine.

Alex released a held breath. So did I.

In the dark, the most distinctive difference was his short hair. In female form, Alex had long hair, which we'd always laughed about getting in my mouth and nose while we slept. Like this, the ends of his hair tickled my face a little, but that was it.

I was aware of the different shape of his body, of his broader shoulders and narrower waist, but I was so relieved to be holding him that it seemed ridiculous to have ever thought this would be awkward or weird. The fingers laced between mine weren't as slim and fine as I was used to, but this was Alex, and I was holding him just like I had every night we'd spent together. Right now, nothing else mattered.

And wrapped up in each other's arms, we both drifted off to sleep.

☿ CHAPTER 17 ♀
ALEX

"Technical support, Alex Nichols speaking."

"Oh, don't *you* sound all professional?" Tabitha's voice drew a chuckle out of me. She was a welcome distraction from the endless whispering and gawking I'd been trying to ignore all damned day.

"What do you want?" I asked.

"Just a quick question. What are you doing tonight?"

"I'm going out with Damon. Why?"

"Because I want to take you out to celebrate your parents going to the big house," she said. "And I want Damon to be there, too."

"Why? So you can ogle him?"

"Maybe."

I laughed. "I can call him. He'll probably be game."

"Tell him dinner's on me."

"Literally or figuratively?"

Tabby snorted. "Keep dreaming, sunshine. Anyway, I'm buying. Now, talk to him, and if he's game, pick me up at the Mat at seven."

"Jeez, you're inviting me out, but I have to pick up the Tab?"

She groaned. "Oh, shut *up*. And speaking of Damon, by the by, how are the two of you doing?"

I smiled to myself, absently twisting the phone cord around my finger. Waking up this morning beside Damon still had me in a good mood. Even if we weren't sexually involved—for now? Forever?—it was nice to be touched again. "We're doing better."

"Glad to hear it. I figured he'd come around."

My heart sank a little. "Well, let's not count our chickens here. It's better, but . . ." I let the cord around my finger unwind itself.

"Give him time, baby. Now get your ass back to work. And I'll see you at seven, assuming Damon's game for a free meal in my fabulous company."

Damon was game, and at seven o'clock sharp, we walked into the Welcome Mat to pick up Tabitha.

"Wow, I didn't think it'd be this busy," Damon said.

"No kidding." For a weeknight, the place was packed. There must have been a private party booked or something, but looking around, I recognized a lot of familiar faces. Many were regulars, but they weren't part of any specific group or club as far as I could tell. Every bartender on the payroll, myself excluded, was behind the bar, and the servers were practically running to keep up with orders.

It surprised me that Tabby was willing to leave for the evening, even if it was just for dinner, when the club was this busy. But then, with every last staff member except the two of us working tonight, maybe it was covered enough for her to bow out for a bit.

"Guess we should find Tabitha and get out of here before she decides to put you to work," Damon said.

"I wouldn't put it past—"

"*There* you are!" Tabby squeezed out of the crowd and approached with her arms out. "Thought you boys were going to stand me up."

"Not when there's free food involved," I said. "Are you nuts?"

"Oh, whatever. Before we go, though, we have something we need to take care of."

I raised an eyebrow. "We?"

"Yes. As in you and me." She grabbed my wrist and started to pull me toward the front of the club. "You, too, Damon. Come on."

Damon and I exchanged puzzled glances. He shrugged. So did I. Then he followed while she dragged me through the crowd. My heart beat faster when she pulled me up onto the small stage beside the DJ's booth. Heads started turning. Conversations died down. Embarrassment heated my face.

"What's going on?" I whispered loudly.

"Just have a little surprise for you, that's all."

"Uh, last time you surprised me, I almost had to—"

"Nothing like that this time, sweetie."

The music cut off abruptly and the whole place fell silent. In an instant, all eyes were on us. My face burned. The DJ handed her a microphone, and my eyes widened.

"Tabby—"

She clicked on the microphone and held it up to her lips. To the crowd, she said, "Everybody, I think you know who this lovely gentleman is, right?"

Everyone applauded and cheered. I looked at Damon, and we once again exchanged clueless shrugs.

"Okay, okay, quiet, all of you," Tabby said, and the room fell silent once more. "I'm going to keep this short and sweet so our bashful bartender doesn't die of embarrassment up here." She turned to me. "Listen, you can call us all a little presumptuous, but everyone's heard what happened, and when we found out how expensive this surgery is going to be, we thought you could use a little help."

My stomach flipped. "You didn't have to—"

"We did, so hush. We passed the hat around, and . . ." She paused. "Well, we got a little carried away."

I swallowed. "Carried away?"

"Oh, just a little. We only expected it to go on here in the club, but then a bunch of people spread the word to their churches, their offices, all over the place. Someone did a website, and I think someone even auctioned their underthings on eBay. Oh, and you should have *seen* the carwash." She winked. "Anyway, after all that, when I counted it all up, it wouldn't fit in the hat anymore."

My lips parted. "Tabby . . ."

She reached into the front of her dress and pulled out a white envelope. "So, I hope you'll accept this instead." She held the envelope out to me.

"You didn't have to do this," I whispered, surprised the words came out at all.

"And you have about five seconds to take it before I decide to go spend it all on shoes."

I laughed and took the envelope from her. To everyone in front of the stage, I said, "You guys are great. I really don't know what to say."

"Open it," Tabby said in a stage whisper.

I looked at Damon. He nodded toward the envelope. Being up here on the stage, in front of all these people, I felt conspicuous. Most of the time, I didn't know what stage fright was, but this was all so unexpected, I was nothing but nerves.

With unsteady hands, I fought to open the envelope. The flap finally came loose, and I pulled out a cashier's check.

"Oh my God." I blinked a few times, certain I was hallucinating. "You guys, you . . . you didn't."

"We did." Tabby squeezed my arm. "Everyone here loves you, baby, and we all felt it when your parents did this. What they did to you was like kicking this entire community in the balls." She nodded at the check in my hand. "So we want to help you kick them back." She turned to the crowd. "Isn't that right?"

The whole place erupted with cheers and applause.

I looked around. At my coworkers. At the customers, some of whom were regulars, some of whom I'd never seen before. At my boyfriend, who'd stood by me when I'd convinced myself a dozen times over he'd be long gone. At people I knew, people I didn't know, all of whom were rallying around me when my own family had made my life hell.

And back at the cashier's check in my hand.

The cashier's check for ninety-five thousand dollars.

And I lost it.

Damon put his arm around my shoulders. Tabby put hers around my waist. I held the check in a trembling hand and struggled to regain my composure, but the dam had broken.

Never in my life had I been so overwhelmed.

Tabby kissed my cheek and whispered over the cheering crowd, "Don't you dare try to say we shouldn't have, or you can't accept it, or anything like that. The money's yours so you can have your life back."

I wiped my eyes and smiled at her. "As corny as it sounds, I really don't know what to say."

She winked and picked up the microphone again. "He says he doesn't know what to say." She eyed me. "How about . . . Thank you, Tabby's the best boss on the planet, and I'm going to go behind that bar and pour everyone in this club a free drink?"

"You don't mind?"

"I *am* the world's best boss, aren't I?"

I wrinkled my nose. "Not in *that* dress, you're not."

She smacked my arm. "Whore."

I laughed. Then I hugged her. "You're the best, Tab." When I released her, I gestured for the microphone, so she handed it to me. "You're all amazing. There is no way I can even begin to thank you enough for this."

"You can start by pouring us some booze," someone called out from the back.

"Free drinks!" someone else shouted.

They started chanting: "Free booze! Free booze! Free booze!"

I laughed again. "Tabby, are you sure you don't mind me pouring free drinks for everyone?"

"Are you kidding?" She gestured at the gathered patrons. "If I said no now, they'd turn into an angry mob." She pointed at the bar. "Now get to work."

I looked at Damon. "Are you cool with staying?"

"After what they just did for you?" He smiled. "Fuck yeah."

I looked at the check in my shaking hand again. "I can't believe it. I really can't."

"Guess it's true what they say," he said. "Times like this, you find out who your friends are."

I met his eyes. "I guess you do, don't you?"

We exchanged smiles, holding eye contact for a long moment. Then I dropped my gaze and gestured toward the bar. "I should, um, get over there. People want their free booze."

He laughed. "Well, don't keep them waiting, then."

"You're sure you don't mind—"

"*Go.*"

While I poured drinks for the gathered patrons, the DJ fired up the karaoke machine, and the whole place came to life. The other bartenders and I struggled to keep up with the demand, but people were patient. No sense being a dick when you're getting free alcohol, after all.

I was surprised that my hands were steady enough to keep the liquor flowing into glasses instead of onto the bar or elsewhere. The check that was now safely in my wallet. The barrage of emotions when I realized what everyone had done for me . . . it all still had me off-balance. My knees weren't shaking, nor were my hands, but they felt like they should have been. There was a tingling aftershock, that reminder that I'd been a trembling mess just minutes ago.

What I'd done, in this life or a past one, to deserve the outpouring of kindness from all these people, I had no idea. They could have easily clicked their tongues over my parents' actions, shaken their heads, murmured that it was a goddamned shame what had happened. But raising just shy of a hundred thousand dollars? Enough to cover most if not all of the cost of the surgery? I was used to people turning their backs on me or grudgingly accepting me for the creature that I was. People who were close to me, who were supposed to love me unconditionally, had rejected me, and it was these people, all these friends and strangers gathered in the Welcome Mat, who'd picked me up, dusted me off, and said, "It's okay, we've got you."

I stole a glance at Damon, who was shooting the breeze with someone at a table not far from the bar. He looked up and caught my eye, and we both smiled.

The rest of the world could kiss my ass. I knew who my friends were.

The music cut off. Over the microphone, Tabby said, "Hey, Alex."

I looked up from mixing a mojito, eyebrows raised. "Yeah, boss?"

"How's your back tonight?"

Oh, no. Tabby, don't make me do this. Not in front of Damon.

"Come on, Alex," she said. "How's the back?"

Chuckling, I yelled back, "Uh, it's okay . . . I guess . . ."

"Good. Why don't you earn your keep, then?" With that, she hit a button on the karaoke machine, and when the intro to "Simply Irresistible" started, three of us—myself, Colin, and Dale—groaned.

"You heard her," I said. "Let's hit it." Damon shot me a puzzled look. Then his jaw dropped when the other two bartenders and I peeled off our shirts and jumped up on the bar.

☿ CHAPTER 18 ♀
DAMON

Up on the bar, Alex and the other two bartenders broke into a dance they'd obviously rehearsed a hundred times over. She'd mentioned in the past that the male bartenders often did this. I supposed it shouldn't have surprised me now that Alex himself was included in that equation, and I whistled and clapped along with everyone else. It was like the bastard lovechild of the Chippendales and Coyote Ugly. Goddamn it, I never knew he could move his hips like that. Well, I did, but . . .

Whatever, Damon, just watch and enjoy it.

Alex glanced down at me and winked. I just laughed and shook my head. Watching him like this, I had to admit that whether I was into men or not, he looked good. He looked damn good. The way he snapped his hips made me shiver, bringing to mind some other things Alex had done with her hips. Apparently certain talents carried over. Did they ever. Jesus.

When the song ended, the patrons stumbled over each other to shove dollar bills into the tip jars.

Alex jumped off the bar and picked up his shirt. Grinning like a little kid, he looked at me. "Sorry," he said, panting and wiping sweat off his forehead. "We . . . um . . . it gets a bit crazy in here sometimes, what can I say?"

"I don't mind in the least." *My God, it's good to see you smile like that.* I nodded toward the end of the bar. "Looks like your fans await."

He glanced in that direction, at the gathered patrons who were still waiting for their free drinks. "Guess I should go take care of them." Our eyes met. "I swear, I'm not ditching you."

"No, you're not. Don't worry about it. I'm enjoying myself. Now go."

He held my gaze a second longer, just enough to raise my pulse a notch, before he left me to go tend to his waiting customers.

And how the hell was he messing with my pulse? My pulse which was already inexplicably racing after he'd been dancing on top of the bar? I shook my head. This was madness. But then . . . it wasn't. After all, he was Alex. Why should it be weird for Alex to have this effect on me?

A hand materialized on my shoulder, and I turned to see Tabitha beside me.

"You'll keep me updated after he has the surgery, right?" she asked.

"Yeah, of course. He has your number, so I'll get it from him and be sure to keep you up-to-date."

"Thank you." She smiled. "I can't even tell you how lucky he is to have you, Damon."

I laughed softly. "I don't know. I probably haven't made things much easier for him lately." I dropped my gaze. "I'm still not quite sure what it is we're doing anymore. And I still feel like an ass for—"

"Damon, darling." She squeezed my arm. "The very fact that you're here at all means the world to him. I don't think he'd dream of asking you for more than that."

I watched Alex as he carried on with some of his customers, laughing and bantering while he poured their drinks. *The very fact that you're here at all.* In the back of my mind, I remembered being drawn toward the door, being tempted to run like hell from all this insanity, but my feet were firmly planted now.

"Damon." Tabitha pulled my attention away from him. "Don't be so hard on yourself just because you've had second thoughts about things. Anyone in your position would have."

"I guess they would," I said with a nod. "Still feel like a dick."

"Well, I can call you one if it makes you feel better."

I laughed. "Thanks, Tabitha. Much appreciated."

"I do what I can." She grinned. "Anyway, I'd better get back to cracking the whip and making my people behave. Have a drink and relax a bit, darling. This is a party."

"Will do." As she turned to go, I said, "Tabitha."

She looked over her shoulder, eyebrows raised.

"Thanks. For what you did for him."

Tabitha smiled. "For Alex, I'd do it again in a heartbeat."

I returned the smile. "Still, thank you. I know it means the world to him, and it does to me too."

She gave a slight nod but didn't say anything else. As she walked away, I watched Alex again. Once everyone had been served and was happily working their way through their free drinks, he came around the bar and joined me.

"Looked like you were getting lonely over here," he said with a grin.

I chuckled. "Oh, I managed. There's enough entertainment to keep me occupied." I gestured at the stage, where a couple of women were stumbling their way through an ABBA song on the karaoke machine.

Alex grimaced. "I don't know if that's entertainment or torture."

"A little of both, probably."

He laughed. He had one of the other bartenders pour us a couple of Cokes, then took me around to meet the various customers, many of whom had stories of people they knew who'd gone through similar ordeals as Alex. Parents, spouses, adult children, even grandparents had found ways to get implants into people who didn't want them. The stories of coercion, manipulation, and—in rare cases, like his—physical force, were unreal.

"My folks have been after me to get one since the things hit the market," someone said. "They forced my brother to get it right before he turned eighteen, and he's miserable. Fuck that."

"My sister-in-law convinced my brother to get it done," one guy told us. "Six months after he put it in? He couldn't take anymore. You can guess what happened."

"I have the implant myself," a redhead said between sips of a cosmopolitan. "But it was *my* decision. I spent three years agonizing over it, and for like a year afterward, I'd have panic attacks when I wondered whether I did the right thing or not. Having someone else make that decision for you?" She shook her head and scowled. "No way."

And somehow the horrifying tales didn't put a damper on the mood in the room. Everyone remained so positive and upbeat, like the combined effort to get Alex's implant out was their way of making things right for him and for everyone else in his shoes. He gave them hope, they gave him hope.

"Wow," I said when we'd pulled away from the crowd for a minute or two and returned to the bar for refills. "People really are hell-bent on getting implants into shifters, aren't they?"

Alex looked up from filling our drinks and nodded. "Unfortunately. And a lot of them have the best of intentions; they just don't realize how much this affects us. It forces us into a neat, tidy little category that's easy for them to deal with, but turns our lives upside down."

"So I've noticed," I said quietly.

The music stopped again, and every head turned toward the stage, where Tabitha stood with the microphone.

"Alex, darling," she singsonged. "Our adoring fans have been begging all evening long for some Alex-and-Tabitha-style karaoke. What do you say?"

A spotlight focused its blinding, blanched light on Alex. His cheeks turned bright red. "Do I have to?" he called back.

"Yes!" the gathered mob answered in unison.

"The people have spoken, my dear," Tabitha said.

"But if they hear me sing, they're all going to take their money back."

"We're going to take it back if you don't get up there and sing," someone yelled out.

He turned to me, eyebrows raised in a "help me" expression.

"Oh, go on." I grinned. "I have to see this."

He glared playfully at me. "Ass."

"Come on, Nichols," Tabitha said. "Don't make me drag you up here by your ear."

Alex groaned. Shaking his head, he dried his hands on a towel, and when he started toward the end of the bar, the crowd roared. They parted to give him a clear path across the room, clapping his shoulders as he walked through the gauntlet of fans.

Onstage, Alex grabbed the microphone from his boss. "Before we do this, can I just say for those of you who've never heard me sing, there's a reason for that."

"Oh, shut up," Tabitha said into another microphone. "No one's expecting you to be the next American Idol."

"Yes we are!" someone shouted.

Alex snickered. "That must be someone who's never heard me sing."

"Well, it's high time they heard you." Tabitha looked at the DJ. "Fire it up!"

The music started, and the two of them launched into a duet of some pop song I'd never heard. They were ridiculously horrible, and no one knew that better than they did. At one point, Alex cracked up so bad he couldn't even sing. He could barely stand, and Tabitha wasn't much better. She couldn't get through the chorus without collapsing into fits of laughter. With the way they leaned on each other and fell into hysterics, if I didn't know any better, I'd have sworn they were both drunk off their asses.

The crowd egged them on, cheering and clapping as the two of them wiped tears from their eyes and tried not to stumble off the stage. When the song was over, everyone begged for more, and Tabitha grabbed Alex's arm before he could make his escape. The intro of another song started, and he pretended to beg for her to let him go, but then gave in and "sang" with her.

As I watched, tears streaming down my face as I laughed as hard as everyone else, something caught my attention. For the first time since I'd seen him as a male, Alex looked truly comfortable in his own skin. His smile was genuine, unflinching, not the kind that was ready to wilt and fade when no one was looking. He didn't look like he was shouldering some massive burden.

He looked *happy*.

He also hadn't touched a drop of liquor. Tonight, he didn't need that escape. Not here. He danced on the bar and sang bad karaoke, and he was surrounded by people who wouldn't have changed him for the world. Maybe I was a slow learner, but I realized now that I was one of them.

This was Alex in his element. Male or female, it didn't matter, this was one hundred percent, unadulterated, uninhibited, unafraid *Alex*. Like I'd never seen him before.

No, like I'd seen him *once* before. In a California king bed with rain pouring down outside. On a beach in the rain. One perfect weekend when the rest of the world didn't matter.

I'd been looking for her in everything he said or did, but there she was. There he was. *That* was the Alex I'd fallen in love with, and the Alex I still loved. I loved him the same as I loved her because they were one and the same. Watching him now, I wondered how the hell I'd missed that all along.

I don't care if you're male, female, or a little of both. I don't care if you can't carry a tune. You're beautiful, Alex.

They finished the song, or at least tried their damnedest to finish it in between fits of laughter.

"Okay, I think he's done his penance, don't you?" Tabitha asked the crowd. "Think we can let him enjoy his own party instead of singing and pouring us all more booze?"

Judging by the applause that followed, the crowd thoroughly approved. Before he left the stage, though, Alex addressed everyone in the club. "I just want to say, one more time, how much this means to me. There is no way I can put it into words, but I am so completely blown away right now. You're all amazing. Thank you."

He and Tabitha shared a quick hug, then he left the stage.

"Now that he's been duly humiliated," she said. "That's enough karaoke for one night. I'm turning things over to Bobby the DJ, and I expect everyone to get your asses out on this floor and dance. Understood?"

As people migrated toward the dance floor, Alex emerged from the crowd. He joined me at the bar, wiping sweat from his forehead and reaching for the Coke he'd abandoned to go onstage.

"You never told me you were a karaoke star," I said, chuckling behind my glass.

He rolled his eyes and groaned. "Oh, God, there's a reason I don't usually do it."

I shrugged. "I don't know, looked like everyone enjoyed it."

"Yeah, the same way everyone enjoys watching a train wreck."

"I enjoyed it."

His eyes met mine. "You like train wrecks?"

Grinning, I said, "Sometimes."

"Birds of a feather, right?"

"Hey!"

We both laughed. Then, Tabitha appeared beside us.

She hooked her arm around Alex's elbow. "Before you get all settled in and relaxed, does your man mind if I drag you out on the dance floor?"

"Hmm, I don't know." Alex looked at me. "Do you?"

I pursed my lips. "Actually, yes. I do."

His eyebrows shot up. "You . . . do?"

"Yes." I slipped my hand into his. "Because I think I'd rather drag you out there myself."

Alex's jaw dropped. "Are you serious?"

"Well, assuming Tabitha doesn't mind?"

She released his elbow. "Of course not. Be my guest." She gestured toward the dance floor.

I squeezed Alex's hand and nodded in the direction Tabitha had. *Come on, let's do this before I lose my nerve.*

He smiled and followed me. It was a slow song, the kind that invited couples to get close under the colorful lights, and my heart pounded as I put my arm around Alex's waist. He rested his forearms on my shoulders. A few inches of breathing room remained between us, but I had a gut feeling that space wouldn't be there for long. I'd never danced with a man before, but like rubbing Alex's feet, I didn't feel weird about this. I couldn't feel weird about it. I was nervous and my stomach was fluttering, but that was an all-too-familiar feeling. It was exactly the way I'd felt when I'd asked Alex to dance back when she was still a stranger.

Hoping conversation would distract me from those fluttery nerves, I said, "You remember the first time I asked you to dance?"

He laughed. "I'm surprised *you* do."

"Oh, come on, I wasn't that drunk."

"Uh-huh."

"Okay, okay, I was. But I do remember."

"Me, too." He smiled. "I was kind of surprised when you called after that."

"I was a bit surprised the number worked."

Alex chuckled. "Normally I wouldn't give my real number to someone who was that plowed, but . . ." He finished the thought with a one-shouldered shrug.

"But what?"

"I don't know. I just had a good feeling about you." His humor faded a little, but the smile remained. "Guess it pays to trust my instincts sometimes."

"Guess it does."

We held each other's gazes.

"Stop looking for the woman you knew," Jordan had said. *"Just look for the person."*

Here he was. Right in front of me where he'd been from day one, and I was just as in love with him now as I was then. No, more than I was then.

I slid my hands over the small of his back and drew him a little closer, shrinking that narrow, temporary space between us. Alex swallowed hard, then dropped his gaze. Though the flashing colored lights above the dance floor made it hard to say for sure, I thought his cheeks darkened.

"Do you remember that weekend out at the coast?" he asked, so softly I barely heard him over the music.

I shivered. "Every minute of it."

"I almost told you that weekend. I wanted to, but everything was going so well, I didn't want to ruin it. But I . . ." He paused and took a breath. Then his eyes met mine. "I don't know, I guess I got scared, but that was the first time I realized I wanted you to know what I am."

I swallowed hard. His eyes were almost too intense, looking back at me in this dim, flickering dance floor light, but God Himself couldn't have made me look away. I moistened my lips. "There were a few things I wanted you to know that weekend, too."

"Such as?"

"Such as . . ." *That was when I knew I loved you. That was when I knew I wanted to spend the rest of my life with you.*

I couldn't find the words then, and I couldn't find them now.

I took my hand off his waist and reached up to touch his face. As soon as my fingertips brushed his skin, Alex closed his eyes. Light stubble gently abraded my thumb as I ran it along his jaw, and a shiver—I couldn't say whose—brought us a little closer together. Alex looked up at me again, and I forgot how to breathe.

Cradling his face in both hands, I leaned down. He raised his chin. Liquid fire surged through my veins with every inch we slowly, slowly, *slowly* gained, and when his breath warmed my skin, I thought my knees would go out from under me.

"You don't have to do this," Alex whispered.

I brushed the pad of my thumb over his cheekbone. "Neither do you."

He held my gaze. Then his eyes flicked toward my lips. When he met my eyes again, I kissed him.

The music faded behind the whisper of his breathing. My heartbeat muted the voices and clinking glasses. Everyone else on the dance floor disappeared, shut out when I closed my eyes and unnoticed when all my senses homed in on one person and one person only.

Oh, God, this really was Alex. The way his lips moved against mine, the way his fingers combed through my hair, the way his breath rushed past my skin as he inhaled through his nose. The kiss deepened, and the soft moan that thrummed against my lips was lower than I was used to, but still undeniably *Alex*.

He wrapped his arms around me. His erection brushed mine through our clothes, and to my dizzy, delirious surprise, it didn't weird me out or make me stop and wonder what the hell I was doing. Instead, it sent cool relief through my veins, knowing he was as turned on as I was, and instead of questioning it or wondering how someone in a male body could arouse me like this, I held him tighter.

I broke the kiss but didn't pull away. Slowly, the rest of the world materialized around us again. Disco lights, people dancing together and alone, roaring laughter.

I touched my forehead to his. "I love you, Alex."

"I love you, too."

I slid my hand around the back of his neck and kissed him again. For all I'd worried about having to force intimacy and attraction, none of it needed forcing. The intimacy was still there from before this had all started, right there waiting this whole time for us to come and get it. I'd had to learn to navigate some unfamiliar terrain, but the desire was there because I wanted Alex. In every way, on every level, I wanted Alex.

We separated enough to look at each other.

He grinned. "Do you want to get out of here?"

Nerves and excitement coiled in the pit of my stomach. "Do you?" I gestured around the room, pretending not to notice the unsteadiness in my hand. "This is your party, I don't want to drag you away."

"Oh, you're not dragging me." He kissed me lightly. "Let me make the rounds and say good-bye to everyone. Then we can get the hell out of here."

We made it as far as my living room before Alex's jacket hit the floor. Halfway down the hall, mine landed on the carpet with a heavy thud. Shoes didn't stay on very long after we crossed into my bedroom. A belt buckle jingled and leather hissed across denim before falling to the floor. Step. Alex's shirt came off. Another step. He untucked my shirt. Another step. I slid my hands up his back, and we both shivered as my palms drifted across his bare, hot skin.

And it was there, skin on skin and an arm's length from my waiting bed, that we slowed down. Breathless, desperate kisses became gentle, tender, sensual . . . and hesitant. His cock pressed against mine. At the club, that had aroused me, and it still did now, but it also made me all too aware of my nerves.

I wanted him, but . . .

I needed him, but . . .

I wanted *this*, but . . .

Alex broke the kiss and looked at me.

"You sure about this?" he whispered.

"Yeah. You?"

He grinned. "I've been wanting this longer than you can imagine." He unbuttoned my shirt with hands far, far steadier than my own. Then he pushed it over my shoulders and down my arms, that motion drawing us close enough for another long, spine-melting kiss.

Alex dipped his head to kiss my neck, and the warmth of his lips and breath on my skin made me dizzy. The brush of masculine stubble across my collarbone, though, sent a very different shiver down my spine. I glanced at the bed, a faint twinge of panic working its way into my consciousness. *We're really doing this? Can I do this?*

He looked at me. Then he looked at my hand on his waist. Gently, he closed his fingers around my wrist and brought it up to his lips.

"You're shaking," he murmured against the backs of my fingers.

"Nerves," I said with a self-conscious laugh.

"Nothing to be nervous about." He smiled. "It's just me."

"I know. But I . . ." I dropped my gaze, my cheeks on fire. "I probably don't have to tell you I've never done this before."

Alex ran his fingers through my hair. "Anatomy's the only difference. It's still me."

"That's a pretty significant difference, isn't it?" He laughed softly and pulled me closer. "You'd be surprised."

"Just don't expect me to do everything right."

"You're doing just fine so far." His lips brushed mine. "But if you want to take things a little slower . . ." Our lips met, and I lost myself in him.

My mind wanted to slow down, to give me a chance to take all this in. My body had other plans. I just didn't know which of the two to obey.

Alex cocked his head slightly, that telltale "I'm reading you" look I'd known for the last couple of years.

"You know," he whispered, "I'm a little sweaty from dancing at the club." He tilted his head in the direction of the bathroom. "I could use a shower if you want to join me."

I nodded. "Yeah, that sounds . . . We can do that."

He smiled and stepped back, taking most of my breath with him. I followed him into the bathroom. The idea of getting in the shower together unnerved me, but it wasn't as intimidating as getting into bed together. We'd get there. Tonight, I had no doubt, but not this minute. We had time. Time to hopefully settle my nerves and convince me I could go through with this.

Getting my own clothes off and starting the shower gave me something to occupy my nervous hands and mind. Once the water was hot, Alex got in while I grabbed a couple of towels.

Then, taking a deep breath, I joined him.

His back was to me, water pouring through his short hair, down his neck, over his shoulders—broader than a woman's, narrower than my own—and down to his slim hips. When he turned around and met my eyes, I could barely breathe.

Jesus, Alex, you are *beautiful.*

He reached for me, but I caught his wrist with a gentle grasp.

"Wait," I whispered.

His eyes widened. "What? Something wrong?"

"No. Just let me . . ." I swallowed. "Just let me see you like this."

He shot me a lopsided grin and put his arms out to the sides, striking a ridiculous pose. "Look all you want."

I laughed. Now if *that* wasn't a flash of the Alex I remembered, I didn't know what was. Forget looking.

I reached for his waist. "Come here, you." I put my arms around him and kissed him, and he slid his arms around my neck. In the space of a breath, our bodies were together, and the heat of his wet skin was as overwhelming as the gentle friction of his hard cock brushing mine.

We let a long, lazy kiss linger for . . . hell, I didn't know. A long, long time. The way we always used to kiss when we had nowhere to be except together, and no reason to hurry except our own desperation for each other. We wanted each other so bad we were shaking, but the only things rushing were our beating hearts and the hot water pouring over us while we slowed everything else down to a gentle, passionate kiss.

When we finally came up for air, I touched my forehead to his and whispered, "I missed this."

"Me too." He pulled away enough to look me in the eye. "How far do you want to take this tonight? I mean, are you comfortable . . ."

"I'm not sure." I forced a laugh. "I hadn't thought that far ahead."

He grinned. "Just tell me if you want to stop."

"Right now, that's the last thing I want to do."

Alex shivered and, without speaking, raised his chin to kiss me again. His hand drifted down my side. When he reached my hip, he stopped. Barely breaking the kiss, he whispered, "Do you want me to keep going?"

Goose bumps prickled up my spine. "I . . . yes, I do."

"You sure?"

"Mm-hmm."

His fingertips drifted over my hip and toward my stomach. My abs contracted beneath his featherlight touch, and I bit my lip when his hand slid downward. One finger ran down the underside of my cock. Back up. Two fingers this time, and when they reached the base, they wrapped around it. A third finger. Fourth. Then his thumb, and as he closed his hand around me, he couldn't have made breathing more difficult if he'd grabbed my throat.

"Still okay with this?" he asked.

"Very much so." My voice shook, but I didn't care, because the gentle strokes of his wet palm over my cock felt too fucking good for me to care about *anything*.

"Just tell me if this is too much."

"Oh, it is. But don't stop."

"I don't plan on it." He kissed me, and as he stroked my cock slowly, gently, I could barely remember how to kiss him back. I hadn't been this nervous since the night I'd drunk myself brave enough to approach her in the first place.

"Give me your hand," he said softly.

When I hesitated, Alex grinned. "Just do it. Trust me." His fingertips grazed the back of my hand, and I moved it enough for him to grasp my wrist.

"If you want to stop," he whispered, "just say so." Without breaking eye contact, he guided my hand toward him. When he closed my fingers around his cock, I closed my eyes and sucked in a breath.

"This okay?" he asked.

"Yeah." The single word pulled all the air from my lungs. "Yeah, it's . . ."

"Look at me, Damon," he whispered.

I opened my eyes, and only then did he encourage my hand into motion.

I couldn't say what was more surreal: touching another man's cock, or touching *Alex's* cock. Or maybe, just maybe, the fact that it didn't bother me. It didn't repulse me. Quite the opposite, especially when he closed his eyes, or bit his lip, or moaned softly.

I experimented a little, trying the things I knew I liked and all the things he did to me. I squeezed gently, my breath catching when his did. When I ran my thumb along the underside of his erection, his moaned "oh, my God" was easily the sexiest thing I'd heard all night.

Then he stroked a little faster, so I did the same, and his shudder mirrored mine. Watching him, touching him, hearing him like this, fascinated me. Turned me on beyond rational thought, pushed the nervousness beyond my reach. Whatever thoughts I'd had about being unable to do this or being too afraid to do it, they were forgotten.

I wanted him.

I needed him.

I wanted *this*.

Alex gently pushed my hand out of the way, and I gasped when he pressed his cock against mine. He stroked slowly with his hand, and when my hips—moving like they had a mind of their own—rocked back and forth, his hand and cock both rubbed against mine.

I closed my eyes. "Oh . . . fuck . . ."

"Like that?" he murmured.

"Yeah. Oh, fuck, yeah."

He squeezed gently. Stroked a little faster. His hand, his cock, his breath against my lips, holy *fuck* I had never been so turned on.

I pushed him up against the wall. He gasped and arched off it for a second but relaxed as we made out and ran our hands all over each other's wet bodies. We kissed hungrily, desperately, and the more our cocks rubbed together in his hand, the farther I went out of my mind.

Alex let his head fall back against the wall. "Oh, God," he moaned. "Oh, God, I'm gonna come."

I could barely breathe. All I could do was watch him unravel while I inched closer to doing the same, and more than his body or his hand or his cock against my own, it was his face—eyes screwed shut, lips apart—that turned my knees to liquid. Soaking wet, trembling in ecstasy, right on the edge, back arching off the wall like it had once arched off a rain-drenched blanket on the sand, and when a shudder forced a helpless whimper from his lips, there was no stopping my orgasm.

My eyes rolled back, my spine straightened, and I had to brace myself against the wall with one arm to keep from crumpling to my knees. I was vaguely aware of my voice vibrating in my throat, of my lips and tongue forming some word or another, but I heard nothing except Alex's desperate gasps for breath as his orgasm peaked and fell.

With one last shudder, it was over.

We couldn't kiss. We couldn't speak. We were lucky we could breathe, and for the longest time, that was all we did. Holding onto each other, both using the wall to keep us upright, we breathed.

"That was intense," he finally slurred.

"Yeah, it was," I said, still panting. "Just one thing I can't figure out, though."

"What's that?"

I pulled him closer, drawing him away from the wall and under the hot water with me. "Can't figure out why I waited this long."

He grinned and kissed me gently. "Guess we'll just have to make up for lost time."

"Mmm, I like that idea."

☿ CHAPTER 19 ♀
ALEX

amon and I stayed in each other's arms in the shower until the water started to cool. Once we'd dried off, we moved into the bedroom and got under the covers.

I rested my head on his shoulder and he laid his hand over mine on his chest. His other arm was lazily draped around my shoulders, and as his fingers drifted absently up and down my upper arm, every gentle stroke made my mind reel with disbelief.

In two years, I had never allowed myself to fantasize about this. I was too certain it would never happen. Even if Damon accepted me as a shifter, he'd never be willing to cross this line, so I'd shut out every last fantasy about touching him in my male form. Why torment myself with something I wanted so badly but could never have?

And yet, here we were. Naked, in each other's arms, letting the lingering afterglow fade away at its own speed after a couple of intense orgasms.

"Still awake?" he asked.

I pushed myself up and looked at him. "I was just about to ask you the same thing."

He touched my face. "I'm tired, but I don't think I'm going to sleep anytime soon."

"Same here." I draped an arm over his waist. "What changed, anyway? About, you know, us?"

"I don't know, to be honest. Maybe I just needed some time to get used to the idea." His eyes flicked up to meet mine and the pad of his thumb traced a gentle arc across my cheekbone. "But seeing you at the club tonight, I couldn't take my eyes off you. You just looked so . . ."

"What?"

Damon moistened his lips and met my eyes. "Happy."

I trailed my fingertips down the side of his face. "I was."

"Are you now?"

I smiled. "Yeah. I am." I kissed him lightly.

"Thanks for, you know, not rushing this," he whispered.

"Rushing it?"

"Yeah. Just kind of letting it happen on its own."

I combed my fingers through his damp hair. "I would never have pushed you, Damon. To be honest, I didn't think would happen at all."

He grinned. "Surprise!"

We both laughed.

Damon's expression turned serious, and he stroked my face with the backs of his fingers. "I think," he whispered, pausing like he had to search for the right words, "this was bound to happen sooner or later."

"I'll admit I had my doubts."

"I did, too, but . . . I think I just had to get past the physical side. Had to get it through my head that it didn't matter what skin you were in, I still felt the same about you."

I swallowed the lump that tried to rise in my throat. "You don't know how long I've wanted to hear you say that."

He shot me a playful grin. "Guess you don't have to wait anymore, do you?"

I smiled. "Guess not."

I moved a little closer to him. Damon slid his arm around me, and when our lips met, I melted against him. He kissed me the way he'd kissed me the very first time we'd been together: no uncertainty, no hesitation, no fear. The way he had when I was a woman, he was a man, and everything between us had been simple and easy. Our situation was neither simple nor easy now, but the tip of his tongue teased my lips apart like it was still simple, and his fingers held onto the back of my neck like it was still easy.

And maybe, if only for tonight, it was.

Every inch of warm skin against mine made my head spin, and every breath of his familiar—if subdued after our shower—scent made me want to just lie here and breathe him in all night.

Whenever my fingertips brushed his skin, the muscles beneath quivered just like they always did, and I couldn't help grinning to myself. I loved having this effect on him, and I'd missed it.

His hand followed the curve of my spine down to my lower back, and with just a hint of pressure, he pulled my hips toward his.

I broke the kiss with a gasp, shivering as his erect cock brushed my own. I pushed my hips against him again, just enough to create the slightest, most delicious friction between us, and Damon moaned into another kiss.

My God, I just couldn't get enough of him. The heat of his body, the taste of his deep, slow kiss, the way he shook as badly as I did the more we touched and tasted each other. I never thought I'd be able to turn him on like this, but every movement of our hips left nothing to the imagination about who I was or how aroused we were. Nor did the hand in my hair that begged me not to pull away or the ragged breaths that alternately warmed and cooled my cheek.

"Oh, God, Alex, I want to . . ." He paused. "I want to fuck you."

I pulled back enough to look into his eyes. "Are you . . . sure?"

"Yes. Please. I want to."

I'm dreaming. No way in hell this is real.

He trailed his fingertips down the side of my face. "Please, Alex. I want you so damned bad right now."

I gulped. Words failed me, so I just nodded. I pushed myself up, and Damon reached for the nightstand.

"Still have any of that lube from a while back?" I asked.

"Hmm, I think so." He rifled through the drawer. "Ah, here it is." He pulled out a small bottle and a condom.

"You sure you want to do this?" I asked as he sat up. "We don't have to do everything tonight."

"We don't have to." He tore the condom wrapper with his teeth. "But I want to."

I didn't even try to come up with a witty comment. All I could do was watch him roll on the condom while I silently pleaded with him not to change his mind. He wanted this. I wanted this. *Please, please, Damon, I want you so bad.*

Once the condom was on, he reached for the lube, and without another word, we changed position. I got on my hands and knees, and the warmth of his hand on my hip made my breath catch. Then came the cool lube. His fingers teased me, pressed in a little, teased me some more. He knew damn well I didn't need careful, painstaking prep to take him, but maybe this was more for him than for me. A way of psyching himself up to have sex with a man. As he slid a finger into me, and then a second one, his breathing became heavier just as mine did. I thought I heard him curse, but maybe it was me. At this point, all I knew was how bad I wanted him and how much I hoped he really wanted me.

His fingers slipped out. Then came the pressure.

And . . . oh God . . .

A little at a time, slowly, gently, Damon slid inside me. I willed myself to breathe, if only to prevent myself from passing out and missing a single second of this.

"This okay?" he asked, and he was out of breath already.

"Yeah." Damn, so was I. "This is . . . this is fine." Fine? That didn't even come close. "I love it," I slurred.

"Good," he breathed. "Because I do, too."

I shivered. He withdrew slowly, then pushed back in. He picked up speed, but not much; maybe he wanted it slow, or maybe he was as overwhelmed as I was and needed to take it slow while he wrapped his head around the fact that this was really happening. I didn't mind either way because he felt so damned good.

"Like that?" he whispered.

I nodded, rocking back against him to encourage him to move a little faster. Every stroke sent more sparks of white light across my blurred vision. It had been ages since I'd done this as a man, and I'd almost forgotten how much I loved it. More than that, knowing this was Damon—that Damon was deep inside me, that it was Damon's fingers twitching on my hips, that Damon was the one who'd moaned like that—drove me insane. It was just as well I'd never let myself fantasize about this; nothing my mind could have conjured would have done the real thing justice.

I only wished I could have seen the look on his face.

"Wait," I said. "Stop."

He stopped. I bit my lip, my body screaming for him to keep going while my mind insisted on this. *God, Damon, you feel so good.*

Running his hand up and down my side, he said, "Is something wrong? Am I hurting you or—"

"No, nothing's wrong." I closed my eyes and took a breath, struggling to stay in control. "I want . . . let me get on top."

Damon didn't speak. He kept a hand on my hip and withdrew slowly, both of us gasping as he pulled all the way out. Changing positions took a little longer than before. We were both trembling too much to move quickly, let alone gracefully, but I didn't give a damn how clumsy we were.

As soon as he was on his back, I was over him, and my mouth was against his before he'd even wrapped his arms around me. His lips crushed mine, and when his tongue demanded access to my mouth, I happily granted it. Fingers dug into skin, mouths moved together with feverish desperation, stubble scraped across stubble. There was nothing gentle or subdued about us now. We breathed each other in and kissed and held onto each other like one or both of us were a flight risk.

All at once, we separated, touching our foreheads together and panting against each other's mouths.

"I want . . ." He swept his tongue across his lips. "God, Alex, I want to be inside you again."

"We're getting there," I said. "Don't worry, I'm—"

"*Please*," he whispered.

The desperation in his voice pulled all the air out of my lungs. "Stay just like that." I sat up and reached for the lube. As I put some more on him, I said, "With everything you've done for me lately, I just want you to lie back and enjoy the ride."

"Oh, I'm enjoying it so far."

"Good." I sat over him. He put a hand on my hip and the other on the base of his cock, and I bit my lip as I lowered myself onto him.

"Oh, fuck . . ." he breathed. When I rose off him, he moaned and closed his eyes. "God*damn* it, you feel . . ." He gave another soft moan.

Then he opened his eyes and reached for the bottle of lube.

I slowed down. "Do we need more?"

"No, you're fine." He poured some on his hand, capped the bottle, and tossed it onto the bed beside us. Then he reached between us and closed his hand around my cock.

"Oh . . . God . . ." I screwed my eyes shut and let my head fall forward. His slick palm and fingers slid up and down my cock, and I almost forgot what I was doing before I found my rhythm again. Damon stroked me at the same speed I fucked him, slowing when I did, gaining speed when I did. Maybe I adjusted my speed to meet his. Didn't know. Couldn't have cared less.

"You're fucking amazing at this," I whispered.

"That doesn't surprise you, does it?"

I laughed softly. "Not in the least, no." *I'm just surprised you're enjoying this, Damon. This is so far beyond my wildest dreams, you don't even know . . .*

I leaned down to kiss him. Our lips brushed. Met. Brushed again. I couldn't concentrate on kissing him while maintaining any semblance of rhythm, so I pushed myself back up on my arms.

We locked eyes as I rode him and he stroked me. The muscles in my hips and thighs burned with exertion, and the bed frame groaned with the force of our rapid movement, but as near as I could tell, everything had slowed down. Every breath lasted an age, every stroke and every shudder happened in extreme slow motion. I couldn't look anywhere but right at him, and he looked right back at me, and everything we did, every way we touched inside and out, was so intense my eyes watered.

Damon groaned. His hand tightened around my cock and his back arched beneath us. "Fuck, Alex, you feel amazing."

His grip tightened a little more, and my rhythm fell apart. So did his. I lost track of who was doing what. If it was his hips or mine that set the pace, if his hand was even moving anymore or if I was thrusting into his tight, slippery grasp. The air around us was alive with the squeak of the bed frame and our delirious moans and desperate gasps for breath. I couldn't say for sure who let go first, but the other wasn't far behind, and every move one of us made drew out both of our orgasms until the room around us had dissolved into spinning sparks of tear-blurred white light.

One last shudder turned what was left of my spine to liquid, and I collapsed over him. Struggling to catch my breath, I held myself up on trembling arms until he pulled me all the way down.

"Guess we'll need to take another shower," he murmured.

"Yeah, we will." I kissed him lightly. "Just . . . give me a minute."

☿ CHAPTER 20 ♀
DAMON

few days after the night at the club, Alex went to see the specialist, and he asked me to come to the appointment with him.

We hadn't been waiting long when they called his name, but he didn't see the doctor yet. A few X-rays were taken and a nurse discussed his medical history, wrote down his vitals, and otherwise ran through the usual procedures. Then she showed us back to the waiting room.

"Dr. Rowland will be with you shortly," she said. "Once he's had a look at the X-rays, he'll call you back in."

So we waited. Minute after minute ticked by. We both flipped through magazine after outdated magazine. Other patients came and went. The receptionist's nails clattered on her keyboard, sometimes while she was on the phone, sometimes not. File drawers slammed, papers shuffled, voices murmured on the other side of the door. A half dozen or so colorful tropical fish swam endless, bored circles around the huge tank. All the while, the second hand on the clock tracked every minute we spent here.

Waiting rooms were like their own special brand of purgatory, especially when so much was on the line. The specialist would have the answers Alex desperately needed, but for now, I felt like the diver in the fish tank who would never get any closer to the treasure chest.

Alex put a magazine aside and leaned forward. He rested his elbows on his knees and clasped his hands together. His head was bowed, almost like he was praying, his thumbs pressing into the bridge of his nose. He'd been optimistic and upbeat ever since the outpouring of generosity and support from people at the Mat, but all morning, he'd been quiet. Not necessarily withdrawn like she'd been during depressions, but he was obviously preoccupied.

I put a hand on his shoulder. "You okay?"

His head moved in a hint of a nod.

"Nervous?" I asked.

"Very."

There wasn't much I could offer in the way of reassurance. I didn't know if everything would be okay. I didn't know if the doctor would have an answer that would let Alex get some real sleep. There were so many ways this appointment could go, and with the knot in my stomach, I could only imagine the one in his.

The door between the waiting room and the rest of the office opened. "Alex Nichols?"

We both looked up to see a stocky gentleman in a shirt and tie. Alex rose. I followed him.

The man extended his hand. "I'm Dr. Rowland."

"Alex." He shook the doctor's hand. "This is Damon, my partner."

"Nice to meet you both." Dr. Rowland shook my hand, then gestured through the door with his clipboard. "Come on back."

We followed him into his office instead of an exam room. There, he indicated the pair of chairs in front of his desk while he went around to the other side.

As Dr. Rowland skimmed over some notes, Alex drummed his fingers on the armrest. Wrung his hands in his lap. Drummed his fingers again. I touched his arm, and he glanced at me. I managed what I hoped was an encouraging smile, and he returned it.

Dr. Rowland sat back in his chair and folded his hands across his lap. "Before we get too far into this, there's one thing I want to make clear. Shifters often distrust my colleagues and me when it comes to these implants." He paused. "With good reason, too. This profession is not always friendly toward things it doesn't understand."

"I hadn't noticed," Alex muttered.

"Which is why I want to make sure you understand that I'm on your side." He closed his eyes and exhaled. Beside me, Alex's chair creaked. I glanced at him, and when his eyes widened, I looked back at the doctor.

My lips parted. I stared in disbelief as Dr. Rowland's features softened. Blurred. Changed. I blinked a few times, trying to focus, but then realized it wasn't my eyes at all. His clothing stayed sharp and clear, as did his surroundings, but his face and hands . . . *changed*.

Then everything solidified again, and looking back at us across the broad desk was a woman. Her clothing was the same, just clinging to her figure a little differently than before, and her long brown hair spilled over her shoulders. I'd never witnessed a shift before, not in person, and it was startling to say the least.

"As you can imagine," she said, her voice bearing no resemblance at all to her male form's, "it's in my best interest to make sure shifters are given correct information and proper care. Especially in situations like this."

"Much appreciated," Alex said.

"Now, I've had a chance to look over your X-rays, and we've identified the specific brand and model of your implants."

"And the verdict?"

"They are definitely a black market variety, but the good news, and I use that expression loosely, is that this particular type is not dangerous if left in place. If you forgo the surgery, it doesn't pose any significant risk to your life or quality of life."

"Aside from being static for the rest of my life."

The doctor nodded slowly. "Yes."

"What about taking them out?"

"That's where we run into some not-so-good news, I'm afraid."

Alex tensed. "Meaning?"

"The surgery is risky to begin with. I make no bones about telling patients this is major surgery, not a minor procedure. But with yours . . ." She looked at her notes again. "The angle, the location, where the implants have lodged themselves, they're even more dangerous to remove. That, and the particular make and model of the implant is a black market variety that frequently fuses to nerves, which can be seriously damaged during removal." She paused. "Further, this kind of device has extremely shoddy construction, and they're very, very delicate. Normal activity, even strenuous physical activity won't damage it, but surgical instruments can. There have been a few cases where, during an attempt to remove it, an implant like yours has shattered."

Alex cleared his throat. "I'm assuming this is a bad thing."

"Very. If one shatters, it's nearly impossible to find and remove all the fragments without causing serious damage to the spinal cord. If fragments are left behind, they begin interfering with other neurological impulses. This can result in paralysis within as little as a few months, and can cause organ failure depending on which nerves are affected."

What little color there was drained from Alex's face. I took his hand, gripping it tightly, and wasn't surprised his palm was damp. So was mine.

Dr. Rowland continued. "The best case scenario for one of these implants is for it to settle itself near the initial injection site. It's not as difficult to get in and remove it." She looked him in the eye. "Two of yours have settled fairly close to each other, and won't be difficult to reach. The third, however, is considerably higher. It appears to have attached itself to either the bone or soft tissue, though we won't know that for certain until the surgery."

Alex exhaled. "Great."

"The fact that you haven't experienced any problems to indicate neurological interference tells me none of the implants have embedded in any way that poses a threat to your health. My concern with removing the third one is, judging by its location on the X-rays, the potential for damaging nerves during the procedure."

"So, leaving them in means no risk at all," Alex said. "Taking them out stands a good chance of causing problems."

She nodded slowly. "I wish I had better news for you."

He was quiet for a long moment. "And if I get it removed, assuming the surgery is successful, how likely is it I'll be able to shift?"

"It's difficult to say. Most patients with medically approved implants are able to shift again without issue after its removal. With black market devices, there aren't many studies."

"What about in your experience?"

"In my experience," she said, two sympathetic creases forming on her forehead, "slightly better than half regain the ability to shift."

"Those aren't very promising odds," he said, probably more to himself than to either of us.

"No, they're not. Especially with the amount of risk involved. It's your decision, though. As a surgeon, weighing the risks versus benefits, I'm inclined to urge you to leave the implants in place." She paused. "As a shifter myself . . ."

Alex raised his eyebrows. "As a shifter . . .?"

She thought for a moment. "I would be willing to perform the procedure if you wish to have it done."

"So as both a shifter and a surgeon, would you recommend the surgery or not?"

"As difficult as it is to suggest this to another shifter," the doctor said quietly, "I would recommend against the operation."

Alex's shoulders sank. I squeezed his hand, but he didn't look at me.

"As I said," Dr. Rowland said softly. "The decision is yours."

"How soon would I know if I can shift again?"

"After the surgery, you'd need to wait about ninety days before you attempt to shift. To make sure everything has fully healed and there are no complications. It's longer than is usually necessary, but that way we're absolutely sure you're in the clear. A shift when there are underlying complications could result in enough trauma to cause serious damage."

Alex shuddered. I wondered if it was the prospect of the dangerous surgery and long recovery, or the idea of being stuck as a male for at least another three months.

"Don't make a decision now, Alex," Dr. Rowland said. "Whether it's a yes or a no, take some time and think it over."

He nodded. "I will."

"Do you have any more questions?" Her eyes flicked toward me. "Either of you?"

I shook my head. Alex said nothing.

On our way out, Alex handed me his car keys but didn't say anything. I didn't press the issue; I was just glad we'd taken one car instead of two.

☿ CHAPTER 21 ♀
ALEX

Sitting on my sofa, I pressed my fingertips into my temples and sighed. "You know, I thought it would be a relief if I found out these implants weren't dangerous. Now it just feels like any chance of getting them out is slipping through my fingers."

"Talk about a double-edged sword." Damon put a gentle hand between my shoulders. "You still going to get it done?"

"I . . . have no idea. With the risk, and the possibility of not being able to shift, I . . ."

"The surgeon said she'll still perform the procedure. That says something, doesn't it?"

"Yeah, she will, but I can't decide if I should ask her to." I glanced at him. "It's a hell of a lot of risk, and I might not gain anything."

"You don't think it's worth the gamble to get your identity back?"

"On the surface, yes, I think it is." I let my head fall forward, closing my eyes as Damon rubbed the back of my neck. "But when I start looking at the pros and cons, I just . . . I just don't know."

"Well, whatever you decide, I'll back you," he said softly. "One hundred percent."

I managed the closest thing I could to a smile. "Thank you."

He smiled back. The hand on my neck went to my shoulder. "Come here."

I leaned into him, and his arm had never been more comforting than it was right then, when he wrapped it around me. I put my head against his shoulder, and he laid his hand over mine on his chest.

"I just wonder how much risk is too much," I said. "I want my life back, but how much more of it am I willing to lose to maybe get that part back? It was easy when there was a chance these implants could do as much damage as the surgery. But now . . ." I shook my head. "Transgender statics risk their lives and well-being all the time to get gender reassignment surgery. Tabby would probably belt me for even questioning whether or not to get this done."

Damon shrugged. "I think she'd understand. She obviously hasn't taken the idea of surgery lightly, any more than she's taken the hormone treatments or anything else lightly. She might wish she could become a shifter, but that doesn't mean she'd expect it to be easy for you to make this decision."

"No, I suppose she wouldn't." After a long, long pause, I said, "What would you do?"

"What?"

"In my shoes. Would you get the surgery?"

Damon gave a quiet chuckle. "Quite honestly, I think I'd have been on the floor in a fetal position a long time ago. Forget trying to make a life-altering medical decision."

I smiled and put a hand over his on my arm. "Oh, you never know."

"No, trust me, I don't think I'd have handled it as well as you have." He kissed the top of my head. "And in all honesty, it's easy for me to say off the cuff that I'd get it done. If I actually had to make the decision, I'd probably have as much trouble with it as you are."

"Do you think it's . . ." I struggled to find the right word. "Do you think it's, I don't know, reckless? To go through that much when it's not actually posing a threat to my life?"

"Would leaving things as is pose a threat to your quality of life?"

I nodded.

"Then I think you have your answer." He paused. "If you'd asked me the same question a few months ago, my answer might have been different, but knowing what I do now . . ."

"What do you mean?"

"I've known plenty of shifters in my life, but I never realized how much it affects you. I guess, being static, I just didn't think about it. Until recently, I didn't get it. And, I don't know how I would have reacted had you told me before. I just don't know. But . . . with the way things have worked out . . ." His thumb drew slow arcs across the side of my hand, and when he spoke again, his voice was low and just a little uneven. "All I know is, whatever happens, surgery or not, my biggest fear is losing you." He held me tighter.

"What if . . ." I paused.

Damon squeezed my hand. "What?"

I lifted my head so I could look him in the eye. "What if the surgery goes all right, but I can't . . ."

"But you can't shift?"

The words gave me chills. "Yeah."

"Then we'll learn to live with it. I'm more worried about you dealing with it than me." He drew me back to him and kissed my forehead. "One way or another, we'll figure it out. I'm not going anywhere either way." He paused, releasing a breath that cooled my skin. "I wish I could offer you more than that, but it's all I've got."

"That's more than enough," I said, whispering in case my voice cracked. "You have no idea." I met his eyes. "I love you."

"I love you, too." He kissed me gently and ran his fingers through my hair. "And I'll be here whether you get this done or not."

That shouldn't have been the most important deciding factor, and I supposed it wasn't. Still, hearing him say it lightened some of the weight on my shoulders.

"I want the surgery. I know it's risky, and it might not even work, but . . . I need it. I need to at least try."

He squeezed my hand. "Whatever you want to do. I'll be here for you."

"You know I could end up a paraplegic man living on borrowed time, right?" I said, my voice wavering.

Damon nodded. "I know." He stroked my hair again and touched his forehead to mine. "And you know, when I kept bringing up marriage before, I meant it. Sickness and health, better or worse." He swallowed hard. "'Til death."

Emotion constricted my throat, but I managed to whisper, "I don't deserve you, Damon."

"Too bad. You're stuck with me."

I laughed in spite of the sting in my eyes.

He kissed me gently. More serious now, he said, "Are you sure about this?"

"Yeah. I am." I paused, moistening my lips. "I'll wait until tomorrow to call and schedule it. Sleep on it, I guess. But yeah, I think I'm going to go through with it."

My mind reeled at all the implications of agreeing to this operation. Time off work. A long hospital stay. Longer recovery time.

I'd never had major surgery, at least nothing like this with its long list of potential complications that could make the most stoic patient blanch. This wasn't a wisdom tooth extraction or an outpatient procedure on my ankle. This was the real fucking deal. I'd have to draw up a living will. And a power of attorney. Someone had to have the ability to give or withhold consent if I was unconscious, sedated, or otherwise unable to decide for myself.

If Damon said no, there was always Tabby. Or Ken. But Damon was the first to come to mind. It was weird, the thought of signing over to someone else the right to say yes or no to medical procedures, especially when it included the right to cut off or continue life support.

I was in this situation because someone had taken it upon themselves to make a medical decision for me, and letting that control out of my hands was unsettling. There was no one I trusted more than Damon to take that control, but it was a strange thought.

And putting this much thought into death is so macabre and morbid.

Maybe it was, but it was a necessary evil. The risk of death wasn't extraordinarily high, but the potential complications were nothing to sneeze at. For that matter, paralysis scared me more than death. At least death would mean not having to struggle with this anymore.

No, Alex, don't think like that again. I shuddered. That line of thinking was one I'd fought to abandon over the years.

"You okay?" Damon asked.

"Yeah. Just thinking, I guess." I chewed the inside of my cheek. "Listen, if I'm going to get this done, I need to have someone to . . ." I hesitated. "Someone with power of attorney. In case something . . . goes wrong."

Damon swallowed. "Right . . ."

"If you're not willing to, I'll understand, but honestly, I don't think there's anyone I could trust more with that than you."

He touched my arm. "Of course I will. If you want me to do it, I wouldn't even think twice."

"You probably should think twice. I'm asking you to shoulder the possibility of having to tell them to cut off life support. I know I can trust you to make the decision, I just want to make sure you trust yourself with it."

He said nothing for a moment. I let him run the situation through his head, and he probably wandered through some of the same catastrophic, unrealistic, snowball's-chance-in-hell scenarios that I did. If he didn't want that responsibility, I fully understood.

But he nodded anyway. "Yes, if you want me to, I will."

"Thank you."

We both fell silent for a moment. My mind tried to wander back into that gauntlet of morbid scenarios, so I quickly changed the subject. "On the plus side, at least I don't have to go anywhere near the office for a while."

"Still pretty bad there?"

"I don't see it changing anytime soon. I'm just learning to ignore the gossip, and sooner or later, something else will come along that grabs their attention."

"True. What about those two asses that were messing with you before?"

I shrugged. "They're around. They're still being asses. I just try to steer clear of them whenever I can."

"You shouldn't have to do that at work, though." He ran the backs of his fingers down the side of my face. "If they're creating a hostile work environment, then . . ."

"I know. Not much I can do about it, though."

He pursed his lips. "Why not quit?"

"If it was that simple, I'd have ditched that place a long time ago. I still have to eat, you know. And if my petition for custody of Sam is approved, then . . ." I sighed. "Losing a chunk of my income when he's living with me? There's just no way."

Damon was quiet for a moment. "Would it help if you were only paying half a mortgage?"

I blinked. "What?"

"When this is all over, do you . . ." He paused. "Would you be willing to consider . . . moving in together?"

"Are you—" I blinked. "Damon, are you serious?"

"Completely serious. That job is sucking the life out of you. You make decent money at the Mat, so why kill yourself with two jobs?" He put a hand over mine. "That, and I want us to. I have for a long time, and that hasn't changed."

I swallowed hard. "What about Sam?"

"He's part of the package deal now, isn't he?"

"Most likely, yeah."

"Well, whichever house we move into, there's room for all three of us. Might be a little tight, and we might have to stretch money a bit, but I don't see why we couldn't do it." He squeezed my hand and looked me in the eye. "It would be a hell of a lot better than watching you continue working at the place when it's making you so miserable. And with as much time as we spend together, why not?"

"Good point," I said. "Just keep in mind, I could still be like this, even—"

"I know. We've been through this, and I know what the risks are." He stroked my face. "And I'm still asking, because none of this changes what I feel about you." His hand stopped, his palm warm as he cupped my cheek. "And especially after everything that's happened, I don't want to lose you."

I swallowed hard. "Speaking of which, you know all those times I didn't want to talk about getting married? Assuming things go well with the surgery and . . ." My heart thundered in my chest. "Anyway, is it too late to, um, be open to that subject?"

Damon smiled. "No. No, it's not too late at all."

I rested my head against his shoulder again. "I'm serious, I really don't deserve you."

He kissed the top of my head. "And I'm serious when I say you're stuck with me."

"I could think of worse things. This whole getting married thing could get a little complicated if I'm still static, though. Being a male and all."

He shrugged. "We'll find a way. I hear Canada's nice in the summer anyway."

I laughed. "I don't know; might be fun if there's ten feet of snow on the ground."

"Maybe so." He chuckled. "Has Sam ever been snowboarding?"

"I don't know. I doubt it."

"Well, it's high time he learned." Damon put his hand over mine again. "Canada it is."

☿ CHAPTER 22 ♀
DAMON

Despite a different fan of outdated magazines on a table and a different diver trying in vain to get to a different bubbling treasure chest, this waiting room was just as close to purgatory as the one in the specialist's office. No, not just as close. Closer. A deeper circle of "please let this be over soon," and there was nothing I could do except wait.

I'd stayed with Alex in pre-op until the drugs started kicking in. When the nurses wheeled him out, I'd headed for the waiting room, but I'd made the mistake of pausing to look back.

For the last two hours, I'd replayed the image of those double doors banging shut with cold finality, cutting off the already fading sound of the gurney's wheels. Over, and over, and over, my mind's eye had watched those doors shut. That was the moment when the nerves set in. That was when he was gone, and there was that small but unsettling fear that he was *really* gone.

Magazines couldn't hold my attention. The diver was about to drive me mad. I finally put the magazine in my hand on the table and got up. I paced the deserted waiting room, desperate to relieve this nervous energy.

With each step, the ache in my hips and lower back reminded me of everything we'd done last night. We'd both been insatiable, even more than I could remember during those scorching nights in our past life. Though neither of us had spoken about it, the thought had lurked in the back of my mind that this could be the last night like this. The last time until he'd recovered from the surgery at least, but possibly the last time at all. I hadn't let myself think of all the things that could happen in the operating room, but from the first article of clothing that hit the floor, I'd done everything I could to make sure Alex had the night of his life.

It was a wonder we'd managed to get out of bed in time for him to get to pre-op at the crack of dawn.

Somehow, we'd made it. Now he was back there, I was up here, and I waited.

Pacing the floor, I prayed to God that Alex came through with the ability to live a normal life. A normal life with the ability to walk and the ability to shift from male to female when he needed to. Knowing what I did now, I understood how Alex's ability to shift had permeated his life on every level, to depths I still couldn't fathom. It may have seemed foolish for him to risk life and limb to *maybe* regain that ability, but going on as a static might well have killed him anyway. Slowly, from the inside out, it would have killed him. At least this way, there was a chance, however slim that chance may have been.

"Mr. Bryce?"

At the sound of my name, I spun around. "Yes?"

A nurse approached with a clipboard in her hand.

"Is he out of surgery?" I asked. No, he couldn't be. He'd only been back there a little over an hour and a half.

"Not yet, no." The seriousness in her expression made my pulse jump. "We've run into some difficulty with one of the implants, and since you have his power of attorney, we need your consent to perform an additional procedure to remove it."

My mouth went dry, and I willed my knees not to collapse under me. "What's wrong?"

"The third implant has moved since the original X-rays were taken," she said. "It's up in his neck now, floating between the sixth and eighth vertebrae."

"It hasn't embedded itself?"

"It's hard to say. Dr. Rowland won't know for sure until he gets in and sees it. But it's possible."

"So, what needs to be done?"

"It's a riskier and more delicate procedure to remove the implant in its current location. It'll require keeping him under anesthesia significantly longer, and because of the device's proximity to the spinal cord, there is a substantially greater risk of damage, including paralysis."

"Or death?" I asked, barely forcing the words out.

She nodded. "Yes. The incision for the other two implants is through his abdomen, but for this one, the surgeon will need to go in through the back of his neck. The risks are listed on this form." She held up the consent form.

With my heart in my throat, I took the clipboard from her. "What happens if I don't consent to it?"

"We'll leave that device in place, and when he's conscious, he can make the decision to have an additional procedure to remove it."

My gut twisted and somersaulted. Alex wanted this thing out. There was no way he could afford a second surgery. But how far was he willing to go? He'd told me his wishes, given me the go-ahead to consent to anything short of prolonged life support. He'd want me to sign the form.

I read over the list of risks, potential side effects, all the things that could happen to Alex if I signed on the dotted line at the bottom of the page. It was impossible to say which complications were likely and which were just listed to save the hospital's ass in a lawsuit, but words like "death" and "paralysis" and "brain damage" jumped out at me like they were written in bright, screaming red.

Forcing my hand to stay steady, I signed the form. *Please, God, don't let me be signing his death warrant.*

I handed it back to the nurse. "How long do you think it'll be now?"

"Difficult to say. At least a few more hours. We'll let you know as soon as he's moved to recovery."

"Thank you," I whispered.

With my written permission to cut into Alex's neck, the nurse left, and I was once again alone with the ancient magazines and the Sisyphean diver. I wanted to pace, but I wasn't sure I could rely on my legs to stay under me. Instead, I sank into a chair, resting my elbows on my knees and clasping my fingers in front of my lips.

"You just found out why I've changed the subject whenever you've brought up getting married," he'd said that night I'd gone to check on my girlfriend and found a man with a spinal headache, *"and right now, you have your hands folded so tight in front of your lips that your knuckles are turning white."*

I pulled my hands apart and leaned back in the chair. Staring up at the ceiling, I pretended not to feel the tingling of blood rushing back into my fingers. It was hard to believe it had only been a couple of months since that night. The rug had been yanked out from under both of us, and if there was any chance of getting that rug back under our feet, this was it. Right here, right now, with whatever happened in the operating room. Whatever happened with my permission.

I gulped.

In my pocket, my phone vibrated. When I pulled it out, there was a text from Sam.

Any word on Alex?

No sense worrying him with the newly complicated procedure, so I wrote back, *Not yet. Hopefully soon.*

I sent the message and waited.

Sam and I exchanged a few more texts. Tabitha called to see if I'd heard anything. Alex's friend and coworker Ken called a little while after that. The magazines got older. The diver didn't get any closer to the treasure chest. The hands on the clock went around and around and around. Every set of approaching footsteps was a nurse coming to give me bad news. Every summons on the hospital intercom was someone urgently needed in that specific operating room.

"Mr. Bryce?"

I almost jumped out of my skin. A different nurse entered the waiting room with another clipboard in hand. My heart beat faster, pushing cold water through my veins.

"Yes?" I said, almost choking on the word.

"I thought you'd like to know Alex is in recovery now."

A rush of relief swept through me. "How's he doing?"

"Still heavily sedated, but he came through the procedure without any complications."

More relief. "Will he be able to walk?"

"Too early to tell," she said. "As far as the surgeon could see, there was no damage to the spinal cord, but we'll have to wait until he's fully conscious to see if he responds to stimuli."

I swallowed. "When can I see him?"

"Soon." She smiled. "I'll come get you as soon as he's awake and settled into his room."

"Thank you."

As soon as she turned to go, I slumped back against the chair and sighed, my head spinning and stomach fluttering as a full day's worth of fear evaporated. I wouldn't know for a while if Alex was absolutely okay—if he could walk, if he could shift—but he'd made it through. As far as I could tell, the worst was over.

Thank God. The worst was over.

♂ CHAPTER 23 ♀
ALEX

My eyes fluttered open. Both mind and vision were still cloudy, and it took a moment to orient myself. Sunlight poured in through huge windows, illuminating my familiar-yet-unfamiliar surroundings. I didn't recognize this particular room, but between the bland pastel walls and the halo of beeping machinery all around my head, I realized after a moment that this was a hospital room.

I tried to turn my head, but couldn't.

What the hell?

I tried again. It wasn't just the pain—and Jesus Christ, there was plenty of pain—at the base of my neck.

I. Couldn't. *Move.*

Panic swept through me. I was paralyzed. I couldn't move. Oh, God, I—

My fingers closed around cool sheets and coarse blankets, and something dug into the back of one hand. The haze of sleep and drugs cleared a little more. I could move and feel my hands, so it wasn't paralysis.

With one hand, I reached up to touch my neck. Ah, that was it. A hard brace kept my head still. As my awareness spread, I realized the brace bit into my jaw and collarbones. How had I not noticed it before? I sure as fuck noticed it now.

I raised my other hand so I could see what was digging in. An IV. That shouldn't have surprised me.

So I could still feel my hands. I could move my arms. What about everything else?

Without thinking about it, I tried to move my hip a little and was rewarded with a fraction of an inch of movement and a blazing hot surge of pain.

Bad idea, Alex. Bad idea.

Wracking my brain, I tried to remember how the hell I got here. There were dreamlike images of people looking down at me, voices that sounded hundreds of miles away, and that vague sense of panic that accompanied being disoriented. The memory might have prompted a shudder, but my body didn't dare let that shudder come to life. Not with the pain already loitering along various parts of my spine and above my hip. That must have been where they'd cut in. I distantly remembered Dr. Rowland saying it was an abdominal incision. At least the drugs had worn off enough for me to realize it would be a bad idea to try prodding the spot to see if it was where the incision had been made.

Footsteps would have turned my head had it not been for the stupid brace. Oh, and the pain.

"Damon?" I murmured. Damn, my mouth was dry.

A nurse leaned over the bed so I could see her face. "We'll bring him in shortly. Just want to make sure you're doing okay first."

"You tell me," I muttered.

She smiled. "Well, you're awake. That's a good sign." She pressed something into my hand and closed my fingers around it. "This is a morphine pump. When you need something for the pain, just press the button, okay?"

I ran my thumb over it, and as soon as I found the button, I pressed it.

"Good," she said. "Don't try to be a martyr about it, either. If it hurts, push the button. Don't wait until it's unbearable."

"Duly noted," I whispered.

"Mr. Nichols?" Dr. Rowland's male voice preceded the appearance of his face by about two seconds. "How are we feeling?"

"Ask me again after you tell me how things went."

He smiled. "It went well. Very well. We were able to remove all three implants."

I exhaled. "Thank God."

"Just waiting on the lab to make sure the devices were completely intact, but I'm optimistic about that. Now, we did have to perform an additional procedure to remove the third." He gestured at my neck. "That's why you're wearing the brace temporarily, to keep from disturbing the incision."

"Lovely."

"All in all, though, as far as I can tell, everything was successful. Since you're awake, I'd like to run through a few quick tests. Then we're going to have you up and out of bed."

I blinked. "You—what?"

"We told you that in pre-op," the nurse said with a laugh. "You'll be up and around within the hour."

I groaned. If the pain was this bad while I was flat, I could only imagine trying to get around.

"We'll get to that," Dr. Rowland said.

"I'm going to go out to the waiting room and let his friend know he's in his room," the nurse said to Dr. Rowland.

To me, Dr. Rowland said, "Are you up for visitors?"

"Yeah. Please, I want to see him."

The doctor nodded at the nurse, and her footsteps faded out of the room.

Dr. Rowland moved to the end of the bed. He squeezed my toes. "Can you feel that?"

"Yes."

"Wiggle your toes."

I did, and his satisfied nod sent a rush of relief through me.

"Can you bend your knee?" He slipped his hand under it and rested the other on my shin, and I grimaced as I pulled my knee up slightly, the effort sending fresh pain from my hip to my side. "There, that's fine for now." He eased my leg back down. Other leg, same deal. He tapped a pen up and down my arms and legs, then had me follow the pen with my eyes. The second part was challenging because the morphine was starting to kick in, but apparently I tracked it well enough to satisfy Dr. Rowland.

"Looks like you made it, kid." He squeezed my arm. "We'll know more once you're up and moving around, but so far the response to stimuli is normal. Doesn't appear to be any paralysis or nerve damage."

I closed my eyes. It remained to be seen if I could shift, but my body was still in one piece. The worst was over.

"You have your schedule of follow-up visits," Dr. Rowland went on. When I opened my eyes, he pointed an emphatic finger at me. "No matter how tempting it is, and I know it will be, do *not* attempt a shift until I give you the all-clear. Understood?"

"Understood."

"Good." He squeezed my arm again. "I'll keep my fingers crossed for you."

"Probably not a good thing to do while you're operating on someone."

Dr. Rowland laughed and patted my shoulder. "Looks like your sense of humor made it through intact, too."

"Might pull through after all, then," I said dryly.

He chuckled and turned to go. The morphine had set in pretty well by then, and my eyelids were heavy, so I closed my eyes again.

It was going to be a long three months between now and when I could try shifting again. I didn't expect to draw an easy breath until that day. At least the implants were out, though. Finally. My body was mine again, even if it turned out to be too damaged to shift.

Footsteps worked their way into the drugged haze. I blinked a few times, wondering if the nurses really expected me to get out of bed now. *Just a few more minutes. Please don't make me walk yet.*

"Hey, you." Damon's voice brought a smile to my lips. When he leaned over me, his face made my heart flutter.

"Hey," I said. "Good to see you."

"Good to see *you* among the land of the living." He leaned down and kissed my forehead. "How are you feeling?"

I moistened my parched lips. "Like shit."

"That's not surprising." He slipped his hand into mine and squeezed gently. Concern furrowed his brow. "Did the doctor say anything about nerve damage?"

"So far, so good. Everything seems to be able to move, and as much as I wish it were, nothing's numb."

Some of the tension left Damon's shoulders. "That's definitely good news."

I grinned. "You just want to make sure the important parts work."

"Well, I want that to work, too." He leaned down again to kiss me lightly. "But I'm really glad to hear it doesn't sound like anything's damaged."

"Me too."

He glanced over his shoulder, then back to me. "Oh, by the way, I brought something for you."

"You didn't have to do that."

"No, but I think you'll like it." He turned toward the door and nodded at someone else.

At the sound of light footsteps, I looked toward the door as much as I could, and my heart skipped.

"Sam," I whispered.

"Hey." She squeezed my hand. "You look like you're ready to run a marathon."

I laughed. "Yeah, I'll get *right* on that. Actually, they're going to make me get up and walk pretty soon. Not looking forward to that."

"Already?" Sam said. "Sadists."

Damon chuckled. "They're not sadists. They gave him a morphine pump."

I held out the pump. "You walk the halls for me, you can have this."

"I wish," he said, laughing. "By the way, I talked to Ken and Tabitha. Ken and his wife will probably stop by this evening if you're up for it, and Tabitha said she'd come by in the morning."

"Cool," I said. "Hopefully I won't be drugged out of my head when they show up."

"If you are," Sam said, "we could always video it and put it on YouTube."

I flipped her off, and the three of us laughed.

"I don't know," Damon said. "I think Tabitha would get a kick out of seeing you fucked up on morphine."

"Yes, she would." I rolled my eyes. "God, that's just what I need."

"It'll be entertaining," Sam said.

"You're both evil."

"That's why you love us," she said.

"Birds of a feather, right?" Damon said.

"Yeah. That."

He chuckled, then leaned down and kissed me gently again. "Well, at least this part's over."

"Thank God," I whispered. "Now we just wait and see if it was worth it."

CHAPTER 24

DAMON

Three Months Later

O ver the top of a magazine I wasn't reading, I watched that plastic diver rocking back and forth, trying to reach the bubbling treasure chest like it had the first time I'd come here with Alex.

Here we were again, waiting for the doctor to call him back so we could find out if the surgery had been successful.

Alex didn't bother trying to read a magazine. He was more nervous now than he'd been before the surgery. He fidgeted. Tapped his fingers. Took a few deep breaths. Played with his wedding band. Stared at the ceiling, the fish tank, the wall.

I put a hand on his knee. "You okay?"

He nodded and rested his hand on top of mine, but didn't say anything. I didn't push the issue. He'd been going out of his mind for the last few months, and it all came down to today. This appointment. Here. Now. Any fucking minute. He'd commented the other night that it was like a cross between watching the ball drop over Times Square and watching the last few seconds run out on a doomsday clock.

There was nothing I could say to settle his nerves, so I just continued watching the plastic diver and trying to read this magazine that was of absolutely no interest. Anything to keep from showing him how nervous I was.

I tried to stay optimistic. His recovery had been encouraging, and the pain from the surgery itself was minimal now. He still had some minor twinges and aches in his back, plenty more in his neck, but all things considered, it wasn't bad. The worst side effect had been a sharp pain in his right foot. Apparently the surgeon had nicked a nerve during the procedure, and it'd left Alex feeling like he had a nail in his foot whenever he walked. After a few weeks, though, the pain had diminished. He wasn't quite ready to dance on the bar yet, and it was only recently that he'd let me give him a foot massage, but it was much better.

Physically, he'd done well, but emotionally, he was a wreck. He needed to shift. *Badly.* Knowing that the only thing keeping him from doing so was the doctor's order had driven him crazy. The more his body recovered, the more he ached to, at the very least, find out if he *could* shift.

Over the last few weeks, it had been painfully obvious when he was uncomfortable in his own skin, and sometimes I wondered how I'd ever *not* known what was going on. He avoided his own reflection. He barely spoke. Physical contact made him shudder. The depression was palpable, and it could last for days. Long, long days when there was nothing I could do for him except remind him I was here.

At least the long weekend we'd spent in Canada two weeks ago had been a bright spot for him. Pity shifters couldn't get married in the States without demonstrating, prior to the marriage license being approved, that they were presently capable of shifting to the opposite gender of their spouse. Oh, well. We were married now. Once he regained the ability to shift, it would be legal in this country.

Alex and I had debated for weeks about which house to keep and which to sell, and he'd finally insisted on cutting his loose.

"Too many memories I don't feel like holding on to," he'd said. "And it'll be a shorter commute for both of us."

A shorter commute to his night job, anyway. Moving in with me had added about fifteen minutes to his drive to the office, but as soon as the house was sold, he had his two weeks' notice written and ready to turn in. The sooner the better, as far as I was concerned. He didn't need any more of that stress.

It was just as well we were living in my place now, since one bedroom wasn't going to be enough anymore. Alex's petition for custody of Sam had been denied at first, but he'd appealed it and gotten a second hearing. The judge was hesitant, but after Alex agreed to regular therapy sessions to deal with his depression, as well as completely giving up the booze, custody had been granted.

The therapy turned out to be very helpful, too. Having Sam around was even better. For both of them. Giving up the booze wasn't easy, but when temptation almost got the best of him, all Alex had to do was remember what was at stake, and he'd realize he didn't want a drink after all. Working in a bar didn't help, but he couldn't drink on the job anyway, and even his therapist eventually agreed that the Welcome Mat's environment was good for him.

"Alex?" Dr. Rowland's voice—female today—turned both our heads. She gestured with her file folder. "Come on back."

We both rose. Alex habitually tested his right foot before putting weight on it.

"How's that foot?" she asked as we approached. "Any more pain?"

"Not recently, no," Alex said. "Habit, I guess. I keep expecting it to hurt."

"Understandable." She led us back to an exam room.

Alex sat on the table, and Dr. Rowland ran him through a quick battery of tests, checking reflexes, mobility, and feeling.

"Any pain?" she asked. "Tingling? Numbness?"

"My back still gets a little sore, but it's better."

Dr. Rowland nodded. "Good, good." She perused Alex's chart, then took a seat on the black fake-leather stool. "Everything appears to have healed just fine, and I think we're well out of the woods for any complications that would be exacerbated by a shift." She smiled. "I see no reason to suggest you can't attempt a shift now." Her expression turned serious. "I'd prefer to have you do it here, with me in the room, just in case there's a problem. Assuming you're comfortable with that?"

"Yeah, that's fine," Alex said.

"Fair warning," she said. "Sometimes it takes a few tries. Even if you can't shift immediately, it might just be your system remembering what to do."

Alex nodded. He glanced at me, back at her, then at the floor. Exhaling slowly, he ran a hand through his hair. His other fingers tapped rapidly beside him on the exam table, his ring clicking on the metal edge.

"Something wrong?" the doctor asked.

Alex's gaze flicked back and forth from me to her. "Right now, it's possible." He swallowed. "I *might* be able to shift. I just need to hold on to that hope for a few more minutes before I find out for sure."

"Take your time," the doctor said. "Whenever you're ready."

Alex looked at me, eyebrows raised in a silent plea for reassurance. I gave him what I hoped was a reassuring smile, and he returned it. Then he closed his eyes and took a deep breath. I watched, my heart pounding in my chest as I hoped and prayed he'd—

"*Fuck!*" Alex's spine straightened, and he gasped.

Dr. Rowland and I both jumped to our feet. She caught Alex's arm and steadied him. "What happened?"

"Nothing." He rolled his shoulders and tilted his head to stretch his neck. "I tried to shift once with the implants in, and it, I don't know, shocked me or something." He laughed softly, his cheeks coloring slightly. "Guess I expected it to happen again."

The doctor and I both returned to our seats.

"How many times did you try it with the implants?" she asked.

"Once." Alex shuddered. "That was more than enough, trust me."

"I'm sure," she said with a slight grimace. "I've heard it's not pleasant, and always advise shifters with implants to not even try."

"Duly noted," he said, chuckling. "Okay, trying again."

Alex closed his eyes. His brow furrowed slightly, and with every passing second that his features remained sharp and solid, my heart pounded harder and harder.

Please, please . . .

He exhaled and his shoulders fell. My heart sank.

"I don't feel anything at all," he said, his voice flat. He gestured at his neck. "That . . . tingle. You know what I'm talking about, right?"

Dr. Rowland nodded. "Of course. Nothing?"

"Nothing at all."

"Try it again," she said softly. "Your body may just need to remember how to shift."

He tried again. And again. And again.

After half a dozen tries, he sighed. "So how many times do I try it before I call it a day and accept that I'm static?"

"As many times as you need to."

"Maybe the question should be, how many times do I beat my head against a brick wall before I decide it's enough of a headache?"

"Depends on when you're ready to accept life as a static."

Alex set his jaw. "I don't think I'm quite ready for that yet."

"Couldn't hurt to keep trying, then," she said, her voice gentle. "Sometimes it just takes a little time. And you could be focusing *too* hard. You know as well as I do how much tension can interfere."

"True." Alex rolled his shoulders a few times. "Okay. I'll try it a few more times and see what happens."

He closed his eyes.

I closed my own eyes. I couldn't watch him any more than I could watch my own clasped fingers blanching as they dug into the backs of my hands.

Please, God, please . . .

Someone released a long breath. Beside me, Dr. Rowland's chair made a soft creak. With my heart in my throat, I opened my eyes.

And I stared.

At her.

Alex looked at her hands, turning them again and again. Her ring, which was a little loose now, caught the light as she reached up to touch her own face. She ran her fingers along her jaw, then through her long hair. Then she looked down at herself. Her T-shirt hung loosely over her narrower shoulders, and the front of her shirt showed the gentle swell of her breasts.

Our eyes met, and when I smiled, so did she.

Carefully, putting one foot down, then the other, and all the while holding onto the exam table in case her legs didn't hold her up, she stepped down.

"How do you feel?" Dr. Rowland asked, grinning.

"I feel . . ." Alex paused, and oh my God, I'd missed that smile. That genuine, heartfelt smile. "Like a woman."

I got up, and as soon as I was on my feet, she threw her arms around me. I kissed her, but then we just held on to each other. I closed my eyes, breathing in her scent as she buried her face against my neck. The only relief I had ever felt that surpassed this was when the nurse had come to tell me Alex had made it through the surgery. This, holding Alex in my arms and knowing she finally had her life back, was a very, very close second.

Alex drew back. "Damon, you're not crying, are you?"

"No." I sniffed and quickly wiped my eyes. "No, I'm not crying."

"Yes, you are," she said. "You're not supposed to cry, damn it."

"Why not? Because I'm the guy?"

"No, because you're making *me* cry." She wiped her eyes, and we both laughed as I pulled her to me again.

After a moment, she broke the embrace and turned to hug Dr. Rowland.

"Thank you so much," she whispered. "For everything."

"You're welcome, Alex." When Alex released her, Dr. Rowland continued. "I do want to run you through some quick tests before I let you go. Just to make sure you're completely in the clear."

Alex nodded and sat on the exam table again.

"Before you do that," I said. "Alex, you want to surprise Sam? Or should I tell him?"

"Tell him. He's probably not paying attention in class anyway."

"Well, he did say he wanted to know as soon as you did, so . . ." I held up my phone. "Smile."

She smiled, striking a typically ridiculous Alex pose, and I snapped a picture of her. While Dr. Rowland ran her through some simple tests, making sure her balance and response to stimuli were normal, I typed *Look who's back* beneath the picture. Then I sent it off to Sam.

Look who was back indeed. I couldn't stop grinning as I watched Alex. Test after test—squeezing the doctor's fingers, pushing her hands apart, pushing them together—verified that she had no lingering damage, no loss of sensation, no loss of movement. Aside from the minor pain she still experienced, she had a clean bill of health.

"Thank you again," Alex said to Dr. Rowland, and they shared another brief hug.

"You're welcome," Dr. Rowland said. "I'm glad we were able to get you back to normal."

Normal. Now wasn't that a term whose definition had changed significantly for me in the last few months? Then again, what *hadn't* changed in my world in the last few months? Goddamn, what a ride. It was hard to believe it had been less than half a year since this whole thing had started. So much had happened, so much had changed, and it had all been leading up to today.

So this is what a moment of truth feels like.

The click of the door brought me out of my thoughts, and I realized Alex and I were alone again.

Our eyes met, and she smiled. "Ready to go home?"

"You better believe it." I put my arms around her and kissed her forehead. "I'm so glad this worked out."

"Me, too." She rested her head on my shoulder. "I swear to God, now that it's all over, I could go home and sleep for a month."

Stroking her hair, I said, "You're not the only one."

She raised her head and met my eyes. "I can't even begin to tell you how much it means to me that you stuck by me through all of this."

"I told you, babe." I sniffed sharply. "You're going to have to try harder than that to get rid of me."

Alex laughed and stood on her toes to kiss me.

"Why don't we get out of here?" I murmured against her lips. "Now that you have your life back, I could think of better places to spend it than in a doctor's office."

"Good point." She grinned. "You know, we still have a few hours between now and when Sam gets home from school."

"Hmm, so we do. What do you think we should do with it?"

"I have a few ideas." She kissed me lightly. "The question is, which Alex are you in the mood for?"

"Whichever Alex is in the mood for me." I pulled her closer. "But something tells me you might feel like spending a little time in this body for a change."

"Oh, God, yes. You never know, though." She winked. "Play your cards right, and one of these days you might get an evening with a little of both Alexes."

Trying to sound serious, I said, "So does that qualify as a threesome, or—"

She smacked my arm playfully. "Oh, shut *up*."

I put up my hands and batted my eyes. "What? It's a valid question, isn't it?"

"I suppose I walked into it, didn't I?"

"Ya think?"

She raised an eyebrow and tried to scowl. "You want to sleep on the sofa tonight?"

"Please. You wouldn't make me sleep on the couch."

Fighting a losing battle against a grin, she said, "Wouldn't I?"

"No." I ran my fingers through her long hair. "You wouldn't."

"Prove it."

A hand under her shirt. A lingering kiss behind her ear. A whisper of what I planned to do to her if she'd please let me join her in bed.

Alex whimpered.

And I was safe from the couch for another night.

☿ AUTHOR'S ♀
NOTE

So . . . *Static.*

In the three years since I wrote this book, I've had numerous people ask me where it came from. After a few dozen gay and hetero erotic romance titles, what in the world possessed me to write transgender science fiction?

The short answer? I had to.

It all began a few years ago when another author, M. Jules Aedin, befriended me. We spent a lot of time instant messaging, and eventually worked together as author and editor. Somewhere in the middle of all of that, over a fairly short period of time in late 2010, Jules educated me on all things gender. I knew as much as the next person about it (in other words, nothing), but after a few months, my brain was suddenly full of this entire new world of human identity.

I needed to do something with that information. There was just so much, and I didn't know what to make of it. It shouldn't have been a surprise when my method of processing everything became "write about it." In fact, I didn't even realize that's what I was doing until after the fact.

In early 2011, I wanted to write about shapeshifters. I hadn't played in that particular genre, and it was intriguing, but I wanted to do something different. So as I often do, I was brainstorming while I drove, and the thought process went something like this:

Werewolves? It's been done.

Were-frogs? Possibility.

Were-worms? Probably not.

What if a shapeshifter could shift into anything?

What if a shapeshifter could turn into another person?

What if they could shift genders?

And I almost ran off the road.

By the time I reached the restaurant where I'd planned to do some writing, I had everything: Characters. Title. Plot. It all just . . . happened. Of course writing it was more of a challenge than that, but the foundation pretty much dropped out of the sky and demanded I drop everything and write it at once.

What followed were three of the most difficult weeks in my writing career. Some books just grab on and won't let go, demanding my full attention every hour of every day. That's a good thing, of course, but it's stressful too, and this one was particularly so for two reasons. One, because the story was ripping my guts out at every turn. This was uncharted emotional territory for me, and Alex—the shapeshifter who'd lost his ability to take his female form—was so, *so* real to me that it was painful to process a lot of the things he was feeling and thinking.

The other reason this book was particularly difficult was that I was afraid of getting the gender issues wrong. Of accidentally using an offensive stereotype, or inadvertently making some horrifically inaccurate assumption. At the time, I typically used one or two beta readers for each book. For *Static*, I recruited nine, all of them identifying as genderqueer of some variety (transgendered, genderfluid, third gender, etc.). To my tremendous relief, all of them gave the book a thumbs up, not to mention loads of feedback.

As I went through the edits, I realized this book had been a subconscious way to process everything Jules had taught me. It wasn't a textbook, just a way of applying all the information to people and a situation so that I could make sense of it all. I still have tons and tons to learn, but by the time I finished *Static*, I had a much deeper and more empathetic understanding of people whose gender identity doesn't fall into the culturally accepted binary of male-bodied men and female-bodied women. I hope my readers can take away the same understanding and, of course, enjoy the story as well.

And this is why *Static* is, and always will be, for Jules.

Dear Reader,

Thank you for reading L.A. Witt's *Static*!

We know your time is precious and you have many, many entertainment options, so it means a lot that you've chosen to spend your time reading. We really hope you enjoyed it.

We'd be honored if you'd consider posting a review—good or bad—on sites like **Amazon, Barnes & Noble, Kobo, Goodreads, Twitter, Facebook, Tumblr,** and your blog or website. We'd also be honored if you told your friends and family about this book. Word of mouth is a book's lifeblood!

For more information on upcoming releases, author interviews, blog tours, contests, giveaways, and more, please sign up for our weekly, spam-free newsletter and visit us around the web:

> **Newsletter**: tinyurl.com/RiptideSignup
> **Twitter**: twitter.com/RiptideBooks
> **Facebook**: facebook.com/RiptidePublishing
> **Goodreads**: tinyurl.com/RiptideOnGoodreads
> **Tumblr**: riptidepublishing.tumblr.com

Thank you so much for Reading the Rainbow!

RiptidePublishing.com

☿ ALSO BY ♀
L.A. WITT

A Chip in His Shoulder
Something New Under the Sun
O Come All Ye Kinky
The Left Hand of Calvus
Finding Master Right
Unhinge the Universe, with Aleksandr Voinov
Conduct Unbecoming
From Out in the Cold

Tucker Springs Novels
Where Nerves End (coming soon)
Covet Thy Neighbor
After the Fall
It's Complicated

Market Garden Tales, with Aleksandr Voinov
Quid Pro Quo
Take It Off
If It Flies
If It Fornicates
Capture & Surrender
Payoff
If It Drives

Coming Soon
Noble Metals
Precious Metals

For a complete list, please see www.loriawitt.com.

⚥ ABOUT THE ⚥
AUTHOR

L.A. Witt is an abnormal M/M romance writer currently living in the glamorous and ultra-futuristic metropolis of Omaha, Nebraska, with her husband, two cats, and a disembodied penguin brain that communicates with her telepathically. In addition to writing smut and disturbing the locals, L.A. is said to be working with the U.S. government to perfect a genetic modification that will allow humans to survive indefinitely on Corn Pops and beef jerky. This is all a cover, though, as her primary leisure activity is hunting down her arch nemesis, erotica author Lauren Gallagher, who is also said to be lurking somewhere in Omaha. L.A. can be found at www.loriawitt.com, as well as exchanging irreverent tweets with Aleks as @GallagherWitt.

FALLING SKY

THE COMPLETE COLLECTION

Liam Lansing is heir to a prominent family of bio-modified vampires. That is, until he chooses the wrong lover and is cast down to the Gutter to scrape for his life. Daniel Harding is heir to Cybernetix and a prince of the corporate Sky. That is, until his ideology drives his father to put a price on his head, forcing him into the Gutter. Years of anger and a heap of mods have kept Daniel and Liam apart. They have no reason to trust each other, but a bargain that began with the simple urge to live soon reminds them of the love they once shared.

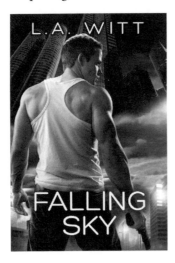

Together, they plan to rip open the hidden corruption that runs the Sky—for vengeance, for justice, and for hope. Only through courage in the face of death—or worse—might Daniel and Liam change the world they live in and create something new under the sun.

Available at tinyurl.com/FScollect
Ebook ISBN: 978-1-62649-040-6

CHAPTER 1

"**W**hy is my son still alive, Liam?" The irritation in Richard Harding's voice set my teeth on edge. "I'm running out of patience."

"Do you want it done quickly, or do you want it done right?" I muttered as I adjusted my cell phone's earpiece. "Choice is yours, but it's one or the other."

"I want it *done*. You're not getting sentimental about this job, are you?"

I stopped dead in my tracks, my boot scuffing on the sidewalk. "I beg your pardon?"

"It's a valid question, don't you think? Given your . . . history with Daniel."

I nearly gave into the urge to grind my teeth. "That was a long time ago. This is business."

"Then get it done. This is taking entirely too long."

I started walking again, taking longer, faster strides. I shoved my hands into the pockets of my duster and nestled my face into the high collar to keep from choking on the downdraft of thick, acrid pollution. "For the record, that UV-resistant mod that's been 'in development' since the dawn of time would have sped up this process considerably."

"That mod is still in the experimental phase," he said. "You know that."

"Then this will take some time. If you wanted it done faster, you might have lit a fire under the asses of the people who could give me the ability to move around in daylight."

He huffed. "Just get it done. I'm a patient man, but—"

"Has the money been transferred?"

"Yes."

I stepped up to the curb and gestured for a cab. "All of it?"

"Yes. All of it. Now get it done, Liam."

I laughed. "Or what?"

Silence. Long, telling silence: Harding was desperate. He had to be. Men didn't put themselves on my radar unless they had no other options. For Harding to contact me and offer up so much money, he had to be beyond desperate. Pity for him he didn't realize I'd have done the job for a fraction of the price. Had I ever crossed paths with Daniel Harding again, I'd have put a few bullets in him for free.

But when a man offers you $10 million to take out his own son, you don't argue.

And neither, apparently, did he, because his end of the line was still silent.

I laughed. "That's what I thought." As a cab nosed toward me and slowed down, I added, "Your son will be taken care of." Before Harding could say anything more, I disconnected the call.

I opened the cab's door and slid into the backseat. The first taste of the air in there made my eyes water; there were disadvantages to an enhanced sense of smell, and enclosing myself in the capsule of filth and sweat that was a taxicab was one of them.

"The microchip factory on Fourth Street," I said, trying not to let on that I was gagging.

The driver grunted an affirmative and pulled out into traffic.

I could walk to the factory in twenty minutes, but the sidewalks between here and there were a gauntlet of thieves. Though muggers didn't scare me in the least, they were an inconvenience. A delay. And every minute wasted was a minute closer to sunrise.

Streetlights glowed halfheartedly along the roadside, yellow clouds of mist swarming around each burning bulb. Passing cars sliced hazy bands of amber and gold into the fog, some with headlamps so dim and old they were barely functional. Even with the horrendous visibility down here, workers could only spend so much of their pittance of a salary on anything they couldn't eat.

There was a time when artificial lights, even this foggy darkness, necessitated a pair of sunglasses to keep from burning my eyes. These days, the caustic air stung, but my most recent optical mod included a self-adjusting tint that kept out even the most brutal fluorescents and mercury vapors. Now if the cybernetic companies could just do something about my skin, I'd be happy. But of course, they'd have to spend less time creating super-soldiers and sex goddesses if they actually wanted to outfit the city's vampires with a mod to keep us from bursting into flames on contact with the daylight.

But of course that was, and probably forever would be, "still in development."

While the cabbie drove, I took off my earpiece and dropped it in my pocket. It was just a decoy device, something to tell passersby and anti-mod activists that no, I was *not* speaking to someone using a communications implant. What they didn't know wouldn't inconvenience me.

With my left hand, I pressed the tiny nodule between the middle and third knuckles on my right hand. Everything in my field of vision darkened except the glowing blue-green displays visible only to me. I moved my hand until the nodule—now glowing the same color—lined up with the option for "display account." I logged in and pulled up the transaction history.

As promised, Harding had made the deposit. I transferred the money to another account, then split it between four others. Harding hadn't been thrilled about having to pay in full upfront, but he wanted me and no one else for this hit, so he'd grudgingly agreed to my terms. I wanted to be damn sure he didn't pull a fast one and try to withdraw the money between now and when the hit was complete.

I couldn't blame him if he did. $10 million was a lot of money, even for a cybernetics tycoon. For me, it was a fortune and then some. After this hit, I'd be out of the Gutter and out of this Godawful line of work.

I closed the display and deactivated the nodule, returning my vision to normal. Through the cab's dingy window, I watched rundown people going about their business beside the line of decrepit cars in front of filthy, vandalized buildings. Third shift employees shuffled into factories, looking just as exhausted and haggard as the second shift shuffling out. This was the part of town where the destitute built the mods that bettered the lives of the wealthy.

I sighed and pulled my gaze away.

The cab lurched to a halt at the base of a brick-front building covered in a spiderweb of graffiti. The buildings in the Gutter were nearly indistinguishable from one to the next, but this was the right place. I'd been here enough times; I knew.

I paid the driver, then stepped out and immediately buried my face in my jacket collar again. Here in the industrial heart of the city, the pollution was even thicker and more acrid. My eyes watered, and on top of the lingering aftertaste of the rancid air inside the cab, every whiff turned my stomach. There were mods on the market now that filtered better than my zipped-up jacket collar, but those compromised senses on which I relied, so I dealt with it.

I looked up at the factory. High above me, the feeble glow of the sixth-floor windows was just barely visible in the haze. The seventh floor wasn't visible at all, but I'd done enough recon to—

Footsteps. Behind me. Three meters to the rear and half a step to the left. All my senses immediately shifted, homing in on the approaching individual. Faulty attempt at stealth. Rapidly decreasing intervals between footfalls. Ambush.

I rolled my eyes. *I don't have time for this.*

I spun, and my would-be attacker skidded to a startled halt, lip curled into a snarl and knife in the air.

"Just gimme your cash, man." His voice shook in spite of his aggressive stance. "I don't want no harm, just—"

"Put that knife away before you hurt yourself. You don't know who you're fucking with." With that, I turned on my heel and started toward the side of the factory. Damned Gutter rat couldn't hurt a vampire if he wanted to.

"Hey! Hey!" The mugger lunged at me, and I spun around again. We collided and the blade bit into my palm, but a swift kick to the idiot's side sent the knife clattering to the pavement and its owner flying into the wall. He hit hard, grunting as his face met brick beneath a yellow spray-painted "Sky Must Fall" slogan. Groaning, he crumpled to his knees on the sidewalk.

I glared at the thin, shallow wound on my hand. What the fuck? Times really were getting dangerous when petty thieves carried weapons that could penetrate a vampire's flesh. My arm tingled as nanobots scrambled through my system to take care of the damage. I shuddered and rolled my shoulder; the microscopic machines had saved my life numerous times, but I never could get used to that skin-crawling sensation when they were on the move. My palm burned, and I flexed and straightened my fingers as the tissue fused back together.

While the nanobots did their job, I turned to go, leaving my would-be assailant to figure out what had just happened.

I made it three or four steps, then stopped and looked back. The mugger wasn't seriously injured, but he was still disoriented. He'd probably have a hell of a headache, but as soon as he was steady on his feet, he'd accost the next passerby. On the other hand, as long as he was down, he was vulnerable to the next thief.

I chewed my lip. I was no stranger to the desperation that drove men to crime, especially down here in the Gutter. This was the cruelest part of a cruel world—a place that had driven me to make my living committing murder—and theft probably wasn't just a hobby for a man with ragged, mismatched sneakers barely held together by fraying laces.

I had no qualms about laying waste to the wealthy assholes who forced the rest of us to live like this, but the Gutter rats were like kin to me. It was us against them, so although I couldn't afford the delay, I backtracked toward the mugger.

When I picked up the knife, his eyes widened. He stared up at me, holding his head in one hand and showing his other palm.

"Don't . . . please . . ." He whimpered, drawing back and cringing like he was looking into the face of death.

If you only knew.

I knelt and laid the knife on the pavement. Then I grabbed his wrist, dug a few tattered bills out of my pocket, and pressed the money into his palm. As I stood, I toed the knife toward him. "Careful where you point that thing. Now get the fuck out of here."

Then I walked away.

I went around to one of the factory's side doors. Through bribery, the black market, and a thinly-veiled threat, I'd obtained an access code and a badge. I glanced up and down the narrow alley, making sure I was alone. Then I swiped the badge and punched in the access code. The kid who'd hooked me up obviously valued his life, because the LED turned green and the door unlatched, just like it had during the other night's test run. I pulled it open and slipped into the factory.

The inside of the building was sweltering. The acrid stench of pollution wasn't as strong, but the air was metallic and stank of brass, industrial lubricants, and heated rubber. Machinery clanged and rumbled. Conveyor belts hummed. Components clicked and clattered. Though I moved with practiced stealth, the factory's noise gave me added insurance as I slipped past the workers.

I made my way to the back stairwell, then up to the seventh floor, where a second access code let me into the maintenance facility for the train station perched on top of the building. From there, I went into the restroom where I'd hidden a briefcase and backpack in the ceiling tiles. I quickly changed into the suit from the backpack, hid the bag and my duster back in the ceiling, and took the briefcase with me.

At the sink, watching my reflection in the mirror, I carefully peeled away the false skin that hid the visible mod on my face. Black silicone and titanium covered my temple and formed a crescent around my left eye. It wasn't all that useful now that I'd had the new display implanted with my ocular mod, and down in the Gutter, it was just the kind of thing that would make me a target of the anti-mods. Where I was going, though, a mod marked me as one of the elite.

I discarded the false skin and scrutinized my reflection. Adjusted my tie. Tugged at my sleeve. Smoothed my hair. Once everything was perfect, nothing wrinkled or out of place, I picked up the briefcase and left the gentlemen's room. Looking like any other businessman on his way home from a late night at the office, I strolled through the thin crowd on the train platform to the stairwell.

At the top of the stairs, I took a deep breath of crisp evening air and looked around. Though the Gutter was less than ten meters below my feet, it was a different world up here. Immense glass and metal buildings strained for the stratosphere all around me, and like crystalline capstones, glass penthouses gleamed and glittered on top of each towering structure. The elite of the elite lived in those. Cybernetics tycoons. Software lords. Heirs and heiresses to this or that empire.

Huge fans below the streets kept the industrial pollution of the Gutter down, and the air up here was perfectly crystal clear.

Everything was perfect here. The people of the Sky would never accept anything less.

Want to read more of the *Falling Sky* collection?
Visit http://tinyurl.com/FScollect

HOSTILE GROUND

L.A. WITT
ALEKSANDR VOINOV

After the deaths of three undercover cops investigating a drug ring in a seedy strip club, Detective Mahir Hussain has been sent to finish the job. He joins the club's security team in the hopes of finding enough evidence to bust the operation before the men in charge find a reason to put him in a shallow grave. Ridley, the cold and intimidating head of security, knows exactly how to test potential new hires. From the minute they meet, Mahir and Ridley engage in a dangerous dance of sex and mind games. Mahir needs to find his evidence before Ridley

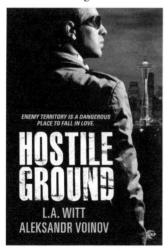

figures out he's a cop—and before they both grow too close to betray one another. As the game goes on, Mahir learns there's much more happening than meets the eye . . . and why every cop who made it this far has been silenced with a bullet.

Avail. at tinyurl.com/hostile-ground
Ebook ISBN: 978-1-62649-125-0
Print ISBN: 978-1-62649-124-3

RIPTIDE
PUBLISHING

CHAPTER ONE

T he bass vibrated through Mahir's bones as a pair of bouncers led him along the staff-only corridor in the nightclub. He caught a line of the rock lyrics—tough luck, tough guy—and thought it ridiculously fitting. He was already seeking conclusions and grasping at nothing, like that meth head from last week who had received messages through the TV, convinced that God spoke to him on the shopping channel.

He walked between two goons who'd hopefully soon be his colleagues, trying not to appear too eager or too relaxed. Saeed, his cover identity, would be alert, but he also needed to radiate competence. He must've done a good job of it to have made it this far.

The goon on his left rapped on the last door of the corridor. The door opened, and the goon waved him in.

The room was half supply cabinet, half office. Boxes piled high against the wall. A water cooler looked out of place between the Formica table and cheap folding chairs. There was only one man in the room, and he stood off to the side.

He was taller than Mahir, though not by much. Just enough that he'd have to look up a little if they were ever standing face-to-face, which Mahir hoped didn't happen anytime soon. That wasn't to say the guy was unattractive. Well dressed, well groomed, dark hair arranged perfectly, and tailored shirt and slacks crisp and smooth. He was slimmer than most of the guys working in this ring but certainly not lacking. His white sleeves were rolled to the elbows, showing off strong, sinewy muscle. And if his forearms were that cut, Mahir could only imagine what the man was hiding under the rest of his clothes.

It didn't help that Mahir knew this guy played for his team. If he was the head of Lombardi's security, he was gay. They all were. That was how Lombardi kept his men from fucking with his girls.

Yeah, he was gay and he was attractive, but there was an air about him that made Mahir more than happy to stay on the opposite side of the room. The guy radiated a menacing intensity. A focused, predatory aura that pulled all of Mahir's nerves taut.

The room was dim, lit only by a single weak bulb over their heads, but the still, silent man wore sunglasses. Dark ones. The slightest motion of his eyebrows said he was looking Mahir up and down. Mahir had seen guys like this before. Some were just douche bags who wanted to look like gangster badasses or action-movie leads, but then there was this kind: the guy who didn't like people looking him in the eye. It probably unnerved the shit out of most people, and Mahir had a feeling that effect was not accidental.

Question was, how much of this was a test? Was Mahir supposed to be intimidated and unsettled or look this guy straight in the eyes—well, lenses—and not back down?

The butt of a high-caliber handgun stuck out of a shoulder holster beneath the man's arm. He didn't play around. Working for a notorious pimp who was likely also a high-powered drug dealer meant he didn't have to play by the same rules Mahir did. Passing whatever test he was currently taking wasn't optional.

Deep, even breaths. "You must be David Ridley."

"And who the fuck are you?"

Mahir swallowed. The guy's voice was smooth but sharp at the same time. He'd probably sound sexy as hell if every word wasn't laced with *give me a reason not to shoot you.*

"I was told you were expecting me."

"I'm expecting someone." The guy raised his chin, drawing Mahir's attention to the flawless lines of his jaw and throat. "You might want to introduce yourself before you start asking questions."

"I'm Saeed." Social protocol suggested he should extend a hand, but he didn't. Probably best to let this guy call the shots. "I was hired by—"

"You Arab?"

Mahir gritted his teeth. That didn't take long. "Syrian."

"I see." The guy paused. "You don't have an accent."

Mahir resisted the urge to roll his eyes. He'd played this game enough times. "My family came here before I was born."

The guy responded with a subtle nod and a quiet grunt of acknowledgment. He pulled off his sunglasses, and when he looked

Mahir in the eye, Mahir caught himself wishing the man had left the glasses on. His clear blue eyes? Piercing. And enough so to make Mahir tongue-tied and off guard.

The guy slid his sunglasses into the collar of his shirt, which had the top button open, and then extended his hand. "To answer your question, yes. I am David Ridley."

Mahir took the hand and shook it. No point showing even a moment's hesitation, and Ridley had one thing going for him already: no jokes about the virgins awaiting him in heaven. Maybe he wouldn't joke about that. "Saeed Hayaz."

The man held on to his hand longer than was polite among straight Western men and kept their eyes locked. Mahir did his best to relax under the challenge. Not give anything away. Levelheadedness usually got him out of tight spots. This would be no different.

"Tell me why you're here." Ridley's grip was strong and dry. Rough skin, like that of an honest worker—or a fighter.

"I need a job. I was told this is a good place for me, considering my skill set."

"By whom?"

"Word on the street." Mahir could see that wasn't enough. "A guy I met in another club. We compared notes, and he said I should come here."

"Who?" He still kept his hand, as if that touch were some kind of lie detector.

"Tommy. Tall, blond, tattooed."

"Tattoos where?"

"Pretty much all over. Two sleeves, one on the neck. Rip tattoo along his left side, looked like the flesh was torn away and you could see the organs below. Pretty gross but a good piece of work."

"Anywhere else?"

"He did have a Prince Albert," Mahir mentioned as if in afterthought.

"Too bad Tommy can't vouch for you. He's dead."

"Damn." Mahir looked down, pretending he had to gather his thoughts. "He did drive like an idiot, but . . ."

"Bullet." Ridley finally let go of his hand, but didn't step back. "That kind of thing happens when guys talk to cops."

Ice trickled down the length of Mahir's spine. "I wouldn't expect any less."

Ridley gave a small nod. His eyes were still locked on Mahir's. "So I don't have to worry about you taking his place as their narc."

Was that a question? A statement? A threat? This guy was impossible to read.

"I don't care for cops," Mahir said. "I just need a paycheck."

Ridley laughed, which was more unnerving than anything else he'd done so far. Any guy who could make a single, quiet sound—and look—that cold was not someone Mahir wanted to spend more time with than necessary. "Well, you'll get a paycheck." He clapped Mahir's shoulder. "As long as you do your job and know what's good for you." He stepped away, allowing Mahir to breathe. Reaching for the door, Ridley added, "Let's go someplace more comfortable."

He pulled open the door, and Mahir followed him into the hallway back toward the nightclub's lounge area. At the edge of the lounge, where the painted concrete floor met plush red carpet, Ridley pulled his sunglasses from his collar and put them back over his eyes. Mahir couldn't blame him. The flickering lights were a migraine waiting to happen.

As they crossed the lounge, Ridley seemed to make a point of taking a winding path that led them right by all three of the round stages where girls danced for sweating, liquored-up patrons. The walls were almost entirely mirrored, and when Mahir glanced at one of the many reflective surfaces, he thought he caught Ridley looking at him. Impossible to say for sure, though, thanks to those damned sunglasses. Mahir had been warned that the pimp didn't play around with making sure all of his security guards were gay, and he had no doubt he was being tested again.

He didn't have to fake being uninterested in the ladies, but he made sure to give a male bartender an exaggerated double take as he went by. And just before they left the red carpet and stepped into another hallway, he exchanged grins with one of the other security guards. Hopefully that would be the extent of his tests in that department.

Out in the hallway, Ridley took off his sunglasses again and hooked them in his collar. He opened another door and gestured for Mahir to go ahead of him.

This room was closer to what Mahir had expected in a place like this. Lavishly appointed with the same rich, red carpet as the lounge and furniture that probably didn't contain a trace of particleboard. Ridley went around behind a broad desk and lowered himself into a red leather chair. Then he gestured at one of the two smaller chairs in front of the desk. "Have a seat. Relax."

Yeah. Relax. Right.

Mahir sat down, leaned back, but kept his legs uncrossed. With his back to the door, he was vulnerable, and he glanced over his shoulder. Showing that it made him uneasy would only show he knew his job.

"Who used to sign your paychecks?"

Mahir's focus returned to Ridley. "Uncle Sam. I did my four years and got out in 2004. Did security ever since then. Odd jobs. Drove deliveries across the country, bounced in bars. Didn't really get settled anywhere."

"Ten years of drifting?"

Mahir shrugged. "They tried to get me to reenlist, so I just stayed on the move."

Ridley steepled his fingers on his belly. Flat, trim, powerful. "Iraq?"

"Yes." Mahir met his gaze. "Fallujah was the last big thing I was involved in."

Why are you working for the infidels, brother?

But the question of which side he worked on was never that easy.

"Where do you live?"

Mahir balked. "I've house-sat recently, slept on couches. Looking at a couple crash pads once I know I can afford them."

"I guess that means you'll need a sign-on bonus?"

"Certainly wouldn't hurt."

"Family?"

"Nobody I still speak to." Making him disposable and vulnerable. Nobody who'd start asking questions if he vanished for good.

"Right." Ridley sat up straighter. "Take off your jacket."

Mahir took off his jacket and folded it over the back of the other small chair. He was wearing a dark, tight T-shirt and jeans he could actually move in but were still well cut. Apart from the heavy steel-toed boots, this was what he wore when he drove to a club to score.

It was nothing special, though people told him he wore it well. He showed off what he had, and that was usually enough.

Ridley stood, walked around the desk, and then sat down on it in front of him, the grip of the pistol almost touching Mahir's face. "Shirt off too."

Mahir didn't hesitate. He wasn't wearing a wire so there was nothing for the man to see. He laid the T-shirt over his jacket and sat back, arms on the armrests so Ridley could see his exposed chest.

"Stand up."

Mahir obeyed, a little unnerved. Not because he thought Ridley might find something damning, but because the two of them were, in spite of the abundance of space in the room, close together. If Ridley so much as pushed out a breath with a little more force than usual, it would probably brush Mahir's chest, and that thought made his flesh prickle with goose bumps.

Focus, Mahir. No point in getting a hard-on.

Though if he did, and Ridley felt inclined to do something about—

Mahir.

"Turn around." Ridley sounded amused. As close to amused as someone like him could, anyway.

Mahir slowly turned so Ridley could see every inch of his torso. Every place he might've hidden a wire. And it dawned on him—he always wore these jeans to clubs because they sat just right on his hips. He wondered if Ridley noticed.

When they were facing each other again, Ridley grinned.

But faint as it was, the grin quickly disappeared. Ridley's expression was carved in ice again, and so was his voice. "How do I know you're not a cop?"

Mahir didn't bat an eye. "You've got a guy running background checks, don't you?"

"Of course."

"Is he good at what he does?"

Ridley's eyes narrowed. "Are you suggesting I hire incompetent fucks around here?"

"No. Quite the contrary."

"What?"

"If he's good at what he does," Mahir said, "then he'd have found anything linking me to the cops. If he didn't, then . . ."

Ridley pursed his lips. After a long moment, he nodded. "All right." Then he put his hands on the edge of the desk and slowly—extra slowly, as if he was doing it deliberately to fuck with Mahir's head—pushed himself to his feet. When he was fully upright, he stood maybe a couple of inches from Mahir. Normally, he would be thrilled to be this close to someone so attractive, but the tightness in his chest had nothing to do with arousal.

"There've been some cops through here," Ridley said. "Undercovers and whatnot."

"They made it past your—"

"Yes, they made it past," Ridley snapped. "They're crafty sons of bitches sometimes. And if you're a cop, if you've ever even dreamed of being a cop in your wildest, most fucked-up fantasies, then I would suggest you turn around and walk out. Right now."

Mahir didn't move. "I'm not a cop."

"So you say." Ridley inclined his head, drawing them just a little closer. "The last three undercovers left this place in body bags."

Mahir didn't let himself gulp or show even the slightest hint of nerves. He also didn't let himself curl his hands into fists as he wondered if the man in front of him had pulled the trigger on any one of them. The memory of their funerals—grieving widows, confused children asking where Daddy was, Mahir himself trying to keep it together in his dress uniform—was still fresh, still raw. The only things keeping him composed now were a shitload of undercover training and the desire to see this investigation through so his colleagues wouldn't have died for nothing.

"I've had enough of serving Uncle Sam. I have my grudges, Ridley, and I don't think ten years is enough to let them go." Planting the suggestion strongly in the man's mind. Fallujah. Massacre. Trauma. Death. Cover-up. Showing him a figment of the truth, making it sound so easy and natural.

He looked up into Ridley's eyes again. "If you believe I'm a cop, tell me to go. I need to work with people who trust me." A gamble. Ridley'd likely not keep him around for his nice torso. "I get enough shit in the rest of my life."

Ridley held his position. Mahir could feel heat radiating through Ridley's shirt. No response to the dare, though. Another test? Something for Ridley's own amusement?

Beads of cold sweat materialized on the back of Mahir's neck, and he gritted his teeth to appear calmer than he was. He was getting irritated, too. Of course, this was part of getting into the organization, but headfucks got old. Fast.

"You might be a good fit here," Ridley said.

"Oh yeah?" Mahir refused to break eye contact. "What else do you need to know?"

Ridley's eyes narrowed again, and Mahir didn't have to look to know that the corners of the man's mouth had lifted. He could feel that fucking smirk.

Mahir lifted an eyebrow. "Is it true what they say about you, Ridley?"

To his immense satisfaction, that prompted the slightest startle out of Ridley. For this man it was probably the equivalent of a sharp gasp. His voice was steady and even as he said, "I suppose that depends. What do they say about me, Saeed?"

Mahir shrugged. "I've just heard you handpick every man on the security team." He added a smirk to match Ridley's, and Ridley folded his arms across his chest.

"Meaning?"

"Meaning I've heard you personally screen all the men," Mahir said. "To make sure they fit all the requirements."

Ridley laughed. "And don't you wish that rumor were true?"

Now that you mention it . . . "Don't flatter yourself."

Ridley's brow creased.

Mahir made a dismissive gesture. "Though I admit I was looking forward to finding out if you're as good a cocksucker as Tommy said you were."

Ridley threw his head back and really laughed this time. "Oh, Saeed." He put a hand on Mahir's shoulder, patting it hard and then pressing down heavily. When he looked Mahir in the eyes again, the challenge was back and stronger than ever. "Do you really think I'd suck your cock to prove you are who you say you are?" Never letting his eyes leave Mahir's, he shook his head slowly. "Other way around, my friend."

"Is that an invitation?"

Ridley's breath caught just enough to suggest that wasn't the response he was expecting, but he recovered quickly. "You aren't the first cocky SOB to walk through here, you know. I guarantee you won't be the last."

"You didn't answer my question."

Ridley held his gaze. He was off guard. Uncertain. Considering the question? Or how to outsmart Mahir and bring the conversation back into his control?

"Well?" Mahir folded his arms, mirroring Ridley. "Was that an invitation or not?"

Maybe he felt a bit smug when Ridley uncrossed his arms and one hand went to his groin to adjust himself. While Mahir was trapped being Saeed, he might as well get something out of it. And if it proved he wasn't a cop, even better. But it had to come from Ridley. The man appeared to respond best when Mahir challenged him. At the same time, though, it should be easiest to bend the man to his will if he allowed Ridley to think it had really been his idea all along.

What Ridley did then surprised Mahir enough to make him jump. He grabbed Mahir's neck and kissed him—one of those open-mouthed, passionate kisses that were all about let's fuck. It caught him by surprise, but his body responded immediately, opened up under the onslaught. Every time Ridley tried to invade his mouth, he countered and tried to claim Ridley's instead. He pushed forward, backed Ridley against the desk, and ground their hips together.

Ridley gasped into the kiss and held Mahir's neck tighter. He put his other hand on Mahir's ass, pressing him closer. Mahir felt naked without his usual stubble. Clean-shaven against clean-shaven was a totally different feeling. He dug his fingers into Ridley's shoulders, keeping the man pinned against the desk with his weight and grinding touch. He could pretend the man wasn't a criminal, just one of his bar conquests, and that helped. Ridley was also incredibly hot—tall, muscular, and smart. Mahir would love to see how he responded to a dick up his ass. Whether he managed to be bossy then, too.

Ridley's hand left Mahir's neck and went up into his hair. He grabbed it, pulled back, and they were suddenly eye to eye and breathless, staring each other down. Okay, this was getting out of control quickly.

Ridley didn't let go of Mahir's hair. His other hand, though, moved between them, nudging Mahir's hips back. Eyes locked, neither of them looked away, but when Ridley's belt buckle jingled, they both pulled in sharp breaths.

Then came the zipper. Oh fuck.

"To answer your question—" Ridley paused to lick his lips. "—yes. That was an invitation." He tightened his grasp on Mahir's hair and shoved downward, but Mahir was pretty sure his own knees dropped out from under him a split second before that pressure came. Whoever's idea it was, the end result was the same: Mahir was on his knees, and he had Ridley's dick between his lips.

Ridley's aggression was as unrelenting as it was hot. He forced himself deep into Mahir's mouth, fists pulling at his hair, which unnerved Mahir because it was so different. Most of his adult life, his hair had been too short to be pulled, but Saeed wore it longer to distinguish him from Mahir. And getting grabbed and having his head controlled did funny things to Mahir, especially in this position.

The man wasn't small by any means, bigger than a lot of guys Mahir had been with, but Mahir didn't let it show that his jaw ached or that Ridley pushed the limit of his well-trained gag reflex. Mahir's own erection pressed against his zipper. How long had he been itching for a man who'd fuck his face like this? Just one split-second mental image of Ridley fucking his ass and Mahir damn near came.

He put a hand on Ridley's hip just to steady himself and wrapped the other around the base of Ridley's cock. Ridley groaned. His other hand hit the desk beside him with a sharp smack, and Mahir stole a glance just to confirm that, yes, Ridley's knuckles really were turning white as he gripped the edge of the desk. The ones in Mahir's hair were probably just as pale if the painfully tight grasp was any indication.

In spite of the way Ridley tried to force Mahir to stay still, Mahir managed to bob his head up and down, taking control of the depth and speed. He stroked with his hand, teased the head and slit and underside with his tongue whenever he had enough space to do so, and he shivered as Ridley rewarded him with a low, throaty groan.

"Oh fuck," Ridley murmured, fingers loosening and tightening in Mahir's hair. "Oh God . . ." His hips fought against Mahir's hand, so Mahir put his arm across Ridley's belly, pinning him in place, and the groan turned to a faint whimper. Mahir couldn't tell if the man was frustrated as Mahir kept eroding his control over the situation or if Ridley was just too far gone to give a fuck. All he knew was that he couldn't remember the last time he'd been this turned on, and he stroked and sucked Ridley's cock like it was the last time he'd ever touch a man.

The whimper became a low growl. Ridley's hips trembled, his fingers twitched in Mahir's hair, and Mahir squeezed Ridley's dick just right. Ridley swore once under his breath before he came hard, nearly choking Mahir, but Mahir recovered and swallowed everything the man gave him.

"St-stop. Fuck. Stop."

Mahir glanced up and pulled off Ridley's dick slowly with a teasing pop. The suction and release made Ridley shudder from head to toe. Seemed he was the type who got oversensitive just after orgasm, the type who'd likely try to shake Mahir off if he came first while fucking. Mahir clambered to his feet again and licked his lips. "Your turn."

Ridley stared at him as if not comprehending, mind still blown from the orgasm, and he tucked himself in, struggling a little to close the zipper over his still mostly hard dick. "Only polite, eh?"

"I'd say." Mahir grinned at him, tasting the man on his tongue, in his throat. He shouldn't have swallowed, but damn, he liked it, and he didn't want to smell of cum when he left this place.

"Fair enough." Ridley grabbed him by the hair and kissed him again, as deeply and passionately as before, likely tasting himself, too. Mahir pressed his groin against Ridley's hip, desperate for some kind of relief. Ridley pushed him toward the desk. "Down. Facedown."

He can't possibly fuck me. Mahir allowed Ridley to bend him over the desk. Ridley was working on Mahir's belt and fly to free him, pressed close and keeping him in place.

Ridley spat in his palm, and Mahir expected the spit-slicked fingers in his ass. Wrong. Ridley's hand closed around his dick, and he pushed up against him from behind, the denim rough against Mahir's bare ass as Ridley began to jerk him off.

Mahir pushed against the desk, not to escape, just to not lie there like a dead fish while that hand tortured him. Ridley was thrusting his hips forward, mimicking fucking, and at that moment, Mahir wished he hadn't gotten him off yet.

"I knew you were a bottom," Ridley whispered low into Mahir's ear, the tickle of breath making every hair on his body stand up. "Imagined I'd fuck you the moment you entered the room, didn't you?"

Mahir shook his head because he hadn't. And calling him a bottom— Now, that was almost funny. "Just get me off." He thrust into Ridley's hand, tried to fuck it, but his range of movement was restricted by Ridley behind him. Unless he pushed back much more, fucking anything was wishful thinking. Not that he needed to. Ridley's strong, wet hand gripped him just right—slow, intense strokes robbing him slowly of breath and control, squeezing the head of his cock with just a spike of pain, the other hand working his balls.

"I'll get you off," Ridley growled, letting his lips and his breath brush Mahir's ear. But then his hands slowed down. "When I'm damn good and ready, that is."

Mahir closed his eyes tight and couldn't quite stop himself from releasing a frustrated groan.

Ridley laughed. He kissed the side of Mahir's neck. "You'd do anything I told you to, wouldn't you?"

That comment from any other man would've made Mahir laugh, but he just bit his lip.

Ridley went on. "If I wanted to fuck you, you'd bend over and lube yourself up before I even took my dick out, wouldn't you?"

He would. Fuck, as much as he'd always thought of himself as a top with the occasional tendency to bottom just for grins, Mahir couldn't argue.

Ridley's hand slowed even more, nearly stopping. "I asked you a question."

Mahir moistened his lips. "Yes. I would."

A chuckle against Mahir's neck, and Ridley's hand picked up speed, stroking him just fast enough to blur Mahir's vision. "I want you to remember that," Ridley whispered. "That no matter what, you'll do anything I tell you to. Because you will. Won't you?"

Mahir nodded. He tried again to fuck Ridley's hand, but the desk and Ridley's weight still kept him from moving.

"I could stop right now." Ridley bit Mahir's neck just hard enough to make him yelp and then shiver. "I could stop, walk away, and leave you to this"—he squeezed Mahir's dick for emphasis—"and you'd thank me for it. Isn't that right? I could fuck you, not finish the job, and you'd be grateful."

Mahir's knees shook. He grabbed the opposite edge of the desk, just for something to hold on to. A power top with all other men, Mahir whimpered a soft, unsteady plea to the man on top of him for the first time in his life. "Please. Fuck, please . . ."

Ridley gave a soft laugh just maniacal enough to make Mahir cringe. Ridley was going to stop. Any second now, he'd stop. Walk away. Leave Mahir with semen on his tongue and an unresolved erection. And if he came back and ordered Mahir to his knees for another blowjob, Mahir would drop to the floor and thank him for the privilege. What the fuck?

"I won't do that to you this time," Ridley murmured, and he stroked Mahir faster. Mahir's whole body tensed, every muscle tightening with the energy of his impending orgasm, and he silently begged Ridley to be true to his word and not leave him hanging.

Ridley kissed beneath his ear again. Then he whispered so softly Mahir barely heard him. "Come."

And damn if Mahir's body didn't respond immediately. He came hard, unable to even exhale never mind make a sound, and shuddered between Ridley and the desk. His grasp on the edge slipped, so he just let go. He didn't have far to collapse, but as his orgasm subsided, he sank onto the desk and felt like he'd just dropped out of the damn sky.

Before Mahir had even caught his breath, Ridley nipped his earlobe and then let him go. He pushed himself up off Mahir. "You're in, Saeed. Be back here tomorrow night at nine o'clock sharp."

Footsteps. The door opened. Closed.

And Mahir was alone. He straightened, heart pounding in his throat, confused as all hell about what the fuck had just happened. He managed to tuck himself back in, then spotted a door leading to a small bathroom where he washed his hands and belly and rubbed the semen out of his jeans. It was invisible, but he knew it was there. Then he pulled his T-shirt on and, looking around, resisted the urge to search this place. He doubted very much that anybody would take a prospect into a room that kept any important papers. The best thing he could do was be "in," gather information, and then make the whole thing collapse.

You're in.

Well, he'd definitely passed the gay test, and quite spectacularly. Even by his own standards, this had been one of the hottest encounters of his life.

He took his jacket and slipped into it, then left the office. He wove his way back through the Friday-night crowd and resisted the impulse to sit for a moment and have a drink to calm down. He'd have to sleep this off, get into the mind-set and stay there while he was Saeed. This leg of the investigation would likely take weeks, if not months, so he'd better get used to it.

Now, whether to drive to his—Saeed's—crash pad or go home. No competition, really. He would likely spend quite a few nights in that one-bedroom shithole that the department kept for him close-by, so for tonight, he'd take the opportunity to sleep in his own bed while he could.

Want to read more of *Hostile Ground*?
Visit http://tinyurl.com/hostile-ground

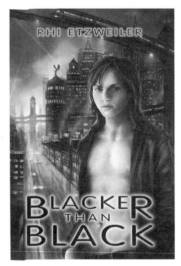